E.R. PUNS
DIABOLIC CAN

CW00455834

ERNEST ROBERTSON PUNSHON was born in London in 1872.

At the age of fourteen he started life in an office. His employers soon informed him that he would never make a really satisfactory clerk, and he, agreeing, spent the next few years wandering about Canada and the United States, endeavouring without great success to earn a living in any occupation that offered. Returning home by way of working a passage on a cattle boat, he began to write. He contributed to many magazines and periodicals, wrote plays, and published nearly fifty novels, among which his detective stories proved the most popular and enduring.

He died in 1956.

The Bobby Owen Mysteries

E.R. PUNSHON

DIABOLIC CANDELABRA

With an introduction
by Curtis Evans

DEAN STREET PRESS

Published by Dean Street Press 2016

Copyright © 1942 E.R. Punshon

Introduction copyright © 2016 Curtis Evans

All Rights Reserved

Published by licence, issued under the
UK Orphan Works Licensing Scheme.

First published in 1942 by Victor Gollancz

Cover by DSP

ISBN 978 1 911413 33 2

www.deanstreetpress.co.uk

INTRODUCTION

"There are bears in the forest."

"There are bears everywhere," Bobby answered.

"There's been a bear at Peter's cottage," she told him.

"Has there?" Bobby said. "What did it do?"

E.R. PUNSHON's seventeenth Bobby Owen detective novel, *Diabolic Candelabra* (1942), appeared on my list *150 Favorite Golden Age British Detective Novels*, published on 2 October 2010 at the website Mystery*File. Blog reviews of the novel by John Norris (Pretty Sinister Books), Les Blatt (Classic Mysteries) and Martin Edwards (Do You Write Under Your Own Name?) followed between 2011 and 2014, making *Diabolic Candelabra* the most reviewed Punshon mystery title on the internet until Dean Street Press began reprinting his books in 2015. It is gratifying to see the novel, one of Punshon's finest detective yarns, now in its turn reprinted by Dean Street Press, for it might be said to be the single book in the author's oeuvre that did the most to effect the modern Punshon revival.

"[H]e reveals a rather manic imagination, fired by powerful emotions and driven personalities," the distinguished mystery scholar Barry Pike once wrote of E.R. Punshon (see John Cooper and B.A. Pike, *Detective Fiction: The Collector's Guide*, 2nd ed., 1994). Nowhere in the author's large body of detective fiction is this quality of "manic imagination" more evident than in *Diabolic Candelabra*, a Grimm's faerie tale in modern dress centering on an ominous forest wherein frightening secrets lie hid. In *The Dark Garden* (1941), the immediately preceding Bobby Owen detective novel, Punshon had briefly alluded to Wychwood, the great forest lying within the boundaries of Wychshire, the English county to which Bobby Owen and his wife Olive relocated from London several books earlier; but it is in *Diabolic Candelabra* that Punshon realized the dramatic possibilities of Wychwood, a strange and ancient realm evocatively described by the author:

> Here the trees grew more thickly, here there reigned a
> deeper silence. It seemed that here the birds did not come,
> nor any living thing, and over all the forest brooded the heavy
> silence of the warm autumn afternoon. They alone might
> have been living as they paced side by side through what

seemed a perpetual twilight, beneath the heavy growth of entwining branches overhead. No breath of wind penetrated here, little sunshine either, only on each side grew the great trees, and beneath them a tangle of undergrowth, so that to Bobby and to Olive it was as though they were compassed in on every side.

(There is, in fact, a remnant of a Wychwood Forest in existence today in Oxfordshire, England, the name having been derived from the Anglo-Saxon appellation Huiccewudu; Punshon's interest in Anglo-Saxon lore would later surface prominently in a 1948 Bobby Owen detective novel, *The House of Godwinsson*.)

Diabolic Candelabra initially concerns a matter of chocolates—not deadly treats, as in *The Poisoned Chocolates Case* (1929), a famous detective novel by Punshon's Detection Club colleague Anthony Berkeley, but what are, quite simply, delicious ones. "They're just the most scrumptious chocolates that ever were, and they're a mystery too, and Mrs Weston gave me some to taste, because she wants a lot more to sell at the bazaar next week, and she wants you to find out," an enraptured Olive rather breathlessly and somewhat incoherently explains to Bobby after popping one of the exquisitely flavored morsels in her husband's mouth. In quest of the recipe for these divine delicacies, the sleuthing knight and his damsel journey into Wychwood to find pretty young Mary Floyd, the maker of the chocolates, who resides at a lonely cottage with her invalid mother and cruel, ne'er-do-well stepfather. Mary has, additionally, an odd younger sister named Loo, who, like Rima in W.H. Hudson's exotic Edwardian romance, *Green Mansions* (1904), dwells in the forest, a child of nature. It is Loo who tells Bobby and Olive that a bear has been to the Wychwood cottage of Peter the Hermit, an elderly herbalist and dear friend of Loo's who created the wondrous essence with which Mary Floyd so lusciously flavors those chocolates. When Bobby and Olive investigate this matter, the couple finds Peter's cottage violently wrecked and Peter mysteriously vanished. Has the old hermit departed for purposes unknown, or has he been murdered?

Additional enigmas arise as the tale continues. What has become of another vanished individual, Charles Crayfoot, proprietor of a prosperous confectionary and bakery business, who on the day of his disappearance is believed to have visited Peter the Hermit's cottage? What, if anything, does precious artwork--two grotesque paintings by El Greco and the so-called "Diabolic Candelabra," a devilishly-designed piece in silver attributed to Benvenuto Cellini— that has gone missing from Barsley Abbey, the ancestral home of the Rawdons, have to do with these human disappearances? Like a classic storybook hero, Bobby Owen must undergo a fearsome ordeal before these puzzling questions are answered.

While there are memorably scary moments in *Diabolic Candelabra*, there are also a number of amusing asides, many of them occasioned by the sudden presence of several businessmen of little scruple in the vicinity of Wychwood, which are splendidly characteristic of the author at his most wryly satirical. At one point Bobby thinks to himself that "business resembles charity in that it covers a multitude of sins." Elsewhere Bobby wonders "why Mr Stone was not a millionaire," as "he seemed to know so well how to transfer money from other people's pockets to his own." Nor do the gentry go unscathed. "I reckon the gentry can go dotty just like anyone else," allows a Wychshire police sergeant, to which observation Bobby bluntly replies: "Or even more." Reflecting his recent experience of the London Blitz, the author notes that the coffee Olive brews to revive Bobby is "of the strength of an R.A.F. bomb and of a blackness to satisfy even an Air Raid Warden on his nightly prowl."

Late in *Diabolic Candelabra* Punshon hearkens back to the first Bobby Owen detective novel, *Information Received* (1933), when, as Olive makes Bobby sandwiches and fills a thermos flask in preparation for her spouse's climactic and potentially quite perilous venture into Wychwood, Bobby recollects sage advice from his early mentor, Scotland Yard's Superintendent Mitchell: "Years before, when he was a raw beginner, a senior man had warned Bobby that a good detective never forgot his sandwiches. ..." Unlike Hansel and Gretel, however, Bobby and Olive never find occasion to leave a trail of breadcrumbs behind them while boldly traversing the forbidding forest of Wychwood.

Curtis Evans

CHAPTER I

CHOCOLATES

OLIVE CAME QUICKLY, even excitedly, into the garden where, on this warm, calm, autumn evening, Inspector Bobby Owen, of the Wychshire County Police, wherein he doubled the parts of head of the somewhat scanty Wychshire C.I.D. with that of secretary to the chief constable, Colonel Glynne, was busily gardening. True, the gardening was being done at the moment from the depths of a comfortable deck chair, but spiritually Bobby was hard at it, digging with fervour, hoeing, sowing, mowing, pruning, weeding, one and all with extreme and extraordinary energy. Not quite realizing what a bustle of work she was interrupting, Olive said:

"Oh, Bobby, shut your eyes and open your mouth." Disappointedly she added: "Oh, they are."

Bobby opened the first named, regarded her severely, spoke with dignity.

"If you are trying to insinuate—" he began, but as to utter these words his mouth had to remain open, Olive saw and seized her opportunity and popped something therein.

"Um-m-m," Bobby concluded his observations.

"Well?" said Olive expectantly.

"Not so bad," said Bobby critically.

"It's heavenly," said Olive conclusively. Then she added: "If you had been more appreciative you could have had this one, too, but now I'll have it myself."

Therewith she popped a second something into her own mouth and contentedly sat down to munch on the grass by his side. Bobby watched her. He said wistfully:

"If you had told me that before—"

"Ah-ha," said Olive.

"What is it?" asked Bobby.

"That's for a good little detective to find out," said Olive.

Scared by even this faint suggestion of work, Bobby sank back into his chair.

"Nothing doing," he said.

"Oh, yes, there is," said Olive, firmly this time. "They're just the most scrumptious chocolates that ever were, and they're a mystery, too, and Mrs Weston gave me some to taste, because she wants a lot more to sell at the bazaar next week, and she wants you to find out."

"Chasing a chocolate to its lair," murmured Bobby. "What's the difficulty, anyway?"

"Mrs Weston always does her shopping in Tombes, or at least most of it, because she says there aren't any queues there, like there are in Midwych, and besides she knows people, and she gets these miracle chocolates at Walters's, the big tea shop, and they cost seven and six a pound, and Walters's say now people know about them they sell out ever so quickly, and they could sell more if they could get them, but they can't. It's the flavour. Isn't it wonderful?"

"Not bad," admitted Bobby.

"Not bad," repeated Olive, surveying him with scorn. "I wish I had kept that one I gave you for myself, instead of wasting it on you. It's absolutely different from anything else I ever tasted, sweet and not a bit sickly and sharp, too, and refreshing and scented as well—makes you think of woods and fields and the early morning and dew and things like that."

"Careful," Bobby warned her. "Careful now, or you'll be dropping into poetry."

"They are poetry," Olive answered with conviction.

"Ode to a chocolate," murmured Bobby, and Olive went on unheedingly:

"You see, they're homemade and Mrs Weston wants the recipe so she can make lots and lots for her stall at the bazaar. She says she'll charge ten shillings a pound, because they're so awfully delicious and you can at a bazaar, can't you? And she says they'll sell like anything and I expect they will, too, because they really are so nice and absolutely different."

"Well," commented Bobby, "I suppose it's no worse giving ten bob for a pound of chocolates than four or five bob for a pound of tomatoes."

"I should like the recipe myself," Olive added thoughtfully.

Bobby composed himself to resume his gardening by lying back in his deck chair and closing his eyes. Olive poked him violently in the ribs. Bobby opened a reproachful eye—only one though, so as to be able to resume his gardening more quickly.

"Here. I say," he protested.

"It's where you come in," Olive told him.

"Me," protested Bobby. "My good girl, I don't know anything about making chocolates."

"You see," explained Olive, unheeding this unnecessary disclaimer. "Walters's say they get them from a Miss Floyd and they don't know her address and they send the money to the Barsley Forest post office, and they are always asking her to send more, and she never does, so Mrs Weston wants me to try to find Miss Floyd and ask her for the recipe."

"Why can't she go herself?"

"It's a long way for them, we're much nearer, and then there's the petrol. Mr Weston wants it all. Mrs Weston says she daren't even fill her lighter. He's a sort of inspector for salesmen or something, and he has to use his car all the time. Besides," added Olive candidly, "I offered, because if I can get the recipe I should like to try myself."

"Suppose this Miss Floyd doesn't want to tell?"

"Well, she mightn't," admitted Olive, "but it would be mean, and besides Mrs Weston said she wouldn't mind paying her. She told Mr Weston and he was awfully interested and said that would be all right, she could pay as much as she liked, as it was for the church bazaar. Mrs Weston was rather surprised, because Mr Weston doesn't take much interest in church work generally."

Bobby mused on this. He thought Mr Weston sounded very generous, but then he didn't know Mr Weston, and quite possibly that gentleman was of a liberal and generous disposition by nature.

He said thoughtfully:

"It may be a girl who lives in a lonely sort of cottage near Barsley Forest village, but right in the forest. I think her name is Floyd and I think there's an invalid mother who has married again. I remember altering the beat of one of our chaps so as to pass by their cottage. It's a lonely sort of place for one thing and the man's a bit of a bad lot, too, or supposed to be, so I thought it might be as well to keep an eye on the place occasionally. He's under suspicion of having been mixed up in a burglary or two, and he's been sent up for petty larceny, I think. I don't remember exactly. Stealing rabbits out of traps, too, I think. Anyhow, I know I thought it might be as well to let him see we existed. Possibly that's why the girl has her money sent to the post office, to keep it safe from step-papa."

"We'll go and see her to-morrow, Bobby, shall we?" decided Olive. "You know, Bobby, those chocolates are really delicious. I've never tasted anything quite like them. I'm sure that girl could sell as many as she liked to make. It's what Walters's said. She could work up a very good business if she wanted to."

"Perhaps she doesn't want," Bobby said. "Are you going to try to cajole her out of her valuable secret?"

He spoke half jestingly, but Olive was beginning to look serious.

"Bobby," she said, "do you think it might really be valuable? I mean, suppose a manufacturer began to make them and advertised a lot and all that?"

"Might mean a fortune," Bobby said, still half jestingly. "It all depends."

"I was only thinking they would be nice to make," Olive explained. She was looking troubled now. "Mrs Weston says Walters's say people are beginning to ask for them and they charge seven and six a pound and that's rather a lot for chocolates."

"Suggests a fair margin for profit," Bobby agreed. Now he, too, was beginning to look interested. "What sort of a chap is Mr Weston?" he asked.

"She'll have to be told," Olive declared. "I mean I don't want the recipe, if it's going to be worth a lot of money. I don't think we'll go, shall we? Mr Weston? I don't like him very much. I've only seen him once or twice, though. I expect he's all right. Only I promised Mrs Weston I would try and get it for her—the recipe, I mean."

Bobby was thinking hard. The official part of him warned him that it was no affair of his and that only the most utter, hopeless fool of a policeman would ever risk seeking trouble when trouble was always so persistently finding him. The human part of him suggested that a girl who might possibly have hit upon some unusual flavouring for her homemade chocolates ought to be given a hint not to part with her secret without due consideration. In the confectionery trade a new flavour might well have its value. Olive's voice broke in upon his thoughts.

"I did promise," she said, for she was one of those rare people who believe that promises should hold.

Possibly it was this remark that influenced Bobby. Or it may have been mere curiosity, a marked trait in his character, so that he could never hear of anything unusual without wanting to get to the bottom of it. Or it may have been even a kind of uneasy premonition that lonely girls in possession of a trade secret of possible cash value might just conceivably come to be in need of police protection. Anyhow, he said:

"We'll go and have a look round if you like. To-morrow's Sunday and I'm not on duty for a wonder." He paused to regard this fact with faint surprise, for it was his deep conviction that he was on duty practically every Sunday. "It's a goodish way, but there's a drop of petrol to spare and if the weather keeps up we could take some lunch and make a sort of picnic of it."

Olive thought this a very good idea. What with war work and threatening air raids and ordinary police routine, it was long since Bobby had had anything even remotely resembling a holiday. Do him good, she decided. Do them both good, for that matter.

"Even if she wants to keep the recipe to herself," Olive went on, "I expect she would be willing to make some for the bazaar. Mrs Weston would love to have them for her stall and she could charge as much as she liked, because you can at a bazaar."

"So you can and so you do," agreed Bobby; and Olive looked at him severely, for she did not altogether approve of the tone in which this last remark had been uttered.

CHAPTER II
WOODLAND RAMBLE

NEXT MORNING, ACCORDINGLY Bobby and Olive started off in their small car, with a basket of provisions as well stocked as the times permitted. As far as the village of Barsley Forest—in peace time a favourite place wherefrom to start for forest picnics—the road was familiar. At the village, for being an inspector of police has its advantages, Bobby parked his car at the village police station—which was the cottage occupied by the sergeant in charge, a man named Turner—and after spending a few moments admiring the garden and expressing his determination to make his own an equal success as soon as he could really get down to it, he explained that he and Olive meant to spend a quiet day in a woodland ramble and what did Sergeant Turner, as a local man, think the best and most picturesque route to follow? One route the sergeant recommended was by Barsley Abbey. The park was open to the public—it was crossed by an ancient right of way—and though picnicking was frowned upon, there were many pleasant spots farther on, beyond the park boundaries. There was also the 'Rawdon Arms' half way on the road to Tombes, and at the 'Rawdon Arms,' the beer, as Sergeant Turner could testify, was of superior quality. Barsley Abbey itself, as Bobby and most other people knew, was renowned for the fine collection of pictures housed there and occasionally thrown open to the public on payment of a small fee for the benefit of Wychshire hospitals. The total value of the pictures was said to be in the order of a vague number of hundreds of thousands of pounds. As, however, they all came under the entail settlement as heirlooms, they could not be disposed of, though it was generally understood that the present owner, Sir Alfred Rawdon, was trying to get the entail broken and permission to sell some or all. This was likely to be a long business, especially as the interests of minors had to be considered, but once the legal formalities were accomplished, the subsequent sale of the pictures and other objects of art was likely to be the sensation of the season. Already it was understood dealers were hinting they would be prepared to make better offers privately than any likely to be secured at public auction.

"Because," it had been explained to Bobby, "if a dealer gives a thousand or so for a picture at public auction, he has to be fairly reasonable in the figure he quotes to a likely purchaser. Whereas if he gives even a few hundred more in private, he can quote any figure he likes and still swear black and blue he is selling at next door to a loss. Then again, many collectors prefer that the amount they have given for their possessions should remain a mystery. That allows them to hint at astronomical sums without the risk of the actual figures being discovered in a reference book."

"There's been a gent from London," Turner was saying now, "asking a lot of questions about those Abbey pictures. He was talking about them in the 'Rawdon Arms' bar. What he said was there was two of 'em stolen fifty years back. Wanted to know if I knew anything about it when he heard me being called 'sergeant', but I told him that was before my time."

"What was it he thought you might know?" Bobby asked.

"Seemed to think some of the folk about here might have them, innocent like. I told him he didn't know the folk about here, if he thought that, but he stuck it out they might think the pictures had just been mislaid like or forgotten. Didn't sound likely to me, not if they were worth all the money he said. I told him so. He had photos of two of them. Lord love a duck," said the sergeant, amused at the memory, "you never saw the like. Nightmares. Fair nightmares. The only thing you saw was an arm as long as a leg and the rest like a jigsaw puzzle, only worse. He said a Greek gentleman did them," and this was evidently regarded by Sergeant Turner as to some extent an explanation or even an excuse.

"El Greco, perhaps," Bobby remarked, interested. "If they are genuine El Grecos they would be worth a bit of money all right, if they did turn up somewhere."

"Not my money," said Turner firmly. "Mr Baker—he's the 'Rawdon Arms' landlord—he said he wouldn't mind having 'em just to show at closing time. Said they would clear the bar in quick sticks. Said anyone seeing them would think it was most like a fit of the D.T.s coming on, and be only too glad to clear off home before it got worse."

"Do you know," interposed Olive quickly, "I remember reading something like that. It was in an article on Spanish art in one of the magazines, about two unidentified paintings, believed to be by El Greco, that were said to have vanished from the Barsley Abbey collection, only it wasn't very certain they had ever been there. Why, they might be worth a small fortune."

"Them things?" asked the sergeant incredulously, and Bobby tried to explain that appreciation of art varied. A painting like, for example, Millet's 'The Angelus', might bring the artist only a comparatively small sum, and yet afterwards be sold for twenty or thirty thousand pounds. Quite possible, Bobby said, that the El Grecos, their worth unrecognized, their strange value not understood, had been hung in some little used room, taken down during some process of cleaning or re-decoration, and then simply forgotten, relegated to a lumber room, and finally lost sight of. Or a dependant of the great house might have taken a fancy to them and they might be hanging peacefully on the wall in some cottage or farmhouse. Or in the course of time they might have got damaged and been disposed of as rubbish.

The sergeant was obviously incredulous and inclined to suspect his superior of the unworthy action of pulling a subordinate's leg. He admitted, however, that he had always considered art a rummy business, anyhow, and was obviously relieved when Bobby agreed with this dictum. Olive remarked that in the same article there had been a reference to what it called 'The Diabolic Candelabra', attributed to Benvenuto Cellini, and supposed to have disappeared about the same time, and when the sergeant understood that candelabra meant many-branched candlesticks and that these would be in solid silver, he was quite relieved.

"Now them things," he said, "would be worth a pound or two and I'll take my oath none of them about here have anything of the sort, or would keep 'em if they had 'em. Straight into the melting pot," declared the sergeant, "silver being always silver, though less so now than when I joined the force."

Olive went a little pale at the thought of Cellini work going straight into the melting pot, but supposed it was a very probable though most awful suggestion. Then the subject dropped, though Bobby wondered vaguely what had brought all this up again after the lapse of half a century, and Sergeant Turner went on to instruct them on the favourite walks in the neighbourhood. Bobby thought the one by Barsley Abbey and the 'Rawdon Arms,' however famous this last might be for its beer, was a little round about, and said they would prefer to get more quickly into the heart of the forest. So Turner recommended another path that led far away from pubs and tea gardens, and other such amenities of civilized life, and on to Heron's Mere, a lovely but also a lonely and unfrequented spot.

"Might walk for miles and never see a soul," declared Turner. "Get lost, too, if you aren't careful, sir, the way the paths in the forest twist and turn."

"No houses anywhere about?" Bobby asked.

"Not a sign of one all the way," answered Turner, "except for Coop's Cottage. And old Peter the Hermit's hut farther on."

"Who is Peter the Hermit?" Bobby asked.

It appeared that Peter the Hermit was a local celebrity, but a celebrity against his will and apt to be vicious if disturbed. There had even been one or two charges of assault against him, though the provocation received had been such that each time he had escaped with a small fine and a warning to keep his temper under better control. He lived in the depths of the forest in a small one-roomed hut he had built himself, though with intervals of wandering that had tended, however, to grow shorter as he himself grew older. How old he was no one knew. Local gossip put his age at a hundred, but that, in the sergeant's considered opinion, was probably an exaggerated estimate. Nor did any one seem to know how long he had occupied his hut. He had come to be accepted in his strange and solitary life as a forest institution. Also he was reputed to have a great knowledge of herbs and their effects, so that his advice was often sought in cases of illness, much to the annoyance of the local medical men, of whom he, on his side, was openly contemptuous. Consultation with him was, however, not easy, as it was never possible to be sure of finding him at home. Even if he were at his hut, it seemed entirely a question of his mood whether he would give the advice asked for and proffer a remedy or whether on the visitor's approach he would vanish into the forest, not appearing again perhaps for many days. How he lived no one knew. Occasionally he would appear in the village to make purchases for which he invariably paid in gold. As this had led to stories that he possessed immense stores of hidden treasure, his cottage, or hut rather, for it was no more, had been ransacked more than once during his prolonged absences, but without result. Nor had he made any complaint, though it was a fact that the residence of one man, supposed to have been responsible for such a search, had been mysteriously burned down. Another man, also held to have been guilty of a similar act, had been found stark naked and generally in sorry plight twenty miles from his home, though how he got there and what had happened he steadfastly refused to say. Other and even more remarkable tales were current and as a consequence no local inhabitant would now ever dream of meddling with the hut or its contents. The hermit's more prosaic appearances in the police court had been largely due to the misguided efforts of a local paper to give him the publicity apt in these drab days to attend anything supposed to be picturesque or unusual. Articles had appeared on the 'Hermit of Wychwood Forest', ill-advised trippers and picnickers had come to stare, and had been driven away with a vigour and an emphasis and a flourished hatchet that had on occasion gone farther than the law approved. Now, however, all that had died down and the hermit was allowed to pursue his own course of life undisturbed save when efforts were made to obtain his advice or some of his herbal remedies.

"If he wanted," said the sergeant, "he could have a crowd there every day. But as like as not if you go you won't find him and if he does give you a bottle of stuff, it's a toss-up if you get another. But they do say it's not often two bottles are needed. One of 'em generally does the trick, not like doctor's stuff you can go on taking for ever and never notice the difference except when the bill comes in."

"Poor old man," Olive said. "Hasn't he anyone belonging to him?"

The sergeant had never heard of any relations, and Bobby, more practical, wondered what the hermit's title was to the land on which, apparently, he had built his habitation. Wasn't most of the forest Crown property, except that portion the town of Midwych had purchased at the end of the last century and a few other parts that were still in private hands?

"Not that there is any need to bother," he added, fearing the question might be misunderstood. "Not our business. I was only wondering."

It seemed, however, that this point had come up during the police court proceedings already mentioned. His was not merely squatter's right. The hut stood at the extreme tip of a narrow, triangular piece of land, belonging to the Rawdon estate, where a strip of Sir Alfred's land ran down into the forest in a kind of peninsula of private property. The hermit claimed to have written permission, dated from long before the first world war, to occupy his hut on payment of a nominal rent that was, as a matter of fact, never demanded. So far, therefore, as occupation went his legal position was secure and he had a perfect title to his habitation. Sir Alfred was also the landlord of Mr Coop, the ill-reputed step-father of the Miss Floyd who turned out such wonderful homemade chocolates. But the rent for the Coop cottage was always duly collected. Indeed the leniency of the Rawdon estate towards the old hermit was the cause of some surprise in the district. Leniency towards tenants had never been a marked characteristic of the Rawdons, who had the reputation, a reputation that went back to early Georgian days, of being harsh and grasping landlords.

Fortified with all this information and with full instructions of the path to follow, passing between the Coop cottage on the left and Boggart's Hole on the right—and of Boggart's Hole they were warned to beware, since it had been the scene of more than one accident— Bobby and Olive set out on the way to Heron's Mere, supposed to be one of the loveliest spots in the forest. It could, however, be reached only on foot and by a somewhat long and tiring uphill walk, so it was not as popular with excursionists and picnickers as were other of the neighbouring beauty spots.

CHAPTER III

UNSEEN FOLLOWER

THE PATH TO Heron's Mere passed close by the edge of Boggart's Hole, the old, long deserted quarry, whence had been cut the stone used in early mediaeval days in building the abbey and, subsequently, many other places in the neighbourhood. From the path above, one looked down on what had become an almost impenetrable jungle of tree and undergrowth, and as the quarry edge was abrupt, unprotected and concealed by bushes, it is little wonder that more than one accident had occurred here, or that the place had acquired an evil reputation. No need to fall back on the evil spirit in the form of a lovely maiden, who, according to local tradition, was supposed to float before belated travellers, enticing them to follow her till, their attention on her and unaware of their danger, they walked over the quarry edge to fall to their death below. The drop down the almost sheer face of the cliff, left by the cutting away of the stone, was at least fifty feet, broken only once by a stunted tree and straggling bushes that somehow or another had managed to cling to, and find sustenance on, a narrow, projecting ledge.

"Don't go too near," Olive said nervously, as Bobby craned forward to look over the edge.

"Nasty dangerous spot," Bobby agreed. "No wonder there have been a few broken necks here. Looks as if something of the sort had been happening recently."

"Why?" asked Olive.

Bobby showed the bark of a tree growing near, slightly bruised.

"Been a rope round there not so long ago," he said. "You can see where it went over the edge." He pointed to where a tiny furrow on the turf at the quarry edge was visible. "Couldn't be bird-nesting at this time of year. Might be something else, I suppose," he remarked.

He peered over cautiously. For twenty feet or so the cliff descent was perpendicular. Then a rough ledge jutted out, widening from a few inches to a couple of feet or so. At the wider end grew a tree, a cluster of tangled bushes. Below, the fall was sheer again and Olive said:

"There ought to be a fence."

"Midwych town property, this part," Bobby said. "You won't catch the corporation doing that. Make them responsible."

"But they are responsible if it belongs to them," Olive declared.

Bobby shook his head.

"Actually," he said, "the quarry remains private property—part of the Rawdon estate. Strictly speaking, you are trespassing if you leave the path. So it's your own look out if you go tumbling over the edge. Up to you to look after yourself. But if the corporation fenced in the path and then you fell over, you, or your heirs rather, could argue the fence was defective and you trusted it and it deceived you or something like that, and the corporation might have to stand a lawsuit and perhaps damages as well. So you don't catch 'em taking the risk."

Olive considered this.

Then she said:

"Is that the law?"

"It is," said Bobby.

Olive drew a long breath.

"How—how mean," she said.

"Oh, just the law," Bobby explained.

They went on their way and when they reached Heron's Mere it proved as charming a spot as it had been described. They spent a little time, resting, eating their lunch, admiring the view, watching the lovely voracious dance of dragon flies like living flashes of light above the surface of the mere, and then turned homewards. Leaving Boggart's Hole, of evil reputation, on their left, they found the path they had been warned to look out for and followed it through what seemed a lonelier and certainly a lovelier part of the forest than that they had traversed before.

Here the trees grew more thickly, here there reigned a deeper silence. It seemed that here the birds did not come, nor any living thing, and over all the forest brooded the heavy silence of the warm autumn afternoon. They alone might have been living as they paced side by side through what seemed a perpetual twilight, beneath the heavy growth of entwining branches overhead. No breath of wind penetrated here, little sunshine either, only on each side grew the great trees, and beneath them a tangle of undergrowth, so that to Bobby and to Olive it was as though they were compassed in on every side.

"It's very quiet, very peaceful," Olive said, "but I don't know that I like it."

"Good place for any hermit chap," Bobby remarked.

They went on, feeling as it were oppressed, as if in this hidden solitude some ancestral awareness of a need for caution had awakened in their souls. On the sea, on the hill-side, man may go upright, ready to face the dangers he can see, but who could tell what might not lurk in these green and silent shades?

"There is someone following us," Olive said.

Bobby had paused to admire an enormous oak, a veritable monarch of the forest, a tree so huge in girth and growth it might well be that beneath its far flung branches Druids of old had celebrated their strange and dreadful rites. Under and near it the ground was clear, as though its majesty tolerated not even the smallest rival.

Olive said again:

"There's someone following us."

"Eh?" said Bobby. "Well, let 'em." Then he asked: "How do you know?"

Olive did not answer a question which indeed did not strike her as very sensible. What did it matter how one knew when one did know? She said:

"There's a bird."

"First I've seen," Bobby agreed. "What do you mean—someone following us?"

"Well, there is," Olive said.

"Perhaps it's the hermit," Bobby said. "I'll have a look."

He went back a few paces and then called:

"Come and have a look. There's a squirrel here."

Olive joined him. In a tree near by, a squirrel perched on one of the branches, chattered at them what seemed its disapproval.

"It doesn't like us," Olive said.

"Thinks it owns the whole place," Bobby said, and was going to throw a twig at it, had not Olive stopped him. "There's that bird again," he added, as with a flutter of wings it passed over their heads. "Bird and squirrel—place getting quite populated. I expect that's what you heard when you thought there was someone there."

Olive looked doubtful and puzzled, but said nothing and they resumed their way. They had not gone far when she said:

"They're still following us, whoever it is."

"See anyone?" Bobby asked.

"No," she answered, "but those bushes moved and there's no wind."

Bobby shrugged his shoulders.

"Oh, well," he said, "if it amuses them. Are you sure? You didn't actually see anything?"

"No," she repeated, "only a movement, only a shadow. But it was someone, something."

"Oh, well," Bobby repeated, and then gave a shout: "Hullo, you there. Do you want anything?"

There was no response. He shrugged his shoulders again and they walked on, seeing and hearing no more till they came presently to where, from the overhanging branch of a tree dangled a roughly scrawled board, on it the word 'Teas'. Beneath the word an arrow pointed at right angles across a narrow glade, towards what seemed as unpromising a wilderness of young trees, bushes, undergrowth, as can well be imagined.

"Funny," Bobby said. "Our chap told us distinctly there was no place about here where you could get anything."

"I should like a cup of tea," Olive said doubtfully, "but it doesn't look as if many people went that way."

They crossed the glade to look and Bobby shook his head. There was no sign of a path, and the dark, close labyrinth of tangled growth suggested that neither entrance nor emergence would be easy.

"Might easily lose your bearings in there," he said. "I don't think we'll try it. Might be hours finding our way out."

They turned to retrace their steps and when they had regained the path and had gone on a few yards, Olive pressed Bobby's arm and whispered:

"There's someone following us again—someone very angry."

"How do you know?" Bobby asked.

Olive did not answer, for again she felt the question useless, since what you know, you know, and what does it matter how?

"Well, if there is, what's the game?" he said, and again Olive did not answer, but this time because she did not know.

"I saw a shadow behind that beech," she said.

"Well, you go that way and I'll go this," Bobby suggested, but Olive put her hand on his arm and stopped him.

"No, it's a child, I think," she said. "You'll frighten it."

She began to try to coax their unknown follower to appear, but without success.

"Oh, well, come along," Bobby said. "We can't wait all day."

"Good-bye," Olive called. "We can't talk to you, you know, if you won't let us see you."

They started to walk on again and a small shrill voice called, startling them a little, as it came from out the stillness of the forest in that warm drowsy afternoon.

"There's a bear."

"Oh, I gobble up bears for supper every night," Bobby called back and Olive laughed and said:

"The funny little thing. I'm afraid we are breaking up some exciting game or another."

A little farther on they came to where there dangled from a tree a notice, old and weather-beaten and reading:

"Trespassers will be prosecuted with the utmost rigour of the law."

"Well, that's what I call being thorough," Bobby commented. "I wonder where it's been pinched from."

When they passed on without heeding this dire warning, Olive declared she could hear an angry scolding behind, and Bobby presently made a sudden leap back and to one side, in the hope of catching a glimpse of their pursuer. But no human creature was visible, nor even so much as the trembling of a twig or the swift passage of a shadow on the ground to tell of the presence of any living creature. Only there was still a squirrel chattering defiance from half-way up a tree, and this time two or three birds fluttering from one branch to another. And Bobby was not sure, but he thought he could see a rabbit, too, peeping from beneath a bush. He was aware of an odd impression that all these creatures were not so much alarmed by his appearance as angered by it. He went back to Olive and she said:

"You mustn't do that again. You'll frighten whoever it is."

"Well, they are trying to frighten us," Bobby grumbled. "Funny thing, it's only when I dodge back that you see anything living—a squirrel and a rabbit this time and birds, too. But for that I should say there wasn't so much as a live mouse anywhere near."

"It's warm and it's afternoon," Olive said. "Everything's asleep."

CHAPTER IV
LOO

BEFORE LONG THE path Bobby and Olive were following, and now without further interruption, brought them to the rear of a small cottage. Its front was to a road that here skirted the edge of the forest where it died away into pasture and open field, with only here and there an ancient tree to give evidence of the woodlands whence this surrounding open land had been rescued. Behind the cottage lay a large, well-cultivated garden. At the end stood a row of hives and the air was heavy with the coming and the going of the bees. From the back door of the cottage emerged hurriedly a short, square-built man, flushed, angry, and gesticulating. Followed him, a tall, thin girl, as pale as the man was flushed, and in her hands she held a large iron pot wherefrom rose clouds of steam.

"You just dare, you just dare," the man was shouting furiously, though, as he shouted, still retreating. "Mind what you're doing. That stuff could scald a man to death."

"I shouldn't wonder," she agreed calmly.

The man waved his arms in furious indignation.

"Murder me, would you? You wait, you little devil," he threatened. "I'll break every bone in—ai-e-e," he concluded abruptly, for with considerable dexterity and unexpected strength of wrist the girl had given the formidable weapon she held, the iron pot of nearly boiling broth, a sudden twirl that sent a splash of its contents on the man's foot.

"Now go," she ordered, "and don't come back till evening."

"You—you," stuttered the man, choking with rage, and adding a few adjectives as he hopped on one foot, clasping at the other with his right hand. "You wait—you wait—when I get my hands on you, I'll show you—"

"Unless you kill me," the girl answered quietly, "you know what'll happen to you afterwards. Another time you might be there longer than a week."

"Aw, shut it," he retorted, though with less vigour.

"As it is, I've a good mind to tell Loo about you," the girl added.

"Aw, shut it, I'm not afraid of her—or you either. Got you," he yelled, for the girl had rashly turned back to re-enter the cottage, so that he saw his opportunity, made a dash forward, and had her in his grasp before she could get the heavy iron pot into position again.

At the same time Bobby vaulted the gate into the garden and called out:

"Now, then, what's all this?"

The man turned, saw Bobby.

"Blasted copper," he said.

Promptly he released his captive and made off at a run.

Bobby scowled. He did hate being called a 'copper', especially and most especially when he was in plain clothes. Besides how did the fellow know? Bobby's firmest conviction was that he didn't in the least look like a policeman, and here was this fellow calling him a 'copper' at the first glimpse. Both puzzling and annoying, he thought. Olive came up to him. She said:

"Bobby, did you notice how that girl looked? She had her pot full of boiling soup and she was quite ready to throw it all over him."

"He would have known all about it, if she had," Bobby remarked. "Just as well she didn't, even if it was self-defence. What do we do now?"

He answered his own question by walking up the path. Olive followed. The girl, going back into the cottage, had closed the door behind her, but closed it hurriedly so that in her haste she failed to make the latch secure. The door swung open and through it they heard a woman's voice saying:

"Oh, Mary, you shouldn't! Oh, Mary, why do you? He didn't hurt me. He'll do something awful."

"He daren't," came the girl's calm voice in answer. "He knows what'll happen if he tries. Next time he got drunk. Unless he kills me first," she added as an afterthought.

The woman said:

"There's a man in the garden."

"I know. It's why he ran away when he had hold of me," the girl answered.

"You wait," Olive said to Bobby. "I'll knock."

She had no need to do so, however, for the girl came to the threshold of the open door. Through it Bobby could see into the kitchen, a clean, comfortable looking room. A fire of pine branches and cones was burning in the old-fashioned grate, giving out a fresh and pleasant smell. On the hob stood the big iron pot that had so recently been so effective a weapon of defence. On a sofa lay a woman, evidently an invalid. The girl said to Olive:

"Won't you come in?"

She went back into the cottage. Olive followed her and so did Bobby, considering that he was included in the invitation. Abruptly the girl said to Bobby:

"That was my step-father. You frightened him. Thank you."

"Oh, well," Bobby said, a little awkwardly.

"Please sit down," the girl said.

She was standing by the head of the sofa, almost as if still guarding the invalid. She was tall and thin, with large melancholy eyes, beneath clearly marked brows. Her nose, her lips, her high cheekbones were all long and narrow, and the beauty that she had was more of line and form than of any perfection of colouring or feature—an austere and even intellectual beauty, unexpected in this poor and lonely cottage. She had one hand held out in a gesture of protection before the invalid, and Bobby, with his instinct for form and pattern, noticed at once its delicacy of structure. Almost, in the light of the afternoon sun shining through one of the windows, were the bones visible under the fine skin. Yet they were strong hands, too, for all their delicacy of appearance, for they had wielded the heavy iron pot with ease. Olive said:

"We have been having a walk in the forest. We thought we would come back this way. You are Miss Floyd, aren't you? My name is Owen and this is my husband."

The woman on the sofa said:

"I am Mrs Coop. Mary is my daughter. That was my husband. He isn't generally like that. He gets so excited. Mary thought he was hurting me. He wasn't really."

"He was shaking you," Mary said. "He was trying to get money from you. That's why he was so angry, because I came in just in time to stop him."

There was a resemblance between them—the tall, pale, upright girl, the worn-looking recumbent woman. Both had the same fineness of bone and structure, the same long and narrow features, the same air of a remote distinction. But the older woman owed it, one felt, to long suffering patiently borne, while with the girl it seemed innate, as though always from her birth she had moved a little apart from the common things amidst which she lived! Yet none the less those common things of everyday life surrounding her showed every sign of receiving a constant and industrious care. Poor they evidently were. Everything showed that. But it was a poverty of simplicity; for as there is a poverty of squalor so there is a poverty of simplicity, and this last can be a lovely thing, a poverty not of want and need but of content.

"I'm inclined to think," Bobby said slowly, "that Mr Coop had better have a warning and I'll see he gets one all right."

"I can look after myself," Mary said, frowning a little, as if she did not altogether approve of this hint of interference.

"Prevention better than cure," Bobby told her.

"There's Loo," Mrs Coop said, and Mary did not answer, but looked troubled.

"I don't expect he'll try to do it again," Mrs Coop said. "It was all so sudden he hadn't time to think or remember. You see, last time, Mary put him in the cellar and kept him there a week and he's always been afraid perhaps she might again."

"If he touches Loo," Mary said, "I think I would put him there and keep him there till he was dead, and never let him out at all."

"What was it you did?" asked Bobby, thinking he could hardly have heard aright, as he surveyed the girl's fragility.

"He beat Mary," Mrs Coop explained. "So when he came home drunk she pushed him down in the cellar with some water and dry bread—at least, not very much water and not very much bread. Only there were potatoes, too, weren't there?"

"Yes," answered Mary. "A lot."

"Of course, they were raw," Mrs Coop admitted. "She didn't let him out for a week, only after we heard him crying and he had promised he never would again. It was awful and he looked worse."

"Served him right," Olive said. "Served him jolly well right. Did he hurt you much?" she asked Mary.

"There are marks still," Mrs Coop said.

"Oh," said Olive.

"I should have again," Mary said gravely, "only longer this time. I mean, if he had beaten me again. It was stupid of me to let him get hold of me. I think he might have killed me this time though," she added reflectively.

"There's Loo," Mrs Coop said again. "Mary says he is too afraid of her to touch her, but you can't be sure, not when he gets like he was to-day."

"I've told him I shall kill him if he touches her and he knows I will," Mary remarked dispassionately.

"Look here," began Bobby uneasily.

"If I didn't, Peter would," Mary said. "Peter has told him so."

"Who is Loo?" asked Olive.

"Who is Peter?" Bobby asked almost at the same time.

Neither question was answered, for a chattering at the window made them all look round. A squirrel was on the sill, peeping into the room, and apparently dissatisfied by what it saw there. It vanished.

"Loo's squirrel," Mary explained. "It's gone to tell Loo there's someone here. Now she won't come."

"Well, I think that's awfully mean of her," declared Olive.

Mary looked offended.

"It's not that at all," she said. "It's because strangers frighten her." Then she added. "If you went and sat in the doorway where she could see you and kept very quiet and still, perhaps she might come. Only you mustn't take any notice."

"I won't stir a finger," Olive promised and seated herself on a rough wooden bench that stood by the door. Sitting there, she said: "What I really wanted to ask you about was those lovely chocolates you make and send to Mr Walters's."

"You haven't come from that man who was here yesterday, have you?" Mary asked doubtfully. "I told Peter about that and he's most awfully angry."

"Who is Peter?" Bobby asked again.

CHAPTER V

STOLEN ESSENCE

MARY LOOKED A trifle surprised, as if not quite sure how to reply to a question to which it might be supposed every one must know the answer.

"Is that the man they call Peter the Hermit?" Olive asked.

"What's he angry about?" Bobby added. "What man do you mean?"

"We don't come from any one," Olive went on, as Mary, still hesitating and a little puzzled, made no answer. "It's just that a friend of mine gave me some of your chocolates she bought at Walters's shop in Tombes and they were lovely."

"Does this Peter the Hermit live near here?" Bobby asked. "He has a cottage somewhere about, hasn't he?"

"Yes," agreed Mary, "only he isn't always there, only sometimes."

"Where does he go when he isn't there?" Bobby asked.

"No one knows. Anywhere. Everywhere. Perhaps Loo knows, but no one else and she promised not to tell."

"Oh, well," Bobby said, remembering now something Sergeant Turner had remarked casually about the old man's wanderings extending at times over the whole country, north, south, east and west.

Olive was interested in chocolates, not in wandering hermits. She said:

"My friend was wondering if you would tell us how you make them so nice. Or is that a secret? The church she goes to is having a bazaar and she thought she would like a big lot to sell at her stall. Could you make them for her yourself if it's a secret?"

"It's a secret in a way," Mary agreed, "only not mine. It's Peter's. That's why he's so angry about the man who was here yesterday."

"Why? What man was that?" Bobby asked.

"He came yesterday," Mary explained. "In a car. He had red hair and his hands were hairy and he was fat and you could hardly see his eyes, and his voice made you think of a frying pan when it hadn't been cleaned properly. I didn't like him, and when Loo came she said there was a nasty smell where he had been, but she often says things like that. I expect it was only fancy. I expect really he is quite nice. People often are, even when they don't look it."

"Oh, yes, quite often," agreed Bobby, "and sometimes they aren't when they do. What happened?"

"He wanted to know about my chocolates and he said he would pay me for telling him," Mary answered and added in a puzzled tone: "I almost think perhaps he didn't quite believe me when I told him I didn't know. He seemed to think I might be telling stories."

"That was very silly of him," said Olive severely.

"Wasn't it?" agreed Mary. "I don't see why he should think such a thing."

"Perhaps," suggested Bobby drily, "he has had occasion to meet people who do tell stories."

"Oh, do you think so?" asked Mary, looking shocked at the idea.

"Perhaps he even tells them himself sometimes," suggested Bobby again and even more drily.

"Oh, no," protested Mary, drawing away from so distasteful an idea. "I know I said I didn't think he looked a very nice man, but I didn't mean anything as bad as that."

"Well, we'll call him Truthful James till we have proof he's otherwise," Bobby said. "What happened next?"

"I brought the little bottle of essence to show him," Mary said. "It's what Peter gives me. I only put a very little with the chocolates when I'm making them and I don't know what it is, but it's what makes them taste like they do."

"Scrumptious," interposed Olive, closing her eyes for a moment to lose herself in a gluttonous dream of the past.

"So I showed it him to let him see for himself," Mary went on, "and he put it in his pocket and walked straight out and I was so astonished at first I couldn't do anything, and then I ran after him and I called, but he didn't take any notice and he got in his car and drove off."

"The—Beast," said Olive energetically.

"He left a pound note, but it was stealing all the same," said Mrs Coop from her sofa.

"It's on the mantelpiece," Mary said.

"Coop took it," Mrs Coop told her. "He saw it there and he put it in his pocket and it excited him because he thought there must be more somewhere. And I told him there wasn't and I told him I would tell you he had taken it and that's what set him off."

"It was my fault," Mary said. "I ought to have known better. We always have to hide any money, but I was so terribly angry, I forgot."

"Can you do anything?" Olive asked Bobby.

"Difficult," Bobby said. "Especially if the pound note he left has been used. Probably he would swear black and blue it was a payment and Miss Floyd agreed to take it. I expect he has had the stuff analyzed by now. If he's got the formula he may fill the bottle up with cold tea or something and give it back and swear he never touched it, and say how sorry he was there had been a misunderstanding."

"I don't think he can really be at all a nice man," decided Mary, though reluctantly.

"I think he's the biggest pig and brute I ever heard of," Olive declared with passion. With a memory of old political associations in her mind and expressing the severest condemnation she could think of, she said: "The sort of thing a dictator would do."

"Only a business man smelling a possible profit," explained Bobby tolerantly. "Money justifies all means, I suppose."

"But it wasn't money," pointed out Mary, who did not quite understand what Bobby meant. "It was an essence from plants and flowers for flavouring."

"Might be used for making a lot of money all the same," Bobby told her.

"Peter wouldn't like that," Mary said. "He says it's good to make things, because that's creation, but not money, because that's destruction. I think that is why he was so very angry at the fat man with the little eyes for taking it. There was only a little of the essence left, though."

"May be enough for him to find out what it's made of," Bobby said. "Your friend Peter never told you?"

"No, I never asked. It's from plants. Peter knows all about plants. He says it's difficult to make and takes a long time. He only does a little at once. First of all he said I was only to use it for chocolates for ourselves or for puddings or tarts, because that was good—I mean, good to have good things to eat. But one year I hadn't any money to pay the rent. It was the year when the spring was so cold it seemed like winter still, and all the summer was wind and rain and there was no sun, so that the fruit didn't ripen and nothing grew and the bees died. You remember?"

Bobby shook his head. Probably that dreadful and disastrous season had meant no more to him than a ruined holiday. No doubt he had been living in a town, secure against the whims of nature. For nature, though she may frown here or there, is sure to smile elsewhere, so that this scarcity may be remedied by that abundance. But for Mary, living by her garden and her bees, nature's frown had been a sentence of death, as so often in days long past it was to our forefathers. She was looking now slightly bewildered by Bobby's shake of the head.

"Oh, you must," she protested. "No one could ever forget that year." She added: "I couldn't pay the rent and so they were going to turn us out."

"Oh-h," said Olive, in long drawn sympathy. "How dreadful."

"Dreadful," echoed the woman on the sofa and Mary, too, echoed the same word, and indeed the dread meaning of that awful sentence she had just pronounced can only be understood by those who themselves have had to fear it.

"It was Loo," Mary went on. "She found Peter and told him, and he said I might make the chocolates to sell, and he gave Loo some more of the essence and the money I got for the chocolates was enough to pay the rent. He said it was primrose root and violets, only other things as well."

"Has Loo birds for pets as well as squirrels?" Olive asked. "Because there are birds flying over where the hollyhocks are growing beyond the marigolds and nasturtiums, and I think I can see the hollyhocks moving."

"If it's her, please don't take any notice," Mary said anxiously. "Or else she may go away and not come back for ever so long. Mother is always dreadfully worried when she stays out all night in the forest."

"You don't mean," Olive gasped, "that you let her do that?"

"We can't stop her," explained Mrs Coop, from her sofa. "She just stays. I tell her she mustn't, but she does. Sometimes she says it got too late to come back, or else she forgot, or there were things she couldn't leave, like that nest of little thrushes just hatched she found deserted."

"Well, it's not safe," declared Olive with energy. "How old is she?"

"Nine," Mrs Coop answered.

"But . . . but . . ." protested Olive, still bewildered. "Aren't you afraid she'll get lost?"

"Lost? Oh, no," answered Mrs Coop in tones of great surprise, and Mary added:

"She knows the forest better than I know this kitchen."

"But . . ." began Olive again, and then gave it up to subside into dismayed contemplation of this vision of a child of nine who spent whole nights alone in the forest and knew it better than her elders knew their own kitchens.

"It's all through Peter," Mrs Coop said, evidently aware of Olive's dismay. "I know it isn't right. Peter encourages her. He says trees are friendlier than people and the forest safer than the town."

"You ought to stop him saying things like that," declared Olive. "It's silly and wicked as well. In a town there would always be some one, and she would be perfectly safe if she stayed at home. You ought to make him stop."

"Yes, I know, only we can't, no one could," Mrs Coop answered. "There's only one way," she added slowly.

"We may have to," agreed Mary. "It's awful to think of. But we've got to, if it's the only way to save Loo."

"The child can't spend all her life running about a forest," declared Olive vigorously.

"No," agreed Mary. "No."

"Well, then," Mrs Coop muttered, half to herself.

CHAPTER VI
BEARS

BOTH MRS COOP and Mary had become very pale, as if at the thought or prospect of some future possibility whereof even the idea filled them with extreme terror and dismay. Olive found herself wondering uneasily what could be in their minds, and wondering still more uneasily if it was the energy of her own protests that had driven them to contemplate some action that hitherto had lain only dimly in the recesses of their minds. Bobby had not been paying much attention to what they were saying though, as was the habit of his mind and training, their words stored themselves as it were automatically in his memory, so that in time to come, when there was occasion, he found himself able to recollect every syllable uttered, every look exchanged. Now Mary was talking in a more normal tone, a little as if she wished to make Olive forget what had just been said.

"You see," Mary was saying, "it's through Loo we got to know Peter. Even when she was quite a tiny she liked to wander out there among the trees and she came across Peter and used to watch him gathering plants and flowers, and she asked him why, and he told her, and he gave her medicine for mother, because Dr Maskell wasn't doing her any good."

Bobby, privately convinced that what Loo needed was a little healthy discipline, though he did not dare say so out loud, had his attention caught by the doctor's name. He had already noticed on the kitchen dresser one or two bottles that looked as though they contained medicine and yet not as though they came from any doctor. He asked now:

"Does Dr Maskell know about your getting stuff from someone else?"

"He was awfully angry when we told him," Mary admitted. "He won't come any more. He said mother would die and she hasn't."

"It stops the pain," Mrs Coop explained. "The pain was awful and all Dr Maskell could do was to send me to sleep. But now the pain's much easier. It doesn't come anything like so often. Peter says he can't make me better, because he doesn't know any plants or herbs to cure what's broken. He says I must do that myself, all he can do is to do his best to make me stronger so that I can try. It was a fall," she explained, "and something snapped in my back and only Peter has ever been able to do me any good."

Bobby reflected that if death occurred there might be a good deal of official trouble resulting both for the hermit and the family. But there seemed no immediate danger of that happening, and anyhow it was their business and not his. Olive still brooding over the strange case of Loo, broke in abruptly:

"Doesn't she go to school?"

"Who? Loo?" asked Mary. "Oh, no. She won't."

Mrs Coop said darkly:

"A man came . . ."

She left the sentence unfinished, brooding indignantly on the memory.

"He kept on asking questions," Mary continued. "He said it was his duty. We told him it would kill Loo to shut her up in school and he said that was nothing to do with him, he had to do his duty, and I asked him why, and he said: 'Well, he had', and then he asked a lot more questions."

"Loo went away into the forest as soon as she saw him coming," Mrs Coop went on. "Afterwards Coop went to the police and said she was out of control and robbed rabbit traps. He said if they thought it was him, they were wrong. It wasn't, it was Loo. He said she was out of control and ought to be sent away."

"It was very wrong of him," Mary took up the tale, "but it was very wrong of Loo, and very naughty, too, to trip him up into a bed of nettles that night as he was coming home. He simply looked awful next day."

"I say, though, did she do that?" asked Bobby, glad he wasn't on duty, or else he supposed he would have had to be shocked.

"What happened?" Olive asked, passing over the deplorable incident of the nettles. "I mean, about school?"

"A lady came," Mary answered. "She had very big boots with square toes, and she made you think she was always saying you mustn't. Loo went into the garden and the lady followed her, and we told her not to, the lady, I mean, but she wouldn't listen, and Loo went out of the garden, and the lady followed, and I told her not to, and she said to hold my tongue, and I did, and Loo went into the forest, and the lady followed, and next morning I had to go to the village to ask them to send to look for her because she hadn't come back, and we still had her bag all full of papers."

"What about Loo?" Bobby asked, interested.

"Oh, we didn't mind so much about Loo," Mary explained. "She sleeps in a tree or somewhere and then she comes home when she is ready. It was the lady we were worried about, because we didn't think she would really like sleeping in a tree."

"One never knows," murmured Bobby, "but perhaps not."

"She was quite all right though when they found her," Mary continued. "At least, not quite all right exactly, because she had fallen into a little stream where it made a pool, and she lost her skirt getting out, and she was scratched all over where she hadn't any clothes any more, because of the bushes, and she had been crying a lot because she never expected to see her home again, and there had been beetles and spiders and frogs crawling all over her all night, she said, but I'm sure that wasn't Loo."

"The frogs might be," Mrs Coop observed, as one who wished to be quite fair.

"Well, the frogs perhaps," conceded Mary. "Anyhow, after the lady had been to a convalescent home for a week or two she was quite all right and it's nonsense to say that was what turned her hair grey, because it was grey before, only dyed."

"Oh, oh-h," said Olive, and then "Oo-oo."

"Why do you say that?" Mary asked.

"Nothing else you can say," Olive countered.

"What happened next?" asked Bobby, more and more interested.

"They said she was a defective child, unsuited for institutional control," Mary explained, "and they've left us alone ever since. Step-father was angrier than ever about it, because when they found him in Mrs Hyman's garden with two of her hens in his pocket, he was sent away for two weeks. He said he was unsuited for institutional control, too, like Loo, but he had to go all the same. He said it wasn't fair, but he's never touched Mrs Hyman's hens since."

"Well, you know," Olive remarked, "Loo does seem rather a dangerous sort of person. Is she rather small, even for a nine-year-old, with her hair long and light brown, and now with the sun caught in it, so that it shines, and her face more oval than yours, but the same sort of look? I think it's the eyes, they're like yours, only not so dark. And does she stand so lightly you think the wind would blow her away, but it doesn't, because really her feet are quite firm upon the ground? Because, if Loo's like that, then it's Loo that's just come out from the flowers by the fence over against the apple trees."

Mary came to the door of the cottage.

"Yes, that's Loo," she said, and called: "Loo, come in to your tea."

But Loo had vanished again.

"You naughty girl," said Mary.

"She must come in when she wants something to eat, mustn't she?" Bobby asked.

"She says the forest is full of things to eat," Mary told them. "She never seems very hungry when she comes back."

"In the winter?" Olive asked.

"It's the same. I think she is like her squirrels and hides away stores of nuts and berries and roots she dries in the sun and other things, too. But I don't know. She never says." Mary raised her voice: "Loo, Loo," she called. "Do come in. I don't want to keep tea waiting any longer and I've made some honey cakes."

Loo, evidently tempted, appeared again, but still hesitated.

"There's a big, bad man there," she explained, looking at Bobby.

"Eh? What? Who? Me?" asked Bobby, even more surprised than hurt.

"Oh, he's not," protested Olive, stung to the depths in her wifely pride. "He's big, but he's not bad a bit."

"Yes, he is," Loo insisted. "He was going to throw things at Henry George only you stopped him. You know he's bad, or why did you stop him?"

And from the branches of the apple tree just behind her a squirrel chattered indignantly, as if in support of this accusation.

"True bill," Bobby admitted, "but look here, Loo, as man to man, Henry George, if that's the name of your friend in the tree, began it. He made an ugly noise at me and that hurt my feelings quite a lot."

Loo appeared to consider this and to be so far impressed as to come forward a little, though still so lightly poised she continued to give the impression of an ability to vanish like a leaf blown on a gust of wind.

"If there's one thing," continued Bobby, perceiving his advantage and determined to follow it up, "that hurts me more than another, it's being chattered at when I've done nothing to deserve it. I think that's much worse than throwing a twig, especially when the twig doesn't get thrown."

Loo came a yard or two farther forward. She looked a little troubled. She was plainly now on the defensive.

"Well, you wouldn't turn back," she said.

"No," agreed Bobby, "we wouldn't. The forest is free to all—at least to those who are not afraid of the forest."

Again Loo appeared to consider this. Presently she said:

"There are bears in the forest."

"There are bears everywhere," Bobby answered.

"There's been a bear at Peter's cottage," she told him.

"Has there?" Bobby said. "What did it do?"

"I don't know," she answered. "I was afraid. I ran away. I couldn't find Peter anywhere and so I ran away."

"And then you tried to frighten us, too, by telling us there was a bear in the way?" Bobby asked.

"I thought it might be you had been there," she explained. "You see, we don't know you. But Henry George oughtn't to have chattered at you till we were sure. Only he was frightened, too, at Peter's cottage. Henry George," she called.

She turned as she did so to the apple tree, but Henry George, apparently feeling that the conversation had taken an unfavourable turn, had removed himself to an upper branch, where only the tip of a depressed and drooping tail was visible. Loo, her hands behind her, gazed upwards into the tree. Two bright eyes showed themselves. Loo said:

"He won't again. Chatter, I mean. It was because of being afraid."

"Why were you afraid?" Olive asked. "You aren't often afraid in the forest, are you? What frightened you?"

Loo made no answer for a moment. Then she said: "Peter wasn't there and we couldn't find him." She repeated, as if wishing to change the subject: "Henry George won't chatter at you ever again."

"And I won't ever even think of throwing twigs at him again," Bobby assured her.

"I wish you would tell me a lot about Henry George," Olive said. "How did you become such friends? Why do you call him Henry George?"

"Because it's his name," Loo explained. By this time she was quite close to the cottage door where Olive was sitting and Bobby standing. "I like you," she said to Olive, but she still seemed a little doubtful about Bobby, and had the air of being ready to leap away at any moment if he were not very careful. "Is he ever angry?" she asked Olive.

"Oh, well," said Olive, slightly embarrassed, and remembering one unfortunate day when their toothbrushes had got mixed, and she was sure, and so was Bobby, and they had both been very cold and dignified about it, after having first been very hot and undignified.

"What about you?" argued Bobby, knowing the best defence is attack. "Aren't you ever angry?"

"Oh, yes," she admitted readily, "but I think when you are angry you are angry like a bear and not like me or Henry George."

"Why do you talk such a lot about bears?" Olive asked. "You've never seen one, have you?"

"We couldn't find Peter," she answered. "He's not at his cottage and he's not anywhere else and we couldn't find him anywhere."

"Well, you don't think a bear has eaten him, do you?" Bobby asked.

She looked at him, hesitated, and then gave a quick nod.

"Well, now then," Bobby said, surprised.

"Tea's ready," Mary called from inside the kitchen where she had been bustling about without paying much attention to their talk. "Come along, or the honey cakes will be spoiled."

CHAPTER VII
FOREST HUT

THE HONEY CAKES duly done justice to—and for all her sylph-like appearance Loo displayed for them an extremely healthy appetite—Bobby and Olive started on their way home. From the cottage door Mary and Loo waved them a farewell. Looking back at those two slight girlish figures, Bobby remarked with a faint grin:

"A formidable pair. They look as if they were made of sugar and spice and all that's nice, and yet one of them will lock a man up in a cellar for a week on bread and water, and the other will take an unlucky school attendance officer into the depths of the forest and just park her there."

"Well, you can't blame—" began Olive, very much on the defensive, but Bobby interrupted her.

"Cops never blame," he said. "Not our job. Only I'm wondering what the pair of them might do if they got really peeved. Sort of if this happens in the dry, what about the green? Or is it the other way round?"

"Do you think—?" began Olive, and once more Bobby interrupted her.

"All I think is that they are the rummiest pair of kids I ever came across," he said, "and I don't know that I should very much care about running up against either of 'em."

"Yes, but," Olive said, "why was Loo afraid?"

"I don't know," Bobby answered, and he looked uneasy. "Something put the wind up her all right," he admitted, "and a kid used to spending all night alone in a place like this—" He waved a hand towards the vast sea of green, silent, impenetrable, lost, that lay all around them. With old ancestral terrors stirring faintly in his mind, the old strange fears the author of *Beowulf* and his fellows knew so well, Bobby found himself wondering what dangers might not lurk in those dim shadows. "Well, you wouldn't expect her to scare too easily," he concluded.

They walked on in silence and presently Olive said:

"Perhaps it was that man going off with the bottle of flavouring that frightened her."

"I don't think so," Bobby said. "She wasn't there at the time, for one thing."

"If he finds out what's in it, can he just make it himself as much as he likes?" Olive asked.

"Nothing to stop him," Bobby answered. "At least, Loo's hermit friend could patent it, I imagine, like patent medicine. But he would have to get in first and you may be pretty sure he hasn't. Most likely he doesn't even know he could."

"Then," said Olive with decision, "he ought to be told. I think it's such a shame. I know how angry I should be if I had a special recipe and someone just came along and snatched it—especially if they used it to make money."

"The world's full of shames," Bobby pointed out.

"No reason why there should be one more," retorted Olive.

"Well, what do you want to do?"

"Find Mr Peter and tell him what he ought to do."

"Loo said he wasn't there."

"You could leave a message. Pin it to the door or something."

"Time we were getting home," Bobby grumbled, but he produced the map with which he had provided himself before starting. The hermit's cottage was not marked, but the boundary between the forest proper and the Rawdon property was clearly shown, and Bobby knew that the cottage stood exactly at a protruding extremity of the estate where it ran down into the forest land. His map showed him it was not far out of the way, and, finding presently a path that led in the required direction, they followed it.

"There ought to be a stream somewhere about and then the cottage shouldn't be more than about a hundred yards away," he remarked.

Immediately afterwards they found the stream, a small, shallow, but quickly running brook, in places so narrow it could be stepped across. Here and there it made small pools of clear, fresh water, a foot or two deep. Bending over one of these pools was a youngish man with black hair and eyes, a dark complexion, a large, prominent nose. He was smartly dressed, rather too smartly, indeed, for a forest ramble, and on the grass by his side lay an umbrella and a small dispatch case. He was busily washing his hands and when he heard their approach he looked round in a quick, startled way. Then without a word, his hands still dripping as he withdrew them from the water, without stopping to wipe them, he snatched up umbrella and dispatch case. But that flew open with the violent jerk he gave it as he caught it up, and the contents, papers and photographs chiefly, scattered on the ground. He scooped them up with a kind of panic-stricken haste, yet not so quickly as to prevent Bobby catching a clear, though momentary, view of one—a large unmounted print or engraving—crammed them into the dispatch case, and dashed away as hard as he could tear. Yet not along the path, but across the stream and into the woodland opposite, where trees and bushes soon hid him from sight, where pursuit, if Bobby had contemplated it, would not have been easy.

"What's the matter with him?" Olive asked, staring after his disappearing figure. "Did we frighten him?"

"Looks like it," said Bobby.

"Why?" asked Olive.

"In my uniform days, in London," Bobby observed meditatively, "I think I should have run after him just to find out why."

"He was only washing his hands," Olive said.

"A symbolic act sometimes," Bobby remarked.

"What do you mean?" Olive demanded. "There's no harm in washing your hands. When he saw us he ran like—like—"

"Like billy-oh," Bobby suggested.

He went a little nearer that clear, shining pool in which the handwashing had taken place. He stared at the water, at the smooth grassy bank. He saw nothing to interest him. The water flowed. The grass had taken no visible print. Bobby said:

"Did you see that photo or something of the sort the chap dropped?"

"Was it a photo?" Olive asked. "I thought it was a picture. I only had a glimpse. He snatched it up in such a hurry before he ran off."

"Photograph of a picture perhaps," Bobby said. "It looked like an El Greco. I didn't see it clearly enough to be sure, but that's what it looked like. I don't suppose I should have spotted it, only for that talk about two El Grecos being missing from Sir Alfred Rawdon's place. But I did seem to catch a glimpse of those elongated arms and legs El Greco used to perpetrate, and there was a kind of huddle of a stormy sky behind that looked his sort of style. I wonder if that's why he was scared, because we saw it."

"He was startled and frightened as soon as he saw us coming," Olive pointed out. "That's why his dispatch case came open, because he snatched it up in such a hurry and gave it a jerk. Besides, why should he mind our seeing it?"

"Only an idea," Bobby answered. "It reminded me of that chap Turner told us about, the one at the 'Rawdon Arms' I mean. You remember? Turner said there had been a fellow there asking questions about El Greco pictures. I wonder if this is the same lad? Something must have started him off talking like that. If he is on the track of lost paintings, so perhaps is someone else as well. If it's like that, he may have thought we were rivals on the same trail, and he didn't want to be spotted himself. Didn't want possible rivals to know he was on the hunt, too."

They thought little more of the incident, which did not in itself seem to be of any great importance or interest. A hundred yards or so farther on they came in sight of a small cottage, if indeed, so small, ill built, half ruinous it seemed, it deserved any other name than that of hovel.

CHAPTER VIII
MISSING AXE

APPARENTLY IT HAD never known the touch of paint. Its walls were of thin boarding that in some places had been patched by what looked like bits of old fencing. Elsewhere the primitive method of moss and dry clay had been used. The one window showed more rags than glass. The roof was of corrugated iron, kept in position by the simple device of placing upon it a number of heavy stones. The door hung half open upon broken hinges, so that there was no possibility of closing it securely. Stove piping poked out from one side and in places was tied up with rope. A roughly built stone oven and fireplace two or three yards away suggested that during the summer at least most of the necessary cooking was done out of doors. Near by was a small pile of sticks cut into convenient size for use as fuel. There was no attempt at a garden. The situation was superb. Close behind the hut, sheltering it beneath wide spreading branches stood a stately beech, a magnificent and lovely tree. In front, open ground, a stretch of level and smooth turf, that in the spring must have been beautiful with cowslip and bluebell and daisy, ran down to the banks of the tiny running brook and then rose again to the denser masses of the wood beyond. Indeed, the only blot upon a peaceful woodland scene was the squalid little hut itself. Olive, viewing it with much distaste, said:

"No one can really live there, can they?"

"Oh, I don't know," Bobby answered.

He had seen as bad, though perhaps never worse. Except perhaps the half-hut, half-cave he had come across once on a dumping ground for London rubbish. And he knew of habitations by the marshy banks of the Thames estuary where the power and the glory of the London docks tail off towards the sea. He was thinking, too, of the building laws. Probably, though, the hut had been put up without notice or permission and now by lapse of time had acquired the status of a *fait accompli.*

"Well, it's no wonder, anyhow," Olive remarked, "that Sir Alfred Rawdon doesn't want any rent."

"Habitation for a hermit," Bobby said, but he spoke absently, for now that they were nearer he could see more plainly through the sagging door of the hut into the interior and what he saw he did not much like. The disorder and confusion within seemed to him greater even than the exterior had suggested. Something, he reminded himself, had frightened Loo. Nor was it only Loo who had experienced fear. The stranger they had seen by the banks of the stream near by had fallen into panic swiftly and easily, as if already he knew of a reason for alarm. The cottage, squat and ugly and deserted looking, crouching there in the shade of the great overhanging tree, as though it lurked in hiding for an evil purpose, began to take on for Bobby a strange, vague atmosphere of apprehension and of fear. Olive, it seemed, felt the same, for she touched Bobby's arm and said softly:

"I don't like this place. It's ugly. Let's go away. There's no one there."

"May as well have a look," Bobby said.

They came nearer and stood in the doorway. They could see then that the place had been carefully and systematically wrecked. Scant and wretched as were the furnishings of the hut, nothing remained intact. The bed had been little more than a heap of rags and now those rags had been tossed hither and thither. The cooking utensils had been three in number—a kettle, an iron pot, a frying pan. They had been flung into a corner with part of what had been the bed. Even the table, though made only of rough boards nailed across two small wooden cases, had been broken and the two wooden cases smashed up. As in the habitations of primitive people, the floor was merely of beaten earth that by long use had grown hard and smooth, but there were marks to show attempts had been made in spots to dig it up or at least to probe it deeply with some sharp instrument. The work of destruction could not have taken long, there was so little to destroy. But it had been thorough. Oddly enough, the most breakable objects in the place, the crockery, a few cups and plates on a shelf had not been touched. Ranged in order still, they looked down from their prim and equal rows upon the ruin beneath.

"What's been happening?" Bobby asked Olive, who was standing in the doorway, looking quite distressed over this scene of what appeared merely stupid, senseless destruction.

"It looks as if a lunatic had been here," she said. "Or has someone been smashing up the poor old man's belongings just out of spite?"

"That wouldn't explain why there's been a start to dig up the floor, or why the crockery hasn't been touched," Bobby remarked. "It looks to me as if the place had been pretty thoroughly searched."

"What for?" Olive asked.

"Gold perhaps," Bobby answered. "It seems there was a story about the old boy paying in gold for all he bought. Stories like that soon get about. Secret hoards. That sort of yarn. Turner said something about attempts at robbery, didn't he? All this looks to me like another. Perhaps that's what scared Loo and made her talk about bears. She may have seen the thieves at work."

"Would that frighten Loo?" Olive asked. "She dealt with that school attendance woman firmly enough. I wonder what's become of the old hermit?"

Bobby was turning over a pile of debris in one corner.

"What are you doing?" Olive asked.

"Looking for an axe," Bobby explained.

"An axe! Why? Whatever for?"

"The old boy must have had some sort of chopper for cutting up firewood," Bobby remarked. "He evidently used wood for fuel, and those bits of dry branches outside are all cut clean to a convenient length. There must have been an axe or hatchet or something like it to do that with."

"He may have it with him," Olive suggested.

"So he may," agreed Bobby. "Anyhow, there doesn't seem anything of the sort lying about. I just thought it a bit queer. Look here," he added, holding out a book, which lay, all torn and battered, the binding half wrenched off, behind the old, rusty, apparently little-used stove. "Horace," he said.

Bobby had forgotten most of the Latin he had once at school and university so laboriously acquired, but he retained enough of it to recognize the *Odes*. The book had been printed in the eighteenth century and the binding had been calf, decorated very richly in the style known as *pointillé*.

"Do hermits read Latin?" Bobby asked. He was turning over the leaves, many of them now torn and soiled from the treatment the book seemed to have recently received. "Look here," he said. "Pencil notes in English. Attempts at translation. Rummy. No one can ever read Horace without having a shot at translating him."

"There's another book here," Olive said, picking it up.

Bobby took it from her. A Virgil this time—the *Georgics*. It was of later date than the Horace, but it, too, had been richly bound, in a fine tooled leather now damp stained and dilapidated.

"Strong on Latin, our hermit," Bobby remarked.

"It doesn't follow that he read them," Olive suggested.

"They have both been read and pretty thoroughly," Bobby remarked. He was turning over the pages, trying hard to remember his Latin, but without much success. He was able to recognize the portions more specially dealing with the care of bees, and these he noticed had often pencil notes against them, as though the old Roman poet's instructions had been studied with some care. Showing them to Olive he told her what they were and added: "I wonder if Miss Mary got handed any tips out of old Virgil. Do you notice anything—the binding, I mean?"

"No. What?" Olive asked.

Bobby pointed to the crest and motto stamped thereon. The crest showed an arm in armour holding a pen. Beneath was a Latin motto. Bobby translated it as 'Both sword and pen'.

"The crest and motto of the Rawdon family," he said. "Looks as if the books came from Barsley Abbey—like the lost El Grecos."

"Well, you don't think the El Grecos are here too, do you?" Olive asked.

"Doesn't look like it," Bobby agreed. "It would be a bit rummy to find a hovel like this with pictures worth a good many thousands on its walls. Though it's quite on the cards they may be on the walls of some cottage or farmhouse round about here. Or for that matter used to stop a hole in a cowshed."

Olive looked suitably appalled by the suggestion and Bobby began to search again through the debris that cumbered the floor of the hut.

"Someone been smoking cigars," he said, presently discovering a small pile of ash. "Do hermits smoke cigars as they read their Horace and their Virgil? Getting curiouser and curiouser, isn't it? Hullo, look at this."

'This' was a visiting card, bearing the name and address of a Mr Charles Crayford, of 'Bellavista', Tombes, the small straggling town, not far away, inhabited chiefly by Midwych business people, so that it was almost a suburb of that great commercial and manufacturing centre. Bobby took out his notebook and copied into it name and address.

"What's that for?" Olive asked.

"Oh, you never know," Bobby answered. "Somehow I don't quite like the look of things. I can't help wondering what scared Loo, and why that chap bolted like a hare when we caught him washing his hands. It seems such an innocent occupation. And why this place has been mucked up the way it has, and what's become of the old man himself, and why the axe he must have used to chop his firewood with doesn't seem to be anywhere about?"

So far he had been paying attention chiefly to the pile of torn and broken articles of one sort and another that had been flung aside against the wall and into the corners of the hut. Now he began to look more closely at the floor of hard-beaten earth. Here and there a beginning, soon abandoned, seemed to have been made at digging it up. Near the door Bobby found something else that sent him down upon his hands and knees, peering closely at the ground.

"What is it now?" Olive asked.

"I don't know," Bobby said. "I don't know for certain, but I think it's blood."

CHAPTER IX

RICHARD RAWDON

BOBBY WAS STILL in the same position, a somewhat undignified position, on his hands and knees, his nose nearly touching the ground, so intently was he examining that strange, dull, discoloured patch he had noticed on the earthen floor of the hut. Olive was still watching him with an uneasiness she did not in the least understand, but that she knew might at any moment swell to panic. On their abstraction broke a sound of footsteps. They both looked round. A tall young man had come to the doorway of the hut and was standing there, staring at Bobby with mingled surprise and disapproval. He was a well-dressed youngster, good looking, fair complexion, fair haired, grey eyed, with the prominent nose and high cheek-bones so often seen in England. There was about him, too, much of that air of superb self-confidence other nations often find in the islanders and are occasionally apt to resent. There was demand and decision in the quick tones of his voice now, as of one who knew he spoke with authority, when he said:

"Hullo, what's all this?"

Bobby did not answer. After that one quick upward glance to see who the new-comer was, he seemed to lose interest in him, and to become again intent on the dull stain he was examining with such care. Very likely it was of no significance whatever. He was by no means sure that it was really blood. Tobacco juice, for example, can produce very similar stains. So can other agents. With the aid of his pocket knife he began carefully to lever up a piece of the stained earth. The young man in the doorway, unused to being thus ignored, said more loudly and more sharply:

"Here, what are you up to? What's the game? Who are you anyhow?"

Bobby paused in his work to regard his questioner with some annoyance. He had not the least wish to proclaim his identity. If it became known, he knew well all sorts of stories would quickly be in circulation concerning visits by the police to the old hermit. Undesirable to allow such stories to get about. If nothing was wrong, then the old man would have reasonable cause for annoyance. There might even be complaints. And if his own vague suspicion that here mischief had been afoot had any foundation in fact, all the more reason for avoiding premature gossip. But this new-comer, Bobby recognized reluctantly, had not the air of one very easily put off.

"Well," the young man demanded, "what are you doing?"

"Do you live here?" Bobby asked.

"What's that to do with it?" demanded the other, his tone getting more and more aggressive.

"I was only wondering," Bobby explained, "who you are and what you are doing here and why you are asking questions?"

By this time the new-comer had advanced from the threshold into the interior of the hut. He became aware of Olive, who hitherto had been outside his range of vision. He looked even more surprised on seeing her. He became aware of the extreme disorder, not to say chaos around.

"What on earth . . . ?" he began. "What's been happening?"

"I should like to know that myself," observed Bobby.

He got to his feet, selected a heavy piece of wood from the debris lying around, and began solemnly to thump the ground round the piece of stained earth he had been about to remove. The new-comer gaped. Bobby had just remembered that in removing a piece of blood-stained earth, it is necessary to be sure that no worm is included, since worms feed on organic matter. If one does lie concealed in the lifted clod, there may presently be nothing left but worm and earth, the blood having disappeared. Worms are, as most people know, very sensitive to earth vibrations, and a hammering on the ground above them will soon send them wriggling off as fast as they can go.

Bobby did not much suppose that there would be many worms beneath this hard-beaten, primitive, earthen floor, but he had long ago learnt that in police work nothing may be left to chance. Naturally the young man in the doorway had no idea of all this, and no doubt Bobby's action seemed sufficiently peculiar as he solemnly pounded away on the ground with the heavy bit of wood he had picked up. The stranger appealed to Olive.

"What's the matter with him?" he asked. "Is he mad?"

Olive considered the point gravely, her head to one side.

"I shouldn't wonder," she decided, "but you see, he is my husband, so I do try to give him the benefit of the doubt."

Bobby heard this and paused in his pounding to look very hurt and offended.

"A calm, cold, calculating sanity is my most marked characteristic," he announced. "It has often been commented on."

"Not by me," said Olive firmly.

"A short-sighted woman," pronounced Bobby, and—the worms in the vicinity having presumably been eliminated by now—he knelt down again and continued with his task of levering up a portion of the earthen floor.

"Look here," said the young man resolutely, "I want to know what all this means. I happen to know this isn't your place—"

"I should hope not," said Olive, and was rewarded for her interruption by a coldly indignant stare.

"It strikes me something precious queer has been going on," the newcomer continued, letting his glance wander round the wrecked interior, "and I'm beginning to think it would be just as well to call in the police."

"Oh, lor'," said Bobby resignedly.

"No need to shout about it, anyhow," commented Olive.

"Madam," said the young man, making an almost superhuman effort to keep control of his temper, "I was not shouting."

"Sir," retorted Olive in wicked mimicry, "I didn't say you were. I said you needn't. Because," she explained, nodding at Bobby, busily engaged packing his slice of earth in an old tin box he had rescued from the wreckage, "because he's one."

"One what?" demanded the now thoroughly exasperated young man, this time making no attempt not to shout.

"Police," explained Olive. "In the more stately language of the popular Press—a cop."

Bobby looked round from his task he was now completing by writing his name across the joining of the paper wrapping, so that the package could not be opened without the fact being apparent.

"Well, now we've been properly introduced," he said, "do you mind reciprocating. Are you Mr Charles Crayfoot by any chance?"

"No. I'm not. Why?"

"He is a recent visitor apparently," answered Bobby. "Left his card here. There it is. I've just found it. Looks as if there was no one here when he called, so he left his card instead. I just wondered if it might be you."

The young man was fumbling in his pockets. He produced various objects, including a cigar case holding two or three cigars and serving apparently also for a card case, since from it he finally produced a visiting card.

"There you are," he said, proffering it.

"Mr Richard Rawdon," Bobby read aloud. "Any relation of Sir Alfred Rawdon of Barsley Abbey?"

"Sir Alfred Rawdon is my uncle," came the stiff reply.

"Oh, yes," Bobby said. "Then unless your uncle marries and has children, you are his heir?"

"For what it's worth, yes," the other answered. "Now perhaps you will explain. Why is the place in such a mess? Where's the old chap himself? Why are police here?"

"Not officially," Bobby explained, answering the last question first, and indeed it was the only question of the three to which he knew the reply. "Just accident. I don't know in the least what's been happening here or what's become of the occupier." He produced his warrant card and showed it. "Mrs. Owen and I," he continued, "have been spending the day in the forest as I happened to have time off for once in a way. A Miss Floyd gave us tea and something she said about chocolates she makes at home for sale made us think of calling here. My wife thought she would like to make some of those chocolates herself if she could get the recipe. It seems an invention of the old chap who lives here on his own—the Wychwood Forest hermit they call him sometimes. Or Peter the Hermit. Historical reminiscence, I suppose. Were you wanting to see him?"

The young new comer hesitated. Till now his gaze had been frank, direct, authoritative. Now it wavered, became hesitating, almost sly. There was a perceptible pause before he said:

"I was just passing. Like you. Been having a walk in the forest. Like you. Accident."

"Oh, yes, indeed," Bobby said, trying to make his voice sound as incredulous as in fact he felt.

Young Mr Rawdon flushed. He evidently realized that he was not entirely believed. Somewhat hastily he said:

"What were you digging up bits of the floor for?"

Bobby left the question unanswered. Too obviously an attempt to change the subject. Besides he had no wish to explain. He asked:

"Have you been here before to-day?"

Again Rawdon hesitated, quite plainly considering what reply to make.

CHAPTER X

OLD BOOKS

BOBBY WAITED PATIENTLY for an answer to come. Rawdon went across to the door and stood there for a moment or two, staring out at the scene beyond, but not much as though he saw it. Bobby almost expected to see him begin to walk away and decided that if he did so, he would not be called back. Instead he turned to face them and began to talk.

"I've always heard a good deal about an old chap living out here alone as a kind of hermit," he said. "The story is he can cure all sorts of things. Gives people stuff he brews from plants. Faith healing very likely, but it works all right. All the doctors round here have their knife in him. Dr Maskell says he is a public danger, says he kills a sight more than he cures. Professional prejudice for all I know, but they do say Maskell has lost half his practice through people coming here instead. The doctors can't do anything though. I believe they actually had a sort of confab about it. Nothing doing. The old man doesn't pretend to be qualified in any way and doesn't even sell his stuff. Gives it away if he likes your looks, and, if he doesn't, chases you off with an axe. At least that's the story."

"Interesting," murmured Bobby. "I don't see any axe lying about though."

"I was told he makes a lotion," the young man continued, paying no attention to this comment. "Awfully good if you're a bit stiff after a game of cricket or anything like that. So I thought I would come along and see if I could get hold of some of the stuff."

"Not entirely accident then," Bobby suggested.

"I mean, its being to-day and coming across you is an accident," Rawdon answered, a little angrily, though whether the flushed cheek he showed was wholly anger, or in part at least embarrassment, Bobby was by no means sure. "This is our land, you know. Part of the Rawdon estate. And it may be sold. It doesn't come under the entail."

"But isn't that going to be broken?" Bobby asked. "I think I heard your uncle was thinking of getting that done. I suppose your consent as heir would be required."

"Oh, I'm joining in," Rawdon answered. "Got to. Hard up and all that, you know. But it's a slow job, and this bit of land will go as soon as there's a purchaser. None in sight at present. No great demand just now for an awkwardly shaped bit of woodland like this. Midwych Corporation ought to want it to join up with the rest, but their idea is a nominal figure or a free gift for that matter. Uncle says he can't afford. If Midwych wants it, it must pay like anyone else. If a private purchaser turns up, the old man may be cleared out. He doesn't pay any rent and so far as I know he hasn't got any lease."

"Squatter's title?" Bobby asked. "I have heard he has some sort of written permission."

Young Rawdon shrugged his shoulders.

"I don't know," he said. "I haven't gone into it at all. It just struck me I would ask the old boy himself if I could find him. I was told that very often he wasn't here. Went off on his own somewhere and no one knew where."

"I suppose he doesn't usually smash up his belongings before he goes off though," Bobby remarked. "You didn't say if this was your first visit here."

"Well, it is," Rawdon declared sulkily, too sulkily indeed for Bobby to feel that his answer was altogether satisfactory.

"Smoke cigars sometimes, don't you?" Bobby asked.

"Suppose I do, what about it?"

"Well, there seems to have been a cigar-smoking visitor here lately, that's all," Bobby answered, pointing to the heap of cigar ash he had noticed.

Rawdon looked at it and scowled.

"Nothing to do with me," he said. "What are you trying to get at?"

"The facts," Bobby answered. "That ash shows there has been a cigar-smoking visitor here recently—that's two, counting yourself. Interesting, because cigar smokers are quite rare birds. Cigarettes generally—or a pipe. Whoever it was must have arrived after the place had been upset the way it is, or the ash wouldn't have stayed undisturbed."

"Do you mean—" Rawdon began and paused. "You don't suppose anything has happened to the old boy, do you?"

"I'm not supposing anything," Bobby answered. "I'm just noticing things. I notice, for instance, that there seems to have been rather a rush of visitors here recently—that is, for a hermit. Two cigar smokers, for instance. Then we met a chap coming away. When he saw us he bolted like a scared rabbit. Police get into suspicious ways, and I wondered why. No apparent reason for scuttling off the way he did. Youngish. City business man by his looks. Dark. Big nose. Umbrella and dispatch case. Know him?"

"A fellow like that called at the Abbey a day or two ago."

"Friend, or on business?"

"You want to know a lot, don't you?"

"Police habit," Bobby explained. "Difficult sometimes, when people won't answer questions frankly."

Mr Richard Rawdon stared, glared, hesitated, then decided to lose his temper.

"I'm not going to answer any more of your questions anyhow," he declared angrily. "I think you've got a thundering cheek. What right do you think you have to go about cross-examining people? Free country, isn't it? Even if some of you police don't seem to notice it."

"Would it be pedantic," Bobby mused, "to point out that this isn't a cross-examination? If it's an examination at all, it's an examination in chief. Of course, it's a free country all right. Every policeman gets that rubbed into him good and hard from the first day he joins. You can't guess till you've tried what a job it is to protect the lives and property of a free people who jolly well don't mean to have their lives or their property interfered with. All the same, as it is a free country, we have the right to ask questions, just as you have the right to refuse to answer them. Understood on both sides? Well, did your visitor at Barsley Abbey ask any questions about those El Greco pictures, said to have disappeared from the Barsley Abbey collection half a century ago?"

The young man stared, gaped, gasped. The question had evidently both surprised and disconcerted him. He began to speak, paused, and then abruptly turned towards the door.

"Oh, go to—" he began, and then seemed to remember Olive and paused just in time, finished his sentence with the word 'Jericho', and was marching angrily away when Bobby called him back.

"One moment, one moment," he called. "There are a couple of books here. There's your family crest on the covers. Do you think they came from the library at the Abbey?"

"How should I know?" Rawdon growled. He glanced at the two battered, torn and soiled copies of what had once been noble tomes, formed for a scholar's delight, made for surroundings as rare and exquisite as themselves, but now only one item more in the heap of strangely assorted odds and ends that cumbered the floor of this squalid, almost primitive dwelling. He picked the books up and thoughtfully turned over the leaves. "Horace. Virgil," he said. "Oh, well, that doesn't prove anything. Someone been having a go at Horace. Notes for a translation in the margin." He read aloud from the well-known lines, beginning 'Vixi puellis nuper idoneus', in which Horace declares his intention of abandoning the lists of love. "Can't turn that into English," he said, "and anyway, nothing to go on. Those scribblings might have been done any time by anyone." He put the books down again and said to Bobby: "Books often get mislaid or lost. Given away sometimes. Or borrowed. Much the same thing generally. I expect every second-hand bookseller in Midwych has something from the Abbey library with our arms on the binding."

He shrugged his shoulders and with a brief nod and word of farewell walked away. Thoughtfully, Bobby watched as he went striding along the path whereby Bobby and Olive themselves had so recently arrived. When he was out of sight Bobby picked up the Horace, wrapped it in a clean handkerchief, and put it in his pocket.

"What's that for?" Olive asked, surprised.

"Oh, I don't know, might be useful some day," Bobby answered vaguely. He scribbled a brief note to the effect that he had borrowed the Horace and that it would be returned on request. "Can't afford to be accused of looting," he remarked as he put the note on the undisturbed crockery shelf, securing it in position with a pin he borrowed from Olive.

"I wish I knew what you had in your head," she observed, watching these proceedings with interest and curiosity.

"I would tell you if I knew myself," Bobby assured her. "What I wish I knew, is whether our young friend is on his way to pay a visit to Miss Floyd."

"Why should he?" Olive asked.

"Oh, I don't know, I only wondered," Bobby answered. "I had an idea he knew who she was when I mentioned her name. Perhaps he didn't. I thought when he went off, he walked like someone with an aim in view. Did you notice he gave two separate and distinct explanations of his visit here? First it was to get one of the hermit's lotions. Then it was to ask him if he had a lease of any sort for this hut. Shouldn't think myself anyone would have the cheek to hand out a lease for a hole like this. But two differing explanations make a policeman's suspicious mind wonder if there is also a third—and a true—explanation."

"Both may be true," Olive pointed out. "I mean, he may have wanted to get the lotion and to ask about a lease as well."

"Yes, there's that," agreed Bobby. "Quite possible. All the same he gave me the idea of being a bit uneasy. I don't much like the look of things somehow—not one little bit, I don't. I wish I had some idea of what it's all about."

"Is that really blood on the floor?" Olive asked.

"Can't say yet, have to get a test made," Bobby answered. "Even if it is blood, it mayn't mean anything. The hermit gentleman may have cut himself shaving. That's the favourite explanation. Or skinning rabbits. Or perhaps he suffered from nose bleeding. When it isn't shaving, it's generally nose bleeding."

"What are you going to do?" Olive asked.

"Nothing. No complaint received. No reasonable cause known for taking action. I'll ask our chaps at Barsley Forest to watch out for the hermit's return though. Miss Floyd will know if he gets back. They can ask her to tell them if he turns up all right. There's nothing to go on. Loo was frightened by something and so she tried to frighten us. There seems to have been rather a rush of visitors round here. For a hermitage, that is. This hut looks as if it had been ransacked pretty thoroughly. No sign of any hermit, but that's not unusual apparently. There's what looks like a stain of blood on the floor. There must have been an axe used for chopping firewood and it seems to have been an eremitical habit—"

"A what habit?" interposed Olive.

"Long word for hermit," explained Bobby. "Got it out of a crossword. Anyhow, a common or garden habit of the old gentleman's to chase away people he didn't like. Using an axe for emphasis. No sign of any axe now. He had hit on some kind of new flavouring that might be worth a bit of money. Or might not. A fifty-year-old story about valuable pictures missing from Barsley Abbey has had a new lease of life recently. That chap we saw washing his hands in the brook dropped a photo that may have been of one of the missing pictures—or again may not. Do you know what strikes me as the queerest part of the whole business?"

"No. What? The way that man ran off when he saw us?"

"No. Bad conscience that might be. Bad consciences are plenty common. No, it's that he was washing his hands. Why should you stop in the middle of a forest stroll to wash your hands?"

"Well, I suppose he had got them dirty," suggested Olive.

"What with?" Bobby asked. "Oh, well, no use guessing. Can't make bricks without straw or guesses with nothing to go on. Then the same chap called recently at Barsley Abbey and young Mr Rawdon didn't one bit like the suggestion that perhaps he had called about the lost El Grecos. Again, Mr Rawdon didn't much like answering questions, wasn't best pleased at finding a policeman here, was rather carefully indifferent to those two books with the Rawdon crest on them. Now, what does all that add up to?"

"Perhaps it all cancels itself out."

"Think so?"

"No."

"More do I. I'll get this bit of earth analysed though to make sure if it's blood or not. There's that Dr Maskell Mr Rawdon mentioned. I believe he is more of a scientific swell than are most G.P.s.

Not so long ago he gave some evidence against us. Expert evidence. Very scientific. Very much the professor to the elementary class. Impressed the jury tremendously. Nasty reference to our excellent police who are probably but little acquainted with scientific matters. The jury giggled."

"Poor little boy," said Olive gently. "Were his little feelings hurt?"

"They were," Bobby answered frankly. "Badly. It wasn't so much the nasty things he said as the nasty way he said them. I should guess that tongue of his had more than the hermit's medicines to do with his losing his patients. I think I'll ask him to see to the job."

"Why not send to Wakefield?" asked Olive, who had heard a good deal of Wakefield as a centre of up-to-date police methods. "Or ask Dr Gibbs," she added, naming the prominent Midwych practitioner who generally dealt with such matters both for the county and the city police.

"Because," Bobby explained, "I may want Dr Maskell and that blistering tongue of his on our side next time, so I may as well get on terms with him. Besides, a local man might be able to give me a good deal of local information if I needed it. Asking him to make the analysis will give me an excuse for going to see him. Low police cunning, I suppose."

With that they went on their way and the next morning Bobby received a report from the Tombes police to the effect that Mr Charles Crayfoot, of 'Bellavista', Tombes, had not returned home that night, that his car, parked at the 'Rawdon Arms', near Barsley Forest, between the village and the Abbey, had not been claimed, and that his wife was seriously uneasy as Mr Charles Crayfoot was a man of regular habits, as indeed befitted the proprietor of the well-known and prosperous confectionery and bakery business, trading as Messrs Walters. It was this last piece of information that disturbed Bobby. As a general rule mysterious disappearances soon explain themselves, but 'Walters', Bobby remembered, was the shop which retailed so successfully Mary Floyd's homemade chocolates with their new and exciting flavour.

CHAPTER XI

DR MASKELL

BECAUSE OF THIS coincidence of lost hermit and missing tradesman, recipe for chocolates as a possible connecting link, Bobby decided to make the preliminary inquiries himself, instead of leaving what seemed on the face of it a routine 'missing' case to the care of his subordinates. At the moment he alone was responsible for such decisions since his chief, Colonel Glynne, was absorbed in perfecting A.R.P.—soon to be terribly tested—in other precautions and preparations for a possible invasion, and in writing passionate letters to anyone who by any stretch of the imagination could be supposed likely to help him to get back into the army. As the colonel was over sixty, the army was, of course, for him for ever an utterly unrealizable dream; but in his quality of good Englishman never recognizing defeat, he continued with his efforts, writing ever more and longer and more passionate letters, seeking ever more insistently more personal interviews, till there were those in authority who paled at the very mention of his name.

As it was likely that in this preliminary inquiry the best results would be attained by informal, friendly talk, Bobby made up his mind to go alone, though generally, when carrying out an official inquiry, it is wise to have a companion at hand for support if necessary. He decided, too, to stop on the way for a talk with Dr Maskell who, he had learnt by making a 'phone call, was the medical attendant of the Crayfoot family and might be able to say something about Mr Crayfoot's state of health. It was just possible, too, though hardly likely, for there had scarcely been sufficient time, that the analysis of the piece of earth from the floor of the hermit's hut had been completed. If so, Dr Maskell would be able to say whether or no there was any sign of the presence of blood.

Bobby found the doctor's house without difficulty, though it lay a little off the main road. It was a sprawling and untidy place. Originally it had been a farm and there were still various outbuildings, ruinous and deserted now except for the one Maskell had fitted up as a laboratory. The door was opened by a deaf, elderly, and sullen-looking woman who only appeared at a second and more vigorous knock. Ill-temperedly she showed Bobby a card giving the surgery hours in the morning and the evening and tried to shut the door in his face.

Bobby, however, had seen that coming and his foot thrust quickly forward prevented the design. In turn he showed his own card, bawled his demand to see the doctor into the old woman's ear and finally succeeded in inducing her to show him into the patients' waiting room, a bare, uncomfortable and draughty place without even the customary supply of back numbers of illustrated papers. After a time the old woman returned, mumbling to herself, and took him into a small inner room where presumably the doctor saw the patients whom he seemed to do so little to welcome.

This room, too, was bare, uncomfortable and draughty, but habitation and use gave it a less forbidding air. Scientific papers—*Science Progress, The Scientific American*, and others—were lying about, and on shelves, and on a table standing against the wall, were ranged various bottles, test tubes, flasks and so on. On this table, too, Bobby recognized by his signature he had scrawled on it the packet he had made up containing the stained earth, and there was, too, a tray carrying a teapot, a half empty cup, and some thick and unattractive looking bread and butter hardly touched. Apparently this afternoon refreshment had been found as little appetizing as it looked. Dr Maskell seemed to care no more for his own comfort than for that of his patients. On another table, that at which he was evidently accustomed to sit, were lying two photographs or prints. These at once caught Bobby's somewhat startled attention, for they were of pictures in El Greco's unmistakable style. Bobby picked them up and was looking at them when the doctor himself came into the room.

He was a tall, powerfully built, broad shouldered man, evidently in first-class physical condition, with piercing light blue eyes under bushy brows; an angry, thrust out nose; a grim looking, tightly closed mouth with a bristling moustache above; and he stared at Bobby with what seemed an habitual scowl. Hardly the best bedside manner, Bobby thought, and yet the man had about him an unmistakable air of power and efficiency. Those huge, gnarled hands, for instance, looked as capable as powerful, the eyes showed bright, intent, and steady; the mouth, ill-tempered certainly, but set in firm, strong lines.

"If he doesn't scare his patients to death, he would probably cure them," Bobby thought, and the doctor's scowl deepened as he saw what Bobby was looking at.

"Thank you," he said, and putting out his hand for the prints, he threw them into a drawer and banged it to.

"Looked like El Greco's work," Bobby remarked, ignoring the doctor's rudeness.

"Those things? Who's he? El Greco, I mean," the doctor grunted. "Know more about paintings than you do about science, eh? El Greco's stuff worth anything?"

"Some of his work is extremely valuable," Bobby answered.

"If it's like those prints, it doesn't impress me," Maskell retorted. "You've sent me some stuff to analyse. Why?"

He asked this question with a kind of wary, angry emphasis that Bobby noticed with some surprise. He supposed, however, the question and the surprise were due to a memory of the passage of arms occurring during the police prosecution that had failed so dismally through Dr Maskell's expert evidence. Possibly that memory, too, accounted for the hostility in the doctor's manner and the abrupt and impolite way in which he had snatched the—presumably—El Greco prints from Bobby to shut them in his table drawer. However, neither the doctor's bad manners nor his possession of El Greco prints were points of any very great importance, and when Maskell snapped out another angry 'Why?' Bobby merely answered:

"Oh, as a general rule we ask local practitioners to help us, and, of course, we know your scientific qualifications."

"I had no idea your spying activities went so far," growled Maskell. "How did you find out? Don't read that sort of paper, do you?" He indicated the scientific journals lying about. "Prefer the *News of the World*, I expect, eh?"

Bobby had far too much training in keeping his temper to be in any danger of losing it over what was evidently a deliberate and purposed offensiveness. He wondered a little what caused it. He even suspected for a moment that the other had been drinking. But he did not think that was the case. Just natural bad temper, he supposed, coupled with a consistent disregard for other people's feelings. Quite possibly, too, the doctor cultivated a grudge against the police, and indeed Bobby remembered now that he had been summoned and fined for a small motoring offence. Some motorists never forgave that, their feelings hurt not so much by the fine as by what they held to be the uncalled for insult to their driving ability. Bobby said amiably:

"Oh, police get to know quite a lot in the course of their daily work without any spying. So do doctors for that matter, I suppose."

"What do you mean by that?" demanded Maskell, looking more formidably angry than ever. "You don't suggest doctors and police—" He did not put much respect into the former word, he put immeasurable contempt into the latter—"work on the same lines."

"I didn't dream of doing so," Bobby answered meekly, disregarding the snorted 'hope not', Maskell interposed, "but medical men can often give information—"

"You don't imagine," roared Maskell at the top of his very loud voice, "that I am going to tell you anything about any of my patients, do you? If that's what you're after you can clear out, and the sooner the better."

"Dr. Maskell," said Bobby, suddenly producing his most official tone, "I am here in my capacity as an officer of police to ask you a question. You can refuse to answer it, of course, but I must ask you to listen to it with ordinary civility."

CHAPTER XII

'HUMAN BLOOD'

A SILENCE ENSUED. A silence fraught as it were with rumbling distant thunders and lightnings only just held back. For a moment or two Bobby fully expected that he was going to be ordered out of the house then and there, if indeed mere ordering was going to content this huge and formidable man. He watched warily, prepared for any show of violence. Something of the sort had been, he was sure, Maskell's first impulse. But then the doctor seemed to change his mind. He said sullenly:

"Well, if that's what you want to know, it's human blood all right." He seemed to notice then that Bobby looked surprised. He said: "That's what you've come about, isn't it? Isn't that why you wanted an analysis made? Simple job. I don't know why you wanted to bother me." Again he looked at Bobby with mingled doubt and suspicion, as if suspecting a trap somewhere. Then he looked angrier than ever and went on: "I suppose our wonderful police know there's no certainty except in a negative sense. Analysis shows it might be human blood. But it can't give certainty."

"Yes, I see, thank you," Bobby answered. "You'll let us have your report explaining that as soon as you can manage it, will you?"

"Yes, if you think you'll understand the explanation," Maskell growled.

Bobby went on unheedingly:

"As a matter of fact, it was something else I wanted to ask. I think I had better explain I am here with the knowledge and the consent of Mrs Crayfoot. I believe Mr Crayfoot is a patient of yours?"

"No, he isn't," interrupted Maskell angrily. "I found he was taking some hogswash he got from a lying old humbug you ought to have run in for a rogue and vagabond long ago. I told Crayfoot he had to choose between us."

"And did he?" Bobby could not resist asking in a tone he made as innocently inquiring as possible.

He half expected an outburst of rage for answer. But Maskell seemed for once a trifle subdued. He had even become a little pale; with anger apparently since there was no occasion for fear. He got up and went to a cupboard in the wall, marked 'Poisons'. Bobby was startled for the moment, but Maskell merely produced a bottle of whisky and a soda syphon. He poured out a liberal allowance of the spirit, added a very little soda, said over his shoulder, 'Like a drink', but did not attempt to implement his offer to which Bobby made no reply. Still speaking over his shoulder, Maskell repeated:

"Rogue and vagabond. Public danger. If you had done your duty—" Leaving the sentence unfinished he emptied his glass and then came back to his seat. He went on: "The fellow ought to have been stopped long ago—killing people. That's what he was doing. Served the fools right. All the same, there's half a dozen in their graves I could name ought to be alive and well to-day. But they went to him and they swallowed his stuff and there you are. They all come to me fast enough if a car turns turtle or a man puts a charge of shot into himself instead of the rabbits. And very likely all the time all of them, behind my back, drinking the filthy muck that old fraud gives them and listening to his lies about vivisection and vaccination and anything else none of them knows anything about."

"Oh, yes," said Bobby, who knew Maskell held a licence to practise vivisection. "I gather at one time you did attend Mr Crayfoot?"

"What about it?"

"Mr Crayfoot," Bobby explained, "didn't return home last night. He left his car at the 'Rawdon Arms' after lunching there and it hasn't been claimed. Mrs Crayfoot is afraid something must have happened. Is there anything seriously wrong with him? Any likelihood of his having had an attack of any kind?"

"I shouldn't think so," Maskell answered. "He was sound enough except for a touch of sciatica. That's all. Painful. So people make a fuss about it. People can't stand pain," he added contemptuously. "He thought it might be cancer. Utter rubbish."

"Do you think there was any nervous trouble?"

"And what," demanded Maskell ferociously, "are you pleased to think you mean by 'nervous trouble'?"

"Well," Bobby answered, though slightly taken aback by this demand, "what was in my mind was a lapse of memory. Sometimes these cases of missing people turn out to be cases of lost memory."

"Lost memory fiddlesticks," snapped Maskell. "I won't say it doesn't happen, especially when there's a physical cause, but it's rare. Very rare. Ninety-nine times out of a hundred, it's merely an excuse. Fellow finds his past inconvenient and decides to cut loose. Business troubles, family troubles, another woman, that sort of thing. Simplest card to play is lost memory. Eyewash. Nervous trouble. Bah! What's it mean? I'll tell you. Mental trouble. When people talk about nervous trouble to me, I tell them what they mean is mental trouble. They don't like it. True though. Tell a man he's nervy and he's as pleased as Punch. Tell him he's weak minded and he's offended."

Maskell paused, apparently contemplating with surprise this not surprising fact. Then he said violently:

"I hate humbug. Fatal. Gangrene. Got to be cut out. Or it kills. Humbug. Gangrene. Fatal both of them."

"Then you know of nothing in Mr Crayfoot's mental or physical condition to account for his disappearance?" Bobby asked.

"Nothing."

"If he really got an idea that he was suffering from cancer, would there be any risk of suicide?"

Maskell stared; and then produced a harsh, rumbling sound that was evidently intended for a laugh.

"Suicide?" he repeated contemptuously. "Far too big a coward—the fellow panicked at the mere thought of dying. Came to me once with a pain in his tummy from eating too much roast pork and wanted to know if there was any danger. Scared to blazes. Goodness knows why—death's a biological necessity. Nothing more. Ends it all and that's all there's to it."

"Some people share Hamlet's doubts," Bobby remarked.

"Coppers quote Shakespeare," the doctor sneered. "Wonders will never cease. Anyhow, you can take it from me—there was nothing wrong with Crayfoot or likely to be, except from swallowing the poisons he was getting from that old humbug in the forest."

"The man they call Peter the Hermit?" Bobby asked, and once more Maskell broke into a fierce denunciation of the old man.

"A murderer," he shouted at the top of his voice, "that's the proper word—a murderer. A murderer you police don't trouble your heads about. Why? Tell me that. Why can't you stop a mischievous old fraud like that? Eh?"

"Police carry out the law, they don't make it," Bobby answered mildly. "I understand he doesn't take money for his stuff?"

"That's what people say," Maskell admitted grudgingly. "Some of them have had the cheek and insolence to tell me that when I send in my bill. You may be sure he gets his pay all right on the quiet—one way or another. I caught one girl making up pots of honey to send him."

"Was that Miss Mary Floyd?" Bobby asked, remembering Mary's bees.

"Why? How do you know?" Maskell asked suspiciously.

"Oh, police, you know," Bobby answered vaguely; and by way of turning the knife in the wound, for though he had kept his temper well under control it was not of so meek a mould as to prevent him from seeing an opportunity to repay the other's rudeness, he added: "The mother was a patient of yours at one time, wasn't she?"

The doctor nodded and, to Bobby's surprise, with more of regret than resentment in his tones, he said:

"An interesting case. Injury to the spine—the nervous system. Unusual reactions. I was trying different remedies and taking careful note of the effect. Then I found that ancient fraud of a so-called hermit interfering again—relieving pain, he called it." Maskell snorted. "I told them I couldn't have my treatment interfered with. My results had to be pure if they were to be of value. I explained that.

They didn't seem to understand the importance. I—" He went very red, he made the admission with evident reluctance. "I even went back after I had said I wouldn't." He paused to glare angrily at Bobby who had small difficulty in guessing that this return had not met with any gratitude or welcome. "There's a little impudent brat there—running wild, ought to be sent to a home. She had the cheek—imagine it. A child of that age. Insolence. She actually stood there between me and her mother and told me to go away—told her mother to send me away. Said I cut up animals alive. I would have boxed her ears for her if I had got hold of her."

"Just as well perhaps you didn't, doctor," Bobby remarked dryly. "Magistrates are apt to be sticky these days about boxing the ears of other people's children."

"Bah," retorted Maskell, getting to his feet; and that was the last impression Bobby had of the doctor that day, a tall, big, formidable loosely-built man of intense vitality, drawing himself to his full height and uttering a 'Bah' of the most concentrated contempt for anything, everything, for all the world outside his own sympathies and activities and understandings.

CHAPTER XIII

PORTRAIT IN OILS

AN INTERESTING MAN and an interesting interview Bobby told himself as he pursued his way, and he thought how odd it was that these two motives, the recipe for chocolates, the lost El Greco pictures, should be so continually crossing and re-crossing each other. Not that there could be any real connection, he supposed.

He came soon to the outskirts of Tombes. 'Bellavista,' the Crayfoot residence, proved to be a prim little villa in a prim little garden, surrounded by other prim little villas in other prim little gardens, all of them taken together giving an impression of an order, peace, and the calm regularity of an established way of life nothing could ever change or challenge. Bobby surveyed the scene with approval.

"Smug," he reflected. "The apotheosis of the philistine."

And he reflected that after all, in a world in turmoil, there is much to be said for the regular and settled life of the philistine as against the sloppiness of the bohemian. A reflection which, of course, stamped him at once as the most philistine of philistines.

Leaving his car by the roadside he walked up a neat gravelled path bordered by standard roses and knocked at the 'Bellavista' door. When he explained his errand he was shown at once into a conventionally furnished drawing-room evidently only used on the rarest occasions. He gave the quick, observant glance round to which he had trained himself—the trick was afterwards to shut the eyes, try to remember as much as possible, then open them again and notice how much had been remembered and how correctly. This time, though, his attention was caught and held by a small oil painting on the wall to the exclusion of all else. It was the portrait of a young girl. The technical merit was small. Bobby had some knowledge of painting, the knowledge acquired by an occasional dabbling in the art, and could tell that at once. The surroundings were conventional, the dress was old-fashioned, yet somehow or another the artist had managed to catch in the expression a hint of the ethereal, a suggestion of a detachment from common things, that reminded Bobby very strangely both of Mary Floyd, and, more especially, of the younger sister, little Loo.

He was still looking at it with a deep and puzzled wonder when the door opened and there came in Mrs Crayfoot, an anxious, worried-looking woman of middle age, a good deal alarmed by this visit, for she had at once jumped to the conclusion that Bobby was there to tell her of some dreadful accident of which her husband had been the victim.

She seemed relieved, and yet a little disappointed, too, that the suspense must continue, when he explained that his purpose was only to obtain what information she could give that might be likely to help the police in their inquiry. It was not much she had to tell, and for her part she still insisted she was sure there must have been an accident. The roads were so dangerous. The papers were full of stories of people being killed or injured. Mr Crayfoot himself was a most careful driver. He made it a rule never to exceed thirty miles an hour. If other people would do the same, these dreadful accidents would be avoided.

Bobby agreed, but pointed out gently that Mr Crayfoot's car was safe and undamaged in the 'Rawdon Arms' garage. That did not make it seem very likely that any road accident had occurred. Mrs Crayfoot was not much impressed by this argument. She thought it very likely that the other person involved, and obviously the one to blame since Mr Crayfoot was a most careful driver, had left his victim by the roadside and garaged the car in order to escape discovery. What else but accident, she demanded tearfully, could account for Mr Crayfoot's failure to return home?

Bobby didn't know. Indeed, from all that was said a picture built itself up of a quietly prosperous business man leading a sober and well-regulated life. Apparently he had no hobbies. His sole interest in life was his business. True, in his youth he had indulged a good deal in rock climbing, but on his marriage he had given it up.

"I wasn't going to have him breaking his neck," said Mrs Crayfoot firmly.

Nowadays his recreations were an occasional motoring trip, an occasional visit to the cinema, an occasional game of family bridge with neighbours. As for forest rambles, whereat Bobby had hinted, Mrs Crayfoot was sure such an idea would never occur to him. They had their car; and if you had a car, declared Mrs Crayfoot, you obviously didn't go 'hiking' as people called it. In Mrs Crayfoot's opinion and experience walking might be all right for boys and girls, and for the poorer classes generally, but most certainly not for prosperous business men.

Bobby felt that she felt that one definitely lost caste by walking. Except young people. They might go 'hiking'. He turned the conversation to the subject of business. Mrs Crayfoot was calmly certain that the business was as prosperous as ever. They had very nearly a monopoly of the best custom in the neighbourhood. The war had helped, if anything. There was more money about and fewer people had been away for those long holidays during which their custom was in abeyance. In nothing that she said could Bobby find the least suggestion of any worry or trouble having recently appeared in Mr Crayfoot's life or manner. A passing reference to chocolates brought no response. Mrs Crayfoot never ate chocolates herself. She considered them fattening. Nor had Mr Crayfoot had any visitors recently— no strange visitors, that is. There had been the vicar, of course, and one or two of the neighbours, and young Mr Richard Rawdon from the Abbey.

The last name came out casually, as if young Mr Richard from the Abbey were so frequent a visitor his call had nearly been forgotten. Bobby left the point for a moment and asked:

"I believe Mr Crayfoot suffered from sciatica and used to take a herbal remedy. Can you tell me where he got it?"

From a Miss Mary Floyd, Mrs. Crayfoot explained. Miss Floyd came to the shop to sell her home-made sweets or cakes or something—Mrs Crayfoot was not sure what exactly. Miss Floyd had heard of Mr Crayfoot's sciatica and had offered to provide a liniment made by an old herbalist she knew. A man who lived alone in the forest and knew all about plants. Very economical; because in the first place Miss Floyd said the herbalist never made any charge and, secondly, one only used an eggspoonful twice a week, so that it lasted a long time. They had only had two bottles and the second was still half full, so Mr Crayfoot could not have been visiting the herbalist to secure more. Besides, if he had wanted a further supply he would have asked Miss Floyd, especially as, so far at least as she was aware, Mr Crayfoot had no knowledge either of the herbalist's name or where he lived. There had been nothing else wrong with Mr Crayfoot's health. The liniment had relieved the sciatica more than all Dr Maskell's stuff and there had been no reason for Dr Maskell to take offence. It was Dr Maskell's business to provide better remedies than others could, just as it was Mr Crayfoot's business to provide better bread and cake than others. If either of them failed, then they lost custom. But Dr Maskell was known everywhere for his domineering ways and rough tongue and no wonder his practice was declining. Even the shortage of doctors since the outbreak of the war had not helped him greatly. People were merely tending more and more to try to get remedies from the herbalist of the forest. That is, when he could be found, which was often difficult. To hear Dr Maskell talk, one would think that the herbalist was a murderer and that to consult him was merely a quick way of committing suicide.

Bobby agreed with all this and came back to the subject of Mr Richard Rawdon's visit. Mrs Crayfoot thought it had been something about those new local defence volunteers. There was talk about putting up some kind of obstruction in the road near Mr Crayfoot's shop and naturally he objected. The road was narrow enough just there as it was, and what was the sense of making it even more difficult for customers and their cars? Not as if it was likely the Germans would ever get that far.

Bobby made no attempt to argue the point, even though he reflected that though it was unlikely the Germans would ever get as far as Midwych, yet this was a war in which there happened only the unlikely—or even, one was tempted to think sometimes, the impossible. So he rose to go and then paused to comment on the portrait in oils that had already caught his attention. He remarked on what a charming study it made, a lovely figure in a lovely frame. Was it, he asked unblushingly, by any chance a portrait of Mrs Crayfoot herself when a girl?

This was meant as cunning flattery but was a good deal less successful than it deserved—or didn't deserve. Bobby had forgotten that the style of dress showed the picture was more than half a century old, and that therefore had it been of Mrs Crayfoot when a girl she must now have been at least seventy years of age. Very emphatically Mrs Crayfoot was not prepared to claim a girlhood beauty at the price of a present and premature old age. Besides, she had never thought much of the portrait anyhow. A washed-out sort of creature, that girl, in her opinion. A dying duck in a thunderstorm, was her own judgment. Of course, it was hand done, she admitted that, not merely given away with the supplement to a Christmas number of an illustrated paper. They were much nicer, too, in her opinion, but with the disadvantage that the picture on your walls you might find also adorning a neighbour's as well. With 'hand done' work that fortunately didn't happen. Still, she had often thought of replacing it by something with more colour and life, only it had been done by Mr Crayfoot's grandfather and so he liked to keep it.

Bobby was interested and asked one or two more questions. Mrs Crayfoot had no idea who the original of the portrait had been and evidently had no more information to give on a subject which had never interested her and about which she knew nothing. Nor had Bobby any reason to press the point, since presumably it had no connection with the puzzle of Mr Crayfoot's disappearance he was there to solve, if possible.

He took his leave therefore, since it seemed there was no more to learn. Everything possible would be done to relieve her anxiety, he assured Mrs Crayfoot. By way of encouragement, he assured her, too, that often what seemed the most inexplicable disappearance had the simplest explanation. A letter unposted, for instance, or a telegram wrongly addressed. Mrs Crayfoot seemed a good deal cheered by what he said and as he went away Bobby wondered whether he had been wise to say what he had done.

For he himself was beginning more and more to be aware of dark and strange possibilities, ominous in the background.

CHAPTER XIV
WALTERS'S

FROM 'BELLAVISTA', BOBBY went on to Walters's, the baking, confectionery and tea shop business owned by Mr Crayfoot. It looked, he thought, a prosperous and well-managed affair. There was someone to come forward at once to speak for each department, but no one with any explanation to offer of their employer's absence. Most unusual for him to be away without due warning. None of them had ever known such a thing to happen before. Nor had any one noticed anything to account for it, any unusual incident, anything strange in manner or behaviour. The senior assistant in charge of the confectionery counter knew all about Mary Floyd and her chocolates, all about the famous liniment, too. It was she, the assistant, who, on her own responsibility, had agreed to put Miss Floyd's chocolates on sale. And it was she who had spoken about Mr Crayfoot's sciatica to Miss Floyd on one of her rare personal visits to the shop—for nearly always she sent her chocolates by post or by carrier. The chocolates had been a great success, she added, and always sold well. They had a distinctive and unusual flavour. People who bought them once often asked for them again and were disappointed if they could not be supplied. But there it was. They were home made and naturally Miss Floyd could only provide limited supplies. Once or twice, she, the assistant, had suggested to Mr Crayfoot that it might be a good idea to offer Miss Floyd facilities for increasing her output and he had seemed interested. But there it was. Nothing had been done. You couldn't have home-made quality and factory quantity. Two incompatibles. There was one customer who liked them so much that her husband had come to ask about them. He had even wanted Miss Floyd's address. Like his impudence. Naturally, he had not been told. Not likely. Walters's were fully prepared to take all Miss Floyd cared to make and to give her as good a price as any one. Bobby wondered a little what that price was and what relation it bore to the price charged over the Walters counter. That lay, however, he supposed, outside the scope of his inquiry. He asked for a description of the disappointed inquirer for Miss Floyd's address. The assistant's memory was not very clear nor her description very precise. But now Bobby mentioned it, yes, she thought he had red hair. His voice—was, well, it was like that of any one else. He might have had hairy hands as well but then so many gentlemen had, hadn't they? Consultation with a junior, however, produced confirmation. The junior's memory was better and she had felt quite sympathetic with the customer's disappointment at not being able to buy his wife her chocolates.

"They're ever so nice," the junior declared. "If I could make such lovely chocolates I should start for myself. You could work up a nice little business."

"That takes capital," said the senior severely, evidently considering this a most disloyal suggestion, "and very likely lose every penny. Rent and all," she said. "People only think of profits, never of the overhead."

This last Bobby felt sure was a quotation from Mr Crayfoot himself and the junior did not look much impressed and said she believed it was something like that which had caused the quarrel between Mr Weston and Mr Crayfoot. Bobby, asking for details, learnt that Mr Weston, known as a customer and known to be a friend of Mr Crayfoot, had been heard quarrelling with Mr Crayfoot in that gentleman's private office. Finally Mr Weston had bounced out, looking awful, and Mr Crayfoot had bounced out after him and had shouted to him never to come near the place again and had ordered them, the staff, not to serve him if he did.

"Only, of course," said the senior assistant, "you can't do that, can you? Because a shop's a shop, isn't it? And a customer's a customer, isn't he?"

Bobby, impressed by the profound truth of these observations, agreed, and remembered, too, that it was a Mrs Weston who had spoken of the chocolates to Olive. He decided that it would be as well to have a talk both with Mr Weston and with the red-headed gentleman, if, that is, he could be traced. He might, Bobby thought, be far away by now, laying his plans to launch on the market a new brand of chocolates, flavoured according to the analysis made of the contents of the hermit's bottle.

From the Walters's shop he drove to the village of Barsley Forest where he knew from his talk on the Sunday with Sergeant Turner that the hermit occasionally made purchases. His inquiry there told him that these purchases were rare, that the chief article purchased was paraffin oil, and that payment was always made in gold. An interesting detail was that the sovereigns produced were always of the date of Queen Victoria's first jubilee—1887.

Bobby's next visit was to the 'Rawdon Arms' where Mr Crayfoot's car was still garaged. The landlord, a Mr Baker, knew Mr Crayfoot slightly, as a fellow business man of the neighbourhood, and remembered having exchanged a few words with him. He had been alone, his manner had been perfectly normal. Afterwards he had been seen walking towards the forest. It was, of course, quite common for people to leave their cars there while they themselves went for a forest stroll. Only when later on it was found that the car had not been claimed was any surprise or uneasiness felt, and then it had merely been supposed that Mr Crayfoot had gone home with friends and that his car would be sent for in due course. The landlord's opinion was that Mr Crayfoot had met with some accident in the forest and that it ought to be searched forthwith. A big job, considering the extent it covered. But there were always the boy scouts, said the landlord hopefully. He agreed, though, that Crayfoot was the very last man in all the world he would have expected to go rambling in the forest or get himself into difficulties there.

Nor for that matter did this idea that the missing man might have got lost in the forest or met with an accident there, much appeal to Bobby. Crayfoot had presumably reached in safety the hermit's hut since his card was there; and there seemed no reason to suppose that he would have had greater difficulty in finding his way back, or any reason why he should have met with any accident during what was no more than an afternoon's stroll. Nor did Bobby think it probable that in this tangle of half-seen motives, half-hinted secrets, there was likely to be thrust the additional coincidence of an unrelated accident. In some way he felt sure Crayfoot's disappearance was linked with the obscure happenings whereof he was securing such vague and tantalising glimpses as of figures seen through a drifting, changing haze of fog.

Since apparently there was no more to be learned from the landlord, Bobby went out to have a word or two with the garage attendant—an attention to detail that earned him a rich reward. The garage attendant always tried to remember which car belonged to which driver. Better tips were often forthcoming if the right car were produced the moment its owner was seen approaching or if the owner were allowed to see it receiving an extra rub up. All trades have their tricks and a smart man could easily double the amount in tips normally taken. When therefore the attendant saw Mr Crayfoot emerge from the inn he became busy on Mr Crayfoot's car but had been disappointed to see Mr Crayfoot walk away towards the forest. And he had noticed that a gentleman who had not been lunching in the inn but had been sitting outside with a glass of beer, had left his beer to follow Mr Crayfoot towards the forest. No, he had not joined him, he had merely walked in the same direction some distance behind. The garage attendant would probably not have remembered or even noticed so trivial an incident but for the fact of that desertion of a perfectly good and practically untasted glass of beer. Bobby was inclined to guess, however, that that beer had not been entirely wasted.

"Would you know him again?" Bobby asked.

The garage attendant thought so.

"Fat man, middle aged, hairy hands, red hair?" Bobby asked hopefully.

The garage attendant shook his head.

"Youngish chap, dark, small moustache, big nose?" Bobby tried again and again the garage attendant shook his head.

He was fairly certain he would know him again but he was quite incapable of providing any sort of verbal description. Bobby gave it up and went back into the inn to interview the waiters. He had not much hope of success. Casual guests come and go and are forgotten the moment their tips have been pocketed, their hats and coats handed to them. They are indeed no more to the busy waiter than the raw material of a livelihood, neither worth nor requiring a personal recollection. But this time Bobby's inquiry met with unexpected success. It was the red hair that did it. One of the waiters had red hair himself, a drawback in a profession in which it is a merit to be inconspicuous. But the fact had made him notice a red-haired stranger who was having lunch with Dr Maskell.

Bobby rewarded this piece of unexpected information with a tip and went outside to think it over. Not with much success. An odd little incident but he did not see how it was likely to fit into the puzzle of the Crayfoot investigation. Very likely there was no connection for that matter. Possibly the red-headed stranger had asked Maskell to make the analysis of the bottle of flavouring stolen from Mary Floyd. The doctor might be asked about that but the questioning would have to be done very tactfully and discreetly and casually. He had the kind of temperament that would probably enjoy refusing to give any information in his possession. Not at all likely to go out of his way to help other people, least of all to help police. Nor could questioning be pressed with authority for there was at present nothing to suggest any connection with the Crayfoot disappearance. He and his guest—or host—had come in late and been almost the last to finish their meal, staying long after Crayfoot's departure. There was indeed nothing to show that the doctor and Crayfoot had even noticed each other.

Discouraging, Bobby felt, even though one little disconnected fact after another kept turning up, and it was just possible that in their totality they might make up something like a coherent whole. Nothing to suggest at present, though, what that picture would be like, if and when it reached completion. He went into the bar for a glass of beer he did not want and from the barmaid learnt that she remembered quite well the incident of the customer who had hurried away, leaving behind an untasted glass of beer. She had in fact caught the garage attendant in the act of drinking it to save waste, as he explained, and she had given him 'what for' for his impudence. Oh, yes, she knew the gentleman quite well, Mr Weston was his name. Her father kept a small shop in Tombes and Mr Weston was an occasional customer.

CHAPTER XV

BARSLEY ABBEY

ONCE AGAIN A glass of beer remained untouched as Bobby sat there on the bench before the inn, wondering what to do next; oddly excited too, by the thrill of the hunt as in this strange, disconnected way one small significant detail after another came as it were slowly into being, presently to form, he hoped, the background against which in time a coherent pattern could be framed. Already it seemed to him that the faint outline of such a pattern was growing into visibility, and yet he was not sure. It might well be, he knew, that what he saw was but illusion, built by too swift imagination out of a misinterpretation of the facts.

Over and over again he considered the things he knew; and once, when he lifted his eyes towards where a few hundred yards away the outward surge of the forest was checked by the open fields whereby men held back the march of the trees, he had the illusion that he saw emerging from the mystery of their green shelter the lost Crayfoot, the missing hermit, arm in arm and laughing together at the thoughts of death and tragedy, past and to come, that had forced their way into his mind.

"All the same," he found himself muttering, "there must have been an axe once—and now there isn't."

Again he began to go over mentally what he knew.

There was the red-haired unknown with his stolen bottle of flavouring and his lunch with Dr Maskell; there was the vanished Crayfoot and his wife's fears and the portrait on his drawing-room wall; there was Weston, his quarrel with Crayfoot and his pursuit of him into the forest; there was Dr Maskell, his grudge against the hermit, his statement that the earth from the floor of the hermit's hut contained human blood, his possession of that print of an El Greco picture he had apparently been studying; there was young Dick Rawdon with his visits to Crayfoot and to the hermit; there was the other unknown, he of the dark complexion and the big nose who had removed himself so quickly from the vicinity of the hermit's hut and who, he also, had been in possession of an El Greco reproduction. Then in the background; firstly Sir Alfred Rawdon, trying to break the entail that he might sell his land and so clear the burden of debt weighing down the estate and also the original owner of the lost El Grecos, indeed presumably the present rightful owner if they could be found; secondly, the hermit himself round whom it seemed so much revolved. Finally, the two young girls at the Coop cottage, so gentle and quiet in manner and appearance, so ruthless in action; together with their stepfather, Coop himself, of the doubtful character.

"Direct action there all right," Bobby reflected, remembering an old political catchword much loved by hotheads.

Again he went over the names one by one, ticking them off on his fingers, trying to assign to each one the probable part each played in this drama of which as yet neither the purpose nor the plot was apparent.

The first idea that came to Bobby was to seek out Weston, since he was the last person, who, as far as Bobby's knowledge went, had seen Crayfoot. Then he reflected it might be better to wait to see if Weston came forward voluntarily. If he did so, a waste of time to seek him out. If he failed to do so, then a presumption of guilty knowledge would be established. A point of departure that might be useful!

On the whole Bobby thought it would be best to try to have a talk with young Dick Rawdon. It might be useful to know why he had paid that visit to Crayfoot. Also Bobby felt he would like to know the name, and, if possible, the address, of the dark young man who presumably had given the first, if not both, when making his call at Barsley Abbey told of by Dick Rawdon.

It was growing late in the afternoon now with blackout time beginning to loom in the distance. So leaving on the bench his still untasted beer—once again the garage attendant was in luck and once again he had to pay for his luck by submitting to a 'telling off' from an indignant barmaid—Bobby started for the Abbey, a short drive of a couple of miles along a lonely road.

It was a handsome, well proportioned house of the early Georgian period, of medium size, only the name remaining of the original building. According to the records, the monks and their tenants had attempted to offer armed resistance to the King's Commissioners at the time of the dissolution of the monasteries. They had had some success at first and had remained in possession of the Abbey till, on the approach of overwhelming forces, abbot and monks had fled to a secret refuge in the forest. So much was history; and legend added that this secret refuge had been discovered, and abbot and monks slain to the last man. The Abbey, too, had been set on fire and burnt to the ground. On its site the new owner of the Abbey lands had erected a dwelling that in its turn had been burnt down, to be succeeded by the present building.

Sir Alfred was at home, Bobby learned, and he was shown into a small, plainly furnished apartment, evidently one used chiefly for business interviews. Sir Alfred, a tall, thin, untidy looking man with a long narrow head and long narrow face, appeared presently, nor was it difficult to see that he was ill at ease. Bobby explained that he had met Mr Richard Rawdon the previous evening in the forest and would like, if possible, some information about a man living there as a hermit and understood to be a tenant of the Rawdon estate. Sir Alfred listened in gloomy silence, leaning against the mantelpiece, his hands in his pockets, looking down distrustfully at Bobby, whose six feet of height he overtopped by three or four inches.

"I don't know anything about the fellow," he said. "No one does. He just squatted there, as far as I know. I believe he claims to have a letter from the estate, leasing him the bit of land he occupies. Whether that's so or not, I've no idea. We've never bothered. Maskell wants me to clear him out."

"Are you going to?"

"No. I don't think so. No. Why should I? What's he been doing, anyway? Getting into trouble? He has once or twice. Harmless if left alone but if he's interfered with likely to go charging about with an axe. At least, so I'm told," he added hastily.

"Well, I hope no one has been interfering with him this time," Bobby said; a little startled by this fresh reference to an axe, the axe that certainly had once been in the hermit's hut and now was there no longer.

"I'm not going to, anyhow," declared Sir Alfred. "Maskell can say what he likes. I don't even know that I could turn him out. Very likely the old man has something he could call a lease. Anyhow, I can't give tenants notice simply because Maskell doesn't like them."

"The doctor does seem to take rather a strong line about it," Bobby observed.

"Calls the old man an unlicensed murderer," agreed Sir Alfred. "I said I supposed doctors were the licensed sort. Made Maskell ratty. Anything makes Maskell ratty. Clever chap. Pulled me through a bad spell once. But he doesn't go the way to make himself popular. Was it Maskell put you on our old man of the woods?"

"Oh, no," Bobby answered. "It's not really the old man I'm so much interested in. We've nothing against him. No harm in his giving—or selling for that matter—his stuff to people who think it does them good. I believe you deal with Walters, the baker in Tombes, don't you?"

"Yes. I think so. Why?"

"The business belongs to a Mr Crayfoot. He has disappeared from his home and his wife is naturally anxious and has appealed to us. The connection is that Mr Crayfoot's card was in the hut—the hermit's hut, I mean—so presumably Mr Crayfoot himself had been there. I saw Mr Richard Rawdon there, at the hut. Perhaps he mentioned it to you?"

"He did say something," Sir Alfred admitted but with hesitation. "I didn't take much notice. Nothing to do with me."

Bobby reflected that this nervous baronet seemed very eager to insist on his own complete detachment from recent events. Nor did his nervousness seem in any way to diminish as they talked. Rather he had more and more the air of one more and more disquieted by the course the talk was taking. Bobby said slowly:

"The hut had the appearance of having been deliberately wrecked."

"Yes. I know, Dick told me," Sir Alfred admitted again. He was rubbing his hands together nervously and Bobby, watching his feet, where nervous movements often show more quickly because people think less of controlling them, noticed how his toes were twitching and working inside the patent leather slippers he was wearing. He said abruptly: "You don't think anything can have happened to the old man, do you?"

"Something certainly happened," Bobby said. "A general knocking about of the contents of the hut. It might have been malicious. Or drink. Or some one might have been looking for something."

"There was a yarn going round that the old man had a secret hoard, in gold sovereigns," Sir Alfred said moodily. "It might be that."

"Was it a story generally known—or believed?"

"I don't know. I don't think so. Most people were a bit scared of the old man. He was inclined to turn violent if people bothered him. There are stories of what happened to people he had a grudge against. Anyhow, you don't suspect a respectable tradesman like Crayfoot of that sort of thing—robbery and burglary, I mean?"

"It doesn't seem very probable," Bobby agreed. "All I have to go on is that Mr Crayfoot is missing, that the last trace of him seems to be his card I found, and that there are signs of violence in the old man's hut."

Sir Alfred looked disturbed, uneasy, more than uneasy, indeed, even frightened. He was silent for a moment or two and then burst out abruptly as though he could no longer keep the fear to himself.

"But, good God, you can't suppose he killed Crayfoot?"

"I don't know enough to suppose anything," Bobby answered, and he wondered if it was this possibility alone that was causing Sir Alfred such evident alarm or whether some other, deeper, fear was in his mind.

"Well, look here," he said abruptly, "you had better have a talk with Dick. I don't know anything about it. Wait a moment."

He went out of the room and came back soon. He said:

"Dick and I were having a talk about estate business. I'm not married, so he's my heir. Mr Hart's there, too—our solicitor. Some of the property's got to be sold. It's mostly settled property, though. Heirlooms as well. We have to get permission from the courts. All that sort of thing. Come along, will you?"

CHAPTER XVI
LAWYER HART

SIR ALFRED LED the way into an adjoining room; a large and imposing apartment, oblong in shape, with wide windows looking out over the forest, its walls lined with books that had not much the air of ever being read. Ponderous tomes most of them, clad in calf, sometimes with bindings more interesting than the contents. At a big table in the middle of the room two men were sitting. One was Dick Rawdon, sprawling in his chair with outstretched legs and hands in his pockets. He nodded a curt greeting when Bobby came in and then seemed to lapse again into that profound meditation Bobby's entrance had apparently interrupted. The other man, sitting facing him, was of a youngish middle age with a square body and a square flat face. Bobby noticed specially his eyes, so pale under pale, scanty eyebrows, as to be almost colourless. Yet they were alert enough; with a trick of giving sudden sideway glances, as though in the hope of catching something or some one unawares. He wore pince-nez or rather held them up in one hand, much as if he used them more to emphasize a meaning or illustrate a point than as an aid to vision. He was introduced to Bobby as Mr Montague Hart, the Rawdon family lawyer. Bobby decided that he did not much like his looks and especially not his mouth, at once, as mouths sometimes are, soft, with its full, red lips, and cruel, with its corners slightly lifted to show a gleam of white, pointed teeth behind.

"Inspector Owen," Sir Alfred explained, "is trying to find out what's become of Crayfoot—you know, Dick, Walters's, the baker's. Apparently Crayfoot has turned up missing."

"He is not supposed to be hiding in the Abbey, is he?" Montague Hart inquired, trying to look amused and evidently very much the reverse. "For that matter, is there any reason for taking a serious view of Mr Crayfoot's absence from home?"

"Mrs Crayfoot seems worried," Bobby answered briefly. "We are making inquiries at her request."

"He may have private reasons of the sort wives don't know about," Hart suggested with a faintly unpleasant grin.

"Oh, quite," Bobby agreed. He added thoughtfully: "One or two things seem a bit odd, though."

He paused. None of the three made any comment but he thought that all three looked not only expectant but a little anxious as well. At least, both with Hart and with Sir Alfred he felt sure there was anxiety. Dick Rawdon puzzled him more. The young man seemed changed in some curious, secret, yet excited way. As if he had been through some recent experience of which his mind was so full he could only bring his full attention to bear by fits and starts on present matters. Bobby spoke to him directly.

"You remember, Mr Rawdon," he said, "when we met, I told you I had picked up Mr Crayfoot's card?"

Dick removed his abstracted gaze from the window and transferred it to Bobby.

"Yes, I know," he said. "What about it?"

"Well, for one thing," Bobby told him, "that card seems the last known trace of Mr Crayfoot. I don't think you mentioned that you knew him, did you?"

"I don't expect so. No, I didn't. Why? I didn't know what you were up to. You weren't looking for Crayfoot then, were you?"

"No, not then," Bobby agreed. "Mrs Crayfoot tells me you called to have a talk with Mr Crayfoot the other night?"

"Well?"

"Did you find him in ordinary health and spirits?"

"Yes. I suppose so. As far as I know. I didn't notice anything."

"Do you mind telling me why you wanted to see him? I take it your call had some special purpose?"

Dick hesitated, frowned, looked at the lawyer. Mr Montague Hart said:

"I suggest the inspector ought to tell us exactly what is in his mind."

"It's almost a perfect blank at present," Bobby answered cheerfully. "I'm merely trying to get hold of something that may help me to relieve Mrs Crayfoot's anxiety. After all, a wife has some reason to be anxious when her husband turns up missing, as Sir Alfred says."

"Is there any reason," demanded Mr Hart, not too pleasantly, shaking his eyeglasses severely in the air and in Bobby's direction, "any reason at all to suppose that this very natural anxiety you speak of would be in any way relieved by your knowledge of what passed during a private interview?"

"That," said Bobby amiably, "is precisely what I am wondering. Would it or would it not? It might, mightn't it?" He paused. No one answered. He felt they did not mean to answer. He said: "Of course, if it was merely a question of a road block—"

He paused once more. He had been watching Dick Rawdon closely. It was easy to recognize the look of surprise this reference to road blocks brought into the young man's eyes. Bobby went on:

"That is what Mrs Crayfoot told me. I rather thought she might have got hold of the wrong end of the story. I believe Mr Rawdon is in charge of the Home Guard at his factory?"

Dick nodded.

"Used to make toys for kiddies," he said. "Model trains, model aeroplanes, that sort of thing—the Summit models. Now we make uglier toys for naughtier children. Supposed to be so important we are all specially reserved."

"That's what made me wonder," Bobby explained. "I mean, why a factory unit officer should be dealing with a road block opposite Mr Crayfoot's shop."

"Surely it is evident," put in Montague Hart in the same slightly aggressive tone, the eyeglasses still raised in minatory fashion, "that Mr Crayfoot was merely satisfying his wife's curiosity?"

"I expect so," Bobby agreed. "A pity. Warning to husbands to be frank. Greater frankness to Mrs Crayfoot might have helped us now. Helped us to know how seriously we ought to take her anxiety—she is certainly very anxious."

"I am aware of the reason for Mr Rawdon's call," Montague Hart put in, slowly and gravely lifting his eyeglasses up and down, a little as if he were beating time to an unheard and invisible orchestra. "It was an entirely private matter. It can have no possible bearing on Mr Crayfoot's disappearance. Indeed, personally, I am rather at a loss to imagine what useful information the inspector thinks he is likely to obtain here. Naturally, there is a most perfect willingness to afford every possible help."

"But not apparently to the extent of answering all questions," Bobby interposed quietly, and left it at that for the time. For one thing he had the impression that the lawyer's remarks were not altogether approved either by uncle or nephew. It seemed to him that they were both growing uneasy, that they did not quite like the somewhat bullying tone the lawyer was adopting. Bobby felt it just possible that if, without appearing too eager or pressing, he let them think it over for a few minutes, they might become more communicative. He said to Dick:

"After you left us in the forest on Sunday, you went on to Coop's Cottage, they call it, don't they? To see Miss Mary Floyd?"

Dick jerked round in his chair, stared, his mouth open, too taken aback at first for any emotion but surprise. He blurted out:

"How do you know?" Then he began to grow angry. "What the devil has it to do with you?" he asked heatedly.

"Are we to understand," demanded Hart, his eyeglasses waggling more impressively than ever, "that you are keeping a watch on my client?"

"Good gracious, no," protested Bobby. "Why should I?" he asked; and then he looked from uncle to nephew and back again as if he were asking himself that question very seriously indeed.

He tried to make these quick looks of his as full of meaning as possible, and he was glad to see the two of them showing signs of increasing discomfort. He told himself that one or other of them would soon be speaking freely and he thanked his lucky stars for the presence of a blundering, bullying lawyer who was really being a great help. But then he began to wonder whether Mr Montague Hart could really be as stupid and incompetent as he seemed or whether perhaps he was pursuing some ulterior aim.

Only what?

A fresh puzzle there, Bobby felt.

He went on:

"I asked about the visit to Miss Floyd because when I was at Mrs Crayfoot's, I noticed a small oil portrait. Mrs Crayfoot didn't seem to know much about it. She thought it was the work of Mr Crayfoot's grandfather and that was why they kept it. Otherwise she would have liked to get rid of it. What struck me was there seemed a curious but quite recognizable resemblance to Miss Floyd."

"My God, so there is," cried Dick Rawdon and leaped to his feet, all sudden animation, "that is why when I saw her, I thought that I had always known her."

CHAPTER XVII
FAMILY HISTORY

During all this time Sir Alfred had been leaning against the mantelpiece, his hands thrust deep in his pockets, looking down at the others in moody silence from his six feet three of height, apparently only half listening to what was being said. But now he straightened himself abruptly and made one long stride from fireplace to table.

"What the devil does that mean?" he demanded.

"I knew I had always known her, always," Dick repeated, but he seemed to be speaking more to himself than to them.

"May I suggest—?" began Montague Hart, and then paused.

Evidently he did not really know what to suggest and as evidently he was as much puzzled as was Bobby himself. Sir Alfred went back to the mantelpiece and stood there, balancing himself on his toes, swinging slowly backwards and forwards.

"Well, look here—" he began and then was silent again. Looking at Bobby, he said: "Are you sure the thing was done by Crayfoot's grandfather?"

"I am sure that is what Mrs Crayfoot said," Bobby answered. "I am sure you understand that all I want is any information that may help me to find out what has happened to Crayfoot. Has the fact that Crayfoot's grandfather painted a not very good portrait which has a likeness to a young lady living not far away any connection with Crayfoot's disappearance?"

"The question answers itself," interposed Mr Hart, and Bobby had the clear impression that he spoke, not because he knew or understood anything of what was passing, but because he wished to play well his part of family solicitor, offering advice and counsel and generally protecting the interests of his clients.

Another impression that Bobby had was that neither of the two Rawdons, neither uncle nor nephew, was much impressed. Sir Alfred said now:

"Any connection? No, I don't think so. I don't see how. Do you, Dick?"

Dick was not listening. He was deep in his own thoughts and Bobby fancied that they had taken him back to that cottage in the forest and the young girl he had seen there.

"There's another point I should like to mention," Bobby went on. "Mr Rawdon told me a stranger had called here, and had made some inquiries about two presumably very valuable pictures—El Grecos. Sergeant Turner in the village says the same man—at least I assume it was the same man—has been making other inquiries in the neighbourhood. The idea seems to be that the pictures may possibly still be about here somewhere. Unrecognized. I suppose it's possible. I have heard of an old master being used to patch a broken window in a garret. It's an odd story and Mr Crayfoot's disappearance is odd, and between two odd things happening at once there may be a connection—they may even be cause and effect."

"Oh, nonsense," said Montague Hart.

"That's what I want to be sure about," Bobby explained. "That's why I want to get in touch with this man—to ask him a few questions. I take it he is the same man I saw near the hut in the forest, a chap who made off in a hurry when he saw me. I suppose when he called here he gave his name and address?"

"I don't think so," Sir Alfred answered. "He said his name was Smith which I didn't much believe. He said he represented the Nelson Art Gallery in New Bond Street in London. That's a lie anyhow. I took the trouble to look it up. There doesn't seem to be any such place. He tried to pump me about the El Grecos. I didn't see why I should answer his questions. I told him what every one knows, that there are no El Grecos in the collection, and that we didn't know anything about them, and if we did most likely we shouldn't tell him. Then I asked him why the Nelson Art Gallery wasn't on the 'phone, since their name didn't appear in the 'phone directory, and he looked rather taken aback and made some silly excuse about keeping the number out of the book for the sake of privacy—rubbish, of course—and took himself off."

"Thank you," Bobby said. "We shall have to try to trace him. I've got his description. I'll have some inquiries made among art dealers and see if he is known at all. Can there be any possibility of any connection between these lost El Grecos and the fact that Mr Crayfoot's grandfather was a bit of an artist himself? Could the grandfather have got possession of the El Grecos?"

"You mean," put in Mr Montague Hart excitedly, "that Crayfoot has suddenly discovered them and gone off with them to sell on the quiet?"

Bobby pondered the suggestion. It seemed a possibility. Sir Alfred whistled softly and appeared to think so, too. Dick looked round. He had seemed entirely lost in his own thoughts but all the same he had evidently heard what was being said. Now he uttered one word—and with emphasis.

"Nonsense," he said.

"Not at all," declared Hart with some heat. "Those paintings might be worth thousands—thousands. Enough to tempt anyone," and the gleam that came so suddenly into those pale and distant eyes of his, made it pretty clear that for him at least, the temptation would be great.

"Rubbish," said Dick, changing the word but not the emphasis. "Crayfoot's a decent little man. He wouldn't do it, and if he wanted to he wouldn't know how to set about it—or have the guts to try. Respectable tradesmen don't go in for tricks of that sort."

"I have known cases," declared Hart, and plainly wished it to be understood that only professional reticence prevented him from giving details.

Bobby had known cases, too. The outwardly respectable are sometimes inwardly very much the reverse. Was not Charles Peace known to all his neighbours as a kindly old gentleman who spent most of his time playing the fiddle? He said:

"Possession still counts for a good deal. Suppose these pictures are in Mr Crayfoot's hands, could you make good to the satisfaction of the courts, that they are in fact your property?"

"Blessed if I know," said Sir Alfred.

"In my opinion, undoubtedly," declared Mr Hart.

"Could Mr Crayfoot's grandfather have had access to the picture gallery?" Bobby asked.

Sir Alfred hesitated. It was Dick who answered. He said:

"The old boy was a footman here. He was chucked out at a moment's notice—without warning, without a character, with a spate of abuse to make your hair stand on end."

"There's our case," said Hart triumphantly.

"Nothing to do with stealing pictures," Dick interposed. "I mean, there's nothing to show he had anything to do with the disappearance of the El Grecos. Oh, you'll keep it to yourself, won't you?—I mean, about Crayfoot's grandfather having been a footman here?"

"Does he know?" Bobby asked.

"I expect so, sure to. He may not want every one else to know, though."

"Big wig locally, you know," interposed Sir Alfred. "I daresay he could buy us up—not that that's saying much."

"We certainly shan't say anything unless it becomes necessary," Bobby said. "Police know many secrets—and keep them. It seems a bit of a coincidence, though, that footman Crayfoot had some artistic gifts. The portrait I mentioned isn't a bad bit of work. The man who did it knew something—may have known enough to recognize El Grecos were a bit out of the way. However I'm not looking for lost pictures, it's a missing man I want to find. At present, I don't see much connection. Do you know why the Crayfoot grandfather was sacked?"

"Family scandal," said Sir Alfred. Then he looked at Dick. "May as well tell the whole story," he said. "Nothing much in it."

"I suggest," began Montague Hart, "it is both unnecessary and undesirable. I give that as my considered opinion."

"All very well," retorted Sir Alfred, "but there it is. Crayfoot's missing, and God knows what's become of the old hermit, and you've only got to look at Inspector Owen to see he is going on digging things up."

"Only material things," interposed Bobby. "Only till I know what's become of Crayfoot."

"You'll go on digging 'em up all the same just to see if they are material," retorted Sir Alfred. "Besides, I could bear myself to know what's become of those El Grecos. They would be worth a pot of money if we could find them and establish our claim. Well, there it is. You had better tell the whole yarn, Dick. It was you started all this about the El Grecos—every one had forgotten all about them. Not going to fall in love with this Miss Floyd, are you?"

Dick stared at his uncle as if such a thing had never occurred to him.

"Fall in love with her?" he repeated vaguely.

"It's the same name," said Sir Alfred. "History does repeat itself." He went across the room to where, beneath the bookshelves were some closed, box like compartments. He opened one and began to rummage within. He produced a manuscript volume, opened it at random, and put it on the table. Bobby saw that the pages were covered with a thin spidery writing. The paper was still in good condition, the ink a little faded but the writing perfectly legible. "There's the only proof," he said, "El Grecos were ever here. Dick routed it out."

Dick took up the story.

"One of a set," he said. "I found them in the muniment room. It's a diary kept for seventy years from 1700 to 1770 by the then vicar of Barsley Forest. His name was Floyd."

"Floyd?" repeated Bobby. "An ancestor of Miss Mary Floyd's?"

"I shouldn't wonder," Dick said. "I don't know. It's odd, though, how everything seems to turn in upon itself in all this business. That's what you are thinking, isn't it? Like a maze with every path you take bringing you back to where you were before and none leading you to the centre."

"There must be one that takes you there," Bobby told them, "and it's my job to find it, because, you see, the centre is a missing man, whose wife is anxious."

"Yes, I know," Dick agreed. "When I found these old manuscript books, all tucked away up there, nothing to show how they ever got there, it struck me they might be worth publishing. I don't know if you remember but a few years back there was a sort of boom in old diaries. There used to be very long, very scholarly articles in the *Times Literary Supplement* about them. I happen to know a chap in the writing racket—and a racket it is all right if half the tales he tells are true."

"Probably they aren't," interposed Sir Alfred. "The fellow's a journalist."

This last word was pronounced with a heavy and final condemnation against which none protested. Dick went on:

"I sent him the whole bally lot of manuscript volumes—seventy of 'em, one to each year. He said they were no good—no juice he said. No human interest. All dry items of every day life. Never even said what he had for dinner. Merely noted the weather and the names of people he visited and the times of the services he took in church and that sort of thing. Lists of names and times and dates. Hardly ever any comment. But there was one entry my friend spotted and wrote me about. Old Mr Floyd remarks that Mr Richard of the Abbey is back that day from making the Grand Tour, as they used to call it, and had brought with him a number of paintings. There's a list of them. The old boy had a passion for making lists. Most of the pictures can be identified. They are up in the gallery here all right. But the last item refers to 'Two pictures in frames of gilded wood, very strange, as though done in Bethlem hospital, said to be the handwork of a Greek, as may well be the case.' The price is put down as three guineas and a half for the pair, and the place of purchase as Seville. And that's all."

Sir Alfred took up the tale.

"You can imagine that set us all thinking. We had a look through the house on the off chance of finding 'em tucked away somewhere. I daresay you've heard the story of the Rembrandt found in a nursery where generations of kids had used it for a target for peashooters? No such luck here. So Dick started another search through the muniment room. There are piles of papers, old household books, leases, letters that have been kept for one reason or another."

"It would take years to make a thorough search," Dick interposed. "I had a brain wave though." He walked across to the bookshelves and took down a substantial looking volume, entitled *History of European Art*. He opened it at the chapter dealing with Spain. At the end of the chapter was a blank half page and on it was a note in a thin faded handwriting. Dick read it aloud: "Richard wrong as usual. No mention of his nightmare favourite and so no loss nor mentioned in the inventory. But the candlesticks are listed and are of value and should be recovered. June, 1887."

"Who is 'Richard'?" Bobby asked.

CHAPTER XVIII
AN EARLIER PETER

BOBBY HAD ASKED this question almost casually, without expecting the answer to be of any special interest. Yet it was followed by a curious pause. Dick and his uncle exchanged quick glances. Mr Montague Hart seemed about to make a protest and then to change his mind. Bobby became aware of an odd impression that somehow this stray question of his had pierced near the heart of things. Yet he could not imagine why. He had the impression, too, that the other three had much the same feeling and yet that they also were not certain why.

"The only Richard in the family at that time, taking it the reference is a family one," Sir Alfred said at last, "was my uncle, Dick's great-uncle."

"The Richard Rawdon who died the same year and is buried in Barsley Forest church," interposed Mr Hart.

Once more Sir Alfred and Dick exchanged quick glances. Then Dick said:

"No. There is a memorial tablet there. If Inspector Owen goes to look at it—"

"He would all right," interrupted Sir Alfred, not so much resentfully as stating an unwelcome fact that had to be reckoned with. "Police johnnies are like that."

"I am sure," said Bobby apologetically, for indeed to go and look at that tablet for himself had been his instant determination, though once more he had no idea why he should do so, "I am sure Mr Hart will agree that all evidence is the better for being confirmed. Memory is a very uncertain guide."

Mr Hart uttered a kind of grunt of unwilling and dissatisfied acquiescence, much as if implying that the statement might be generally correct but should not be applied to distinguished and wealthy clients.

"Well, if he does," Dick continued, "he will see the tablet only says 'departed this life', and the date and a long Latin inscription detailing the virtues of the deceased and the grief of his family." Yet a third time uncle and nephew exchanged glances, a little this time as if the younger man were asking permission and the older were disclaiming all responsibility. Dick apparently made up his mind. "The date is June, 1887," he said, and Mr Montague Hart got up and walked across to the window and stood there with his back to the room and an air of finally washing his hands of the whole affair.

"June, 1887," Bobby repeated and glanced at the open *History of European Art* and at the scribbled note bearing the same date.

"Exactly," said Sir Alfred.

Hart came back from the window and began to waggle his eye-glasses again.

"All this seems to me entirely beside the point," he said. "If there is a point," he added. "How is this piece of family history going to assist the inspector?"

"I suppose," observed Sir Alfred, "Dick's got to explain why he went to see Crayfoot and why he was visiting the hut in the forest?"

"It is always of the greatest possible help," Bobby said, "when we are given the background of any investigation. It's an enormous assistance to get some idea of what's behind it all. We do have some idea then at least of how to set to work." He spoke more directly to the lawyer. "Of course, I agree absolutely," he said, "that the whole point for me is the anxiety of a wife over the disappearance of her husband. The Mr Richard Rawdon who died—"

"Departed this life," interrupted Sir Alfred.

"Well, departed this life," Bobby said, accepting the correction with a touch of impatience, "is, as I understand it, buried somewhere else, not in the church here?"

"The family story," Sir Alfred answered, "is that he died on a walking tour in France, somewhere between Paris and Lyons. There seems no record of the exact place. It might be found perhaps if a search were made."

"A difficult undertaking, very costly too," commented Mr Hart.

"You see," Dick continued the story, "there had been a fine old family row. That's where Crayfoot's footman grandfather and the portrait you spotted in his drawing-room come into it. The Richard of the memorial tablet fell in love with a Miss Mary Floyd and wanted to marry her. There was an awful upset. Her father was a farm labourer, rather a superior sort, a foreman on a biggish farm in fact, but still clearly a working man. Our family threw fits. So did the Floyd family apparently. Quite outside their idea of the eternal fitness of things for one of their girls to marry a future baronet and squire."

"Fifty years ago," Sir Alfred reminded them. "They were pretty stuffy about that sort of thing then. Are now for that matter. Still, to-day it's not quite the same as the skies falling as it was then."

"I expect we're more used to the skies tumbling about our heads," remarked Dick grimly. "The world's not the snug, safe, secure place it used to be. Anyhow, it seems hell popped loose. There wasn't much could be done about great-uncle Richard except kick him out; and as he was the second son, and the eldest son, the heir, was an invalid, there was every chance that he might come back again—strict entail."

"My father was the third brother," Sir Alfred explained. "I inherit through him. Dick's father was the youngest son—the fourth."

"Anyhow, as they couldn't do an awful lot about great-uncle, the joint offensive of both families combined was concentrated on the unlucky girl," continued Dick. "I suppose she wasn't strong enough to hold on. Girls did as they were told in 1887 probably. Queen Victoria's jubilee, and her shadow still long in the land. Well, the girl was married off to some one more suitable to a farmer's foreman's daughter than a probable future baronet was thought to be. Good tactics because that disposed of them both. Girl and boy, too. The girl safely married and the boy done in. Because he 'departed this life' as the tablet says, within a few months. Family legend is that it broke him up for good when he found the girl had let him down. No more interest in life, all women a bad lot, and glad to die when he fell ill on his French walking tour. Rosalind says 'Men have died but not for love'. She didn't know great-uncle Richard."

"It's a tragic little story," Bobby said; for somehow the telling of that tale of past despair and grief had a good deal affected him and then he found himself reflecting that probably the Mary Floyd of to-day, the one he had met the preceding Sunday, would not give in so easily or so soon."

"It's how it came about," Dick was saying now, "that the third son succeeded to the title and estates, and unless uncle marries—"

"Not me," interjected Sir Alfred.

"—I shall succeed to them some day," Dick continued.

"To title and estates?" asked Bobby.

"To title and debts," corrected Sir Alfred.

"Whereas, I suppose," continued Dick, paying no attention to the interruption, "if those two poor young devils hadn't been messed about the way they were and allowed to marry, he would have remained a younger son with a younger son's portion and neither title nor estate—nor debts—would have come uncle's way or mine."

"But what had the Crayfoot you said was footman here at the time to do with it?" Bobby asked. "Why was he dismissed without a character?"

"It was through him great-uncle Richard met his Miss Floyd. He and great-uncle were rather pals, apparently. Great-uncle had rather a way of going off on his own—you remember he was on a walking tour in France when he 'departed this life'. Taste for nature, taste for low company, whichever way you like to put it. 'The wind on the heath, brother.' That sort of idea. Somewhere or other he picked up Crayfoot. It seems likely they met in gaol, doing seven days' hard as rogues and vagabonds. On one of his tramps great-uncle got into a row with local police, and was fined twenty shillings or seven days. He had lost all his money in the row, and preferred to do his seven days rather than let the family know. Afterwards he brought Crayfoot back with him to the Abbey, got him fixed up as a footman or valet, or something, and it was through Crayfoot that he met Miss Floyd. Crayfoot apparently had a bit of an artistic gift. Great-uncle thought he had discovered a genius and paid for him to have lessons. The family probably didn't like that; a footman's a footman and an artist's an artist. Much the same, but you don't mix 'em. But his real offence, of course, was his aiding and abetting great-uncle in his love affair; and there's a vicious note, probably libellous, in the household accounts for June, 1887, accusing him of dishonesty."

"The same date," observed Bobby.

"Yes. When things came to a head," agreed Dick. "The note goes on to say he was dismissed without a character and so can go back to his gipsy life in the forest."

"Oh, yes," said Bobby, interested. "Did he, I wonder?"

"Don't know," answered Dick. He added casually: "Footman Crayfoot's first name is given as Peter."

CHAPTER XIX

DIABOLIC CANDELABRA

MR MONTAGUE HART was the first to make any comment. Bobby had received the remark in silence. The other two were trying to look unconcerned but he knew that all the same they were watching him closely. Shrugging his shoulders, the lawyer said, a kind of angry impatience in his tone:

"Peter is a common enough name."

"So it is," agreed Bobby. He looked up at Sir Alfred, still leaning against the mantelpiece with his hands in his pockets, at Dick, who now removed his own gaze from Bobby to direct it out of the window towards the forest, visible in the distance like a vast strange sea of green. Bobby said:

"You mean you think it possible this man they call the hermit may be the Crayfoot who once was a footman here?"

Nobody answered. Bobby continued:

"You think it possible when he left he took the El Greco pictures with him? You think it possible he has them still?"

"Oh, I don't know," said Sir Alfred vaguely.

"There was no sign of them in the hut when I was there," Bobby said.

"No, I know," agreed Dick. He added: "The place was all upset."

"Probably always is," suggested Hart.

"Not like that," said Dick.

"Oh, well," Hart said.

"That's why you went to the hut?" Bobby asked Dick, who removed his gaze from the window and the distant view for one brief moment but otherwise made no reply.

"If he had the pictures there," Bobby said, "you would think some one would have noticed them and said something. I suppose he might have kept them covered up. If he has got them, he might easily claim they were a free gift, and it might be difficult to prove anything else." He paused and said slowly: "Very much a case in which possession would be nine-tenths of the law, more than nine-tenths very likely." When again none of them answered, he said: "There's something about candlesticks, too, isn't there?"

"Supposed to be Cellini's work," Sir Alfred said. "Silver. Candelabra, really, each with six branches. Heirlooms. Always fully described in the old inventories and still solemnly stuck in, though they can't be found. There's that scribble now Dick has come across, if it means anything."

"Nothing much to go on," Dick pointed out. "Candlesticks aren't candelabra. A candlestick is only for one candle. It may mean something quite different."

"If candelabra answering the description in the settlement inventories were found, they could be identified?" Bobby asked.

"Oh, yes," answered Sir Alfred. "They are quite well-known things. Or were. Quite likely somebody stole them and they've been melted down long ago. But there are plenty of references to them up to about fifty years ago. They are known as the 'Diabolic Candelabra'. Cellini mentions them in one of his letters. He doesn't say so but the story is they were made for use at celebrations of the Black Mass."

"Cheerful idea," observed Bobby.

"They look like it all right," Dick said. "At least, the photos do."

He went across to the bookshelves, found another volume, opened it and showed Bobby a photograph of two great spreading candelabra, enormous things, each one of the twelve branches, six to each stem, terminating in a grinning, fiendish head that seemed even in this pictorial representation as if it could have come only from the depths of some tortured, hell-inspired imagination. Bobby stared at them curiously. There was about them a kind of awful fascination that even this mere photograph managed somehow to convey.

"Pretty things, aren't they?" Dick remarked. He closed the book, replaced it on the shelves and all three of them were aware of a certain relief as though an evil thing had been put away. Dick went on: "Another story about them is that Cellini conceived them after committing one of his murders and celebrated their completion by another, and that this time the murdered man, as he was dying, laid a curse upon them, so that ever after whenever they are lighted, murder follows. Two or three times in the old inventories there is a note, 'Let these never be used or lighted, for they are evil things and death follows'. A third version is that Cellini made two almost identical sets. One with heads of the twelve apostles, for the pope of his time, and one, in a kind of devilish caricature, with these heads of fiends. Only stories, of course, but if the originals are anything like that photo, you can understand what started them."

"So you can," agreed Bobby heartily. "Enough to start anything. Anyhow, all that means they can easily be identified. They would be valuable, too?"

"Yes, rather, jolly valuable," declared Sir Alfred. "Fetch a big figure any day. Curiosity value added to Cellini workmanship. American millionaires would tumble over themselves to buy."

"In spite of the legend that when they are lighted, murder follows?" Bobby asked.

"Oh, they would call it a tradition and be willing to pay double," Dick put in. "They've not been found yet, though, and most likely uncle's right and they were melted down long ago. Mr Hart thinks the description in the inventories would be good enough proof of ownership though, if they did turn up."

"Oh, undoubtedly," agreed the lawyer.

"But you don't think the El Grecos could be identified and proof of ownership produced?" Bobby remarked thoughtfully.

"Doubtful," said Mr Hart. "Very doubtful. One could try."

"We don't know much about them," Dick pointed out. "We've no idea of subject or title or anything. Apparently no one thought much of them or thought them worth entering in the inventories."

"Didn't this man who called to see you and said his name was Smith show you what he said were reproductions—prints?"

"The idea was to show the style," Sir Alfred explained. "An El Greco is pretty distinctive. No one else ever turned out stuff quite like his. I think the Smith man meant to ask if we knew of anything of the sort."

"Is it known when the candelabra disappeared?"

"All we can say is that they were missed when the fresh inventory was drawn up on my father's succession—that was in 1897. No reference to them can be traced for a good many years before that. There is one note saying they had been placed in the bank for safe keeping, but there is no receipt, no date, and no entry in the bank records. The last dated reference is the one Dick found there."

He nodded as he spoke to the still open *History of European Art* with the pencilled note at the end of the chapter on the art of Spain.

"The inspector seems very interested in candlesticks," observed Hart with his usual scarcely concealed sneer.

"It seems to link up with something else I came across," Bobby explained. He added formally: "Naturally, if candlesticks or pictures are found, or any information concerning them comes to our knowledge, you will be informed." He went on: "Is there any reason to think that the Miss Floyd who very kindly gave me and my wife some tea on Sunday is descended from the Floyd who was vicar here and kept the diary you showed me, or from the other Miss Floyd you mentioned?"

"It's not an uncommon name about here," Sir Alfred said. "I should think it's very likely there's some connection. The parson had a dozen children or thereabouts. They all had in those days."

"There is certainly a resemblance between the young lady and the portrait I saw," Bobby remarked.

"I must have another look at it," Dick said. "I expect it's the same family. The Miss Floyd who didn't marry my great-uncle died very soon after her marriage and left no children. I do know that. I suppose there may be some relationship."

Bobby got to his feet.

"Thank you very much for all you've told me," he said. "I think it may be a great help. I think I must visit Mrs Crayfoot again and see if she can tell me anything more. May I say that, grateful as I am, I should be more grateful still if you had told me—more."

"Eh?" said Sir Alfred, straightening himself abruptly. "Oh, well, clever, aren't you?" he asked moodily. "Well, we shan't, you know."

"What do you mean—more?" Dick asked.

"In my opinion," declared Montague Hart, his eyeglasses more minatory than ever, "the inspector should explain his meaning fully."

CHAPTER XX

BURGLARY

BY NOW IT had grown late, but all the same Bobby decided to drive straight back to Tombes. It would be as well, he thought, to try to secure at once a further talk with Mrs Crayfoot. He drove slowly, for the night was dark and the 'blackout' strictly enforced. Even the lights of passing vehicles were barely visible. He stopped, too, to ring up Olive, to tell her he would be late home, whereon a small and distant voice asked wearily if he were ever anything else. So Bobby said he was sorry but there it was. In reply to a further inquiry he answered with some indignation that of course he had had something to eat—or at least was just upon the very exact point of so doing. One thing he never forgot, he said, was his dinner; to which the reply was a sniff so eloquent of such contempt for such a claim that he hurriedly hung up and departed. Thus reminded, however, he did delay so far as to spare time to get himself some bread and cheese and a glass of beer, all the nourishment a small wayside inn he came to could provide.

The pause for this refreshment gave him, too, a chance to think over more carefully his recent talk at the Abbey, and more and more strongly grew the conviction in his mind that while uncle and nephew had seemed almost unnecessarily communicative in the long story they had told him of those unlucky lovers of half a century ago, yet that this communicativeness had had behind it a cause and purpose they had kept concealed. Certainly, it was natural enough that police help should be wished for in the recovery of things of such value as the lost paintings and the Cellini candelabra. All the same, Bobby felt very certain that there was some other fact of extreme, perhaps of vital, significance, whereof they had not thought fit to inform him.

What this might be, however, he found it hard to imagine. Was it possible, he asked himself, that they knew or suspected what had happened to Crayfoot? Or again, had Dick Rawdon's visit to the hut in the forest no other purpose than to attempt to identify the hermit as the one-time footman? And was it his first visit?

He finished his meal and resumed his journey; only soon to discover that as before he had been lost in a maze of speculation, so now he was lost, and quite as thoroughly, in another sense, since he had no idea where he had got to. After a time, however, a passer-by put him on the right path and presently he was able to draw up before the gate of the narrow drive leading to the Crayfoot residence. He decided to leave his car in the road, since that narrow and curving drive would not be easy to negotiate in the darkness of a 'blackout', and as he was in the act of pushing open the gate to enter the drive he heard a stealthy, rustling movement in the hedge close by. It had a furtive sound, a warning and suspicious sound, this stealthy rustling. Bobby turned abruptly. Only just in time, for a voice called:

"Take that, you red-headed swine."

At the same instant something heavy—a stone or half a brick perhaps—thrown with force, passed so close it grazed his shoulder. He made a dash forward in a swift pursuit, not likely in that darkness to have much success. He heard someone running away. He ran, too. The sound of running feet that he was following, ceased. Either his assailant was standing still, trusting to the mantle of the night that covered him as with a cloak of invisibility, or else perhaps he had dodged into one of the gardens of these neighbouring houses where the soft earth of flowerbeds or lawns deadened his footsteps.

Bobby gave up the chase after he had nearly knocked all the breath out of his body by colliding with a post it had been impossible to see. A case of mistaken identity, he supposed, since, while he hoped he was not a swine, he knew for a fact that he was not red-headed. He went back to his car, found his electric torch, and by its aid discovered presently an ugly-looking half-brick lying near the entrance to the Crayfoot drive. A very ugly-looking object indeed, Bobby thought, as he weighed it reflectively in his hand, and he was exceedingly glad that he had not in fact 'taken it'. The thing was capable of killing had it struck aright. He tossed it aside. There was no hope of finding fingerprint markings—'dabs'—on that rough and broken surface. It came back to him that the epithet 'red-headed' had been used, a fact of which, until now, in the excitement of the chase and the assault, he had not fully grasped the significance. But now he reminded himself that the stranger, the first stranger, the one who had made inquiries for chocolates at Walters's, who had run off with Mary Floyd's bottle of flavouring, who had lunched with Dr Maskell at the Rawdon Arms, had been described as having red hair.

Was he, then, this unknown, this elusive and vanishing figure, coming back into the story? Was he, as it were, yet another path in the maze, a path like the others leading back apparently and yet that somehow, somewhere, sometime, must join with that other which led to the secret centre of it all? Again, who was it who so much disliked this unknown as to lie in wait for him in the dark with murderous intent? And for what reasons?

"Chocolates? Crayfoot? Chocolates?" Bobby muttered to himself. "We had the lost El Greco motive up at the Abbey and now have we got back to the chocolate motive?"

He shook his head, gave up the puzzle for the time, and went on towards the house, occasionally flashing his torch on the ground to show him his way. He knocked and rang; and as the echo of knock and ring died away, a clamour broke out within the house, a shouting, a sound of heavy trampling, of blows exchanged. There followed, loud in the still night, a pistol shot. Bobby flung himself against the door, but it was strong and securely locked. He flashed his torch on the windows near and saw they were secured by shutters, put on, no doubt, because of the 'blackout' regulations. The sounds within continued. They came, Bobby thought, from the back of the house, and when he ran round the corner of the building, he saw, coming from behind it somewhere, a ray of light, surprising and startling and conspicuous in the dark night whose complete supremacy, in these days of savage war, must not be challenged or broken. Even now a voice in the distance was shouting:

"What's that light doing? What's that light?"

With the ray from the rear of the house as a guide, with the light of his torch on the ground to show him the path, Bobby raced round the house. There, behind it, from the disturbed curtains over one of the windows of a room on the ground floor, light shone out. Bobby ran towards it. Two more pistol shots rang out. Bobby made a leap at the window and balanced himself on the sill. A heavy, well-directed blow, sent him off again. He fell backwards, alighting fortunately on soft earth but for an instant dazed by the fall. He began to get again to his feet. People were running towards him, shouting to each other. One of them made a grab at him and caught him by the arm. He said sharply:

"Let go. I'm a police officer."

"He's not in uniform," someone called suspiciously, and the man who had hold of Bobby's arm tightened a grip he had begun to loosen.

Bobby had no time to waste in argument. He tripped his captor up very neatly, deposited him in the same flower-bed with which he himself had recently become acquainted, made another dive for the window, paused to shout from the sill:

"Go round to the front some of you, see no one gets away."

The voice of authority had its effect. One or two of the newcomers obeyed. The man Bobby had tripped up, less amenable than the others or angered by his fall, shouted:

"See that chap doesn't, anyhow," and began to follow Bobby through the window.

Within, the room was in extreme disorder. Broken furniture, smashed and scattered bric-à-brac, was everywhere. The struggle that had taken place there had been sufficiently destructive in its effects. Only the pictures hanging on the walls seemed undisturbed, though one had its glass smashed. It had been pierced by a bullet. Bobby noticed, too, in the one quick glance he threw around, that the portrait which bore so marked a resemblance to the Mary Floyd of Coop's Cottage was hanging askew, as though some one had recently taken it down to examine it more closely and then had replaced it in a hurry and awkwardly. Before the fireplace a man lay supine, and Bobby gasped with amazement when he saw who it was. He was bleeding from a wound in his side and from a head injury. Bobby knelt to look more carefully at his injuries. To the man who had scrambled in after him, Bobby said:

"I saw a 'phone in the hall. Ring up the police first and then a doctor. Dr Maskell. Hurry. Hurry, I tell you."

"Yes, but—" began the other, apparently still doubtful and suspicious, perhaps still ruffled by his fall whereof face and clothing bore some evidence.

"Do what I tell you," Bobby roared, with an accent of such mingled authority and anger that this time he was quickly obeyed. He shouted after the other's disappearing figure: "Tell the police Inspector Owen is here. Tell Dr Maskell it's urgent."

More people appeared on the scene. Bobby was doing his best to stop the injured man's wound from bleeding. The head injury seemed less serious. Some one offered brandy and was hurt and indignant when Bobby refused to allow it to be poured down the unconscious man's throat.

"No need to choke him as well," he said.

The man who had been sent to 'phone came back into the room and stood looking doubtfully at Bobby. It seemed he was still not quite satisfied.

"You are Inspector Owen?" he asked. "Well, the police will be here as quick as they can get."

He said this with a slightly warning manner, apparently suggesting that if Bobby were not what he claimed to be, then his pretensions would soon be unmasked. Bobby looked up at him. He was a fattish man with a round bullet head and a wide mouth. He had an 'A.R.P.' badge in his button-hole. A taller man, older, wearing a short beard, pushed forward.

"What's going on here?" he demanded. "What's all this?"

"Some of you search the house," Bobby said. "You won't find anyone but you had better make sure. The fellow who did this was probably off and away the second he had knocked me off the window-sill. Does anyone know where Mrs Crayfoot is?"

"She's gone to spend the night with a friend," the man with the beard said. "My name's Mulholland. I live next door. She told me. Is that a burglar?" he asked, looking mistrustfully at the prostrate man by whom Bobby was still kneeling.

To the man who had been 'phoning, who wore the 'A.R.P.' badge, Bobby said:

"Are you a neighbour, too?"

"Next street," the other answered. "I'm an air raid warden. I was going my round as usual. I saw that light." He went over and adjusted the curtain which was still allowing light to escape. "My name's Weston," he said.

"Oh, yes," Bobby said, and knew the name was familiar, and then remembered it was that of the husband of the lady who first mentioned Mary Floyd's chocolates to Olive and had said, too, that her husband thought that the recipe for their preparation might be of value. "Oh, yes," he repeated, and wondered if now Weston also came into the story.

"Who is it?" Mulholland asked again, peering closely at the prostrate man. "He looks like—he doesn't look like a burglar."

"I don't think he is," Bobby answered. "He is Sir Alfred Rawdon, of Barsley Abbey."

CHAPTER XXI

NOCTURNAL VISIT

THERE WAS MUCH routine work to be done. The house had to be carefully examined and the fact was soon made clear that it had been hurriedly but effectively searched. Mrs Crayfoot had to be sent for. She arrived in a highly nervous and excited condition but was able to say that there was nothing missing. A sleepy fingerprint expert appeared and began a task that was long, tedious, and unsuccessful. Dr Maskell came, shook his head over Sir Alfred's condition, and superintended his removal to the local cottage hospital, where, Maskell thought, an immediate operation would be necessary.

It was long past midnight before Bobby, the routine work well under way, was able to depart. Even then it was not home that he went but to the bungalow, not far from his factory, where Dick Rawdon lived alone, the wife of one of the factory employees coming in each day to do the necessary cooking and cleaning. It was not without some difficulty that Bobby found the place and then he had to knock and knock again before at last a window opened and a voice inquired with some adjectival emphasis who he was and what he wanted.

Bobby, who had his reasons for wishing to give his news in person rather than through the local police, explained briefly. Dick, startled out of his sleepiness, admitted Bobby then and listened in apparent complete surprise and bewilderment to his story.

"What on earth," Dick asked, "was uncle doing there and who in thunder could possibly want to attack him like that? You don't mean the wound's dangerous, do you?"

"Dangerous, yes," Bobby answered. "Dr Maskell wouldn't say more than that. The head wound isn't so bad, but he was shot in the side as well. Dr Maskell wouldn't give any opinion. He seemed to think it was impossible to say how it would turn out. He said he could tell better after the bullet had been extracted. Can you tell me what your uncle's movements were after I left?"

"No. I left almost immediately."

"You didn't stay for dinner?"

"No. I said I left immediately."

"Dinner must have been ready," Bobby commented. "Was there any reason why you should hurry away? Didn't Sir Alfred suggest your staying?"

"Well, as a matter of fact, I don't think he did," Dick answered. "Hart said he must be going. I think he said something about some appointment and I said I would give him a lift. I knew dinner would be waiting for me here and I can't say I care for night driving in blackout conditions."

"As a matter of fact," Bobby remarked, "it was much lighter after about eleven when the moon had risen than it was before—pitch black it was earlier on. You and Mr Hart left together immediately after I did. Where did you leave him?"

"I put him down at the Besly tram terminus. I knew he could get a tram there."

"Then you drove on here? And had dinner? There was some one to cook it, I suppose? You would be a bit late and I daresay she would notice what time you got here?"

Dick scowled. He was beginning to look a little uneasy, a little wary, under this examination. He said:

"If you mean you don't believe me—"

"Oh, not at all," Bobby interposed. "Only it's an elementary police duty to check every statement as far as possible. The most honest, best-intentioned witnesses often make the most unreliable statements. Gives us entirely wrong ideas unless we can check up on them. Probably your cook is sure of the time you arrived. Cooks waiting to serve dinner often keep an eye on the clock—a very close eye, in fact. I speak," said Bobby feelingly, "as a married man."

"Well, if you want to know," Dick answered, now with a touch of defiance in his manner, "Mrs Ball looks after the place for me but she has a husband to look after, too. So she never waits after seven. Ball's on late shift and gets home at nine. Anything warm she has for me she leaves in the oven with the gas turned down or else just simmering. I'm afraid you'll have to take my word for it or not just as you like. I can't prove when I got here and I can't even say exactly. I didn't notice."

"Thank you," said Bobby. "May I just repeat that we don't necessarily disbelieve what we are told because we like to get it confirmed if we can. I gather Sir Alfred also left the Abbey very soon after I did. I rang up to tell them he had met with an accident. I didn't think it necessary to give details. I asked if he had dined at home and when he left. I was told only about half an hour after you left—and after me. As soon as you had gone he ordered his car to be brought round. There isn't a regular chauffeur, apparently. Sir Alfred always drives himself, I understand, but there's a man to clean the car and generally look after it. He can and does drive when necessary. Sir Alfred's dinner seems to have been a very hurried affair. I got full details because I asked what he had had to drink and of course they jumped to the conclusion that there had been a road accident and I suspected he might have taken too much. They were quite naturally and loyally and properly indignant. I was told he hadn't touched the fruit tart that was the sweet course and hadn't even stopped for his coffee. You see, Mr Rawdon, it does seem just a trifle odd that three of you should have left the Abbey in such apparent hurry so immediately after our talk."

"I don't see why," Dick answered, still with that touch of defiance in his manner. "Hart said he had an appointment and I wanted to get home. We're all working under pressure at the factory. I've no time to hang about. Got to be up early, too. I don't know about uncle. We had been in conference on business matters. When it was over we all cleared out. I don't see anything peculiar in that."

"I mightn't either in other circumstances," Bobby agreed. "When so much seems peculiar, perhaps I am inclined to think everything more peculiar than it is. May I ask if any differences of opinion developed during your conference?"

"Plenty. Why not? People don't always think alike. Nothing serious, if that's what you mean."

"Are you generally on good terms with your uncle?"

Dick scowled, hesitated, said angrily:

"You want to know a hell of a lot, don't you?"

"I do," Bobby agreed emphatically. "To put it another way. There's a hell of a lot I want to know. One man has disappeared. His wife comes to us for help. I can't get in touch with the owner of the hut where the last trace of him was found. The interior of that hut has been wrecked. Another man is found shot in the house of the wife of the missing man during her absence. I think a certain amount of curiosity on my part is natural. After all, I am an officer of police charged with the preservation of the king's peace. Shooting people is a very definite breach of that peace. Especially just now, we all have reason to know that the preservation of peace is about our most important interest. When peace goes, all goes. Of course, you are not obliged to answer my questions. But just as I am doing my duty as an officer of police, so it is your duty as a citizen to help me. I daresay you know that if a policeman meets with resistance he can call on any passer-by to help him and that a refusal is a criminal offence. Naturally answering questions is on a different footing but you told me so much this evening I had hoped you would be equally ready to talk to-night. I agree you would be within your rights in telling me to shut up and get out. When that happens, as it does sometimes, police have to obey. It's apt to make them think, though, and they generally try other means. So I'll ask you again, have you any objection to telling me whether you and Sir Alfred were on good terms?"

"Oh, good enough," Dick answered. "He's all right. I suppose I had better explain. You would be sure to hear, anyhow. Uncle and I had a blazing row just before the war broke out."

"Will you tell me what it was about?"

"Oh, money, of course. What do you suppose? I put all I had into Summit Models, Ltd. The place was a bit on the down grade when I took over. I had a dandy idea for a model aeroplane I wanted to develop. Uncle promised to come in, too, if things looked good. Perhaps I overspent a bit, trying to get my model aeroplane on the market. Actual figures weren't too good because of overhead, but I thought prospects were fine. Uncle wouldn't see it. He said his promise had been conditional on results, not prospects. Well, I suppose we both got a bit hot. It looked like ruin to me. He said he wasn't going to risk what he had left to please me. I daresay it's true enough that the Rawdons all have a bit of a temper. Well, it ended with his heaving a glass inkwell at my head. Luckily it missed. The thing was heavy enough to lay you out if it caught you fair. I sort of saw red. It's happened to me once or twice before. It doesn't last. Once at Oxford it did for a bit and I slung a chap into the river and then I had to dive in and fetch him out. Silly as you like. He never forgave me. Said he might have drowned. So he might, I suppose. Only he didn't because I hauled him out. Luckily this time I got my senses back before I laid hands on uncle. I think he was a bit scared, though. Of course, the servants had heard us rowing at each other, and as the inkwell had gone through the window, they couldn't help guessing things had been a bit lively. We made it up afterwards. For one thing the money business settled itself. When the war broke out I got contracts enough to satisfy the bank, so they increased the overdraft instead of calling it in. Now it's mostly paid off and butter won't melt in their mouths when they see me coming. Besides, I knew I had made a fool of myself. Uncle felt a bit the same way. Anyhow, we shook hands and agreed to forget it. Only you know how people talk. Stories got about. Uncle was supposed to have said I was a young devil and I had tried to kill him, he supposed I wanted to be Sir Richard in a hurry. Tasty bit of gossip for every old woman's tea party. Silly enough, for who wants to be a blooming baronet without a penny to the title? May be a bit different now, though, if these pictures turn up, or the candelabra, and if we get the entail broken."

"Is there likely to be any difficulty about that?"

"Oh, there's a cousin, Andrew Rawdon. Stockbroker johnny. Pile of money. He wants the collection of paintings kept intact. I think he has some deep scheme for getting hold of them himself in block. I don't know. Anyhow, he is making trouble. He has kids and possibly he thinks they may inherit. So uncle and I are on one side, and Cousin Andrew on the other. I expect that helped us to make friends again after our row though I still think it was a bit mean of him to let the servants think it was I who slung that inkwell at him, instead of the other way round. I know it makes us sound a couple of the damnedest fools going."

"Oh, yes, it does," agreed Bobby amiably, "but then I never knew any one who wasn't sometimes. Thank you for telling me."

"Shouldn't have," admitted Dick grinning, "only I jolly well knew someone else was dead sure to tell you—with trimmings. Police find out everything, don't they?"

"I wish we did," sighed Bobby. "You can understand it was a big surprise to me to find your uncle at Mrs Crayfoot's. Can you suggest why he went?"

"Haven't the foggiest notion," Dick answered. He looked really worried. "It might be something about those El Greco paintings. You told us you were going to see Mrs Crayfoot again. Uncle may have thought he would, too. Sort of get in first idea."

"I had thought of that," Bobby agreed. "Mrs Crayfoot tells me she is sure she locked up carefully before she left. So there is the question of how Sir Alfred got in. My own idea is that he rang, got no answer' went round to the back to see if he could make any one hear there and found a window open. The latch has been forced expertly. There was clearly some other person in the house and there was nothing in Sir Alfred's pocket he could have used for forcing the window. He did have a small penknife but I compared it with the marks on the window frame and there was certainly no identity. Presumably, therefore, the other person was there first and was responsible for forcing the window. Burglars always leave two ways of retreat. One in the front, one in the rear. Possibly this burglar, whoever he was, was surprised in the act by your uncle. He may have mistaken him for the householder returning and attacked him in an attempt to escape. That would explain the struggle that evidently took place and the shooting. Did you see Sir Alfred arrive or had you left before that? I imagine you saw nothing of the burglar?"

CHAPTER XXII

FINGERPRINTS

SUDDEN AND DIRECT as had been this assault, this swift and probing question, Dick showed no sign of discomposure. He looked at Bobby calmly and after a very brief pause he said equally quietly:

"Is this the celebrated police method of pretending to know what you don't know, in the hope of making the victim betray himself?"

"Are you a victim?" Bobby asked.

"Is that what is called a leading question?"

"No," Bobby answered. "For one thing, 'leading question' doesn't mean an important or significant question, as most people seem to think, any more than 'cross examination' means any closely pressed questioning. I asked what I did because there is evidence to suggest you were in Mrs Crayfoot's drawing-room shortly before your uncle arrived. I know you weren't there afterwards because the house was thoroughly searched. So it seems you must have left either after he got there or shortly before."

"Does all this mean I am suspected of having shot uncle?" Dick asked, more uneasily than ever. "Why should anyone think I would do a thing like that?"

"Well, there is a story of an inkwell, isn't there?" Bobby retorted. "I am afraid you must expect more gossip at more tea tables. I don't mind telling you frankly that if you had shown any signs of having been knocked about recently, I should have arrested you at once. It was chiefly in order to make sure of that that I made this, I am afraid, very late call. You see, Sir Alfred put up quite a good fight. The other fellow didn't get away unmarked. Probably your uncle was getting a bit the best of it. That's why the other man started pistol play. We found two bullets in the drawing-room wall, one had gone through a picture. Both had travelled in an upwards direction. As I see it, the man who fired them had been knocked down and was on the floor or getting to his feet again when he fired."

"Uncle is pretty hefty, unusually so for his age," Dick agreed. "I dare-say it was like that. But if you know I wasn't there before or after—"

"No," Bobby interrupted. "What I said was during or after. There's evidence to show you were there before your uncle arrived."

"I've played poker," Dick said quietly. "I'm a fair hand at it. Good enough to spot a bluff. I think you're lying."

"Not a very polite remark," commented Bobby, equally quietly. "Sometimes people try to make police lose their tempers. By using insulting language, for instance. But not people with nothing to hide. Have you anything to hide, I wonder?"

"I wasn't trying to be insulting," Dick answered, looking now a trifle abashed. "I was only telling you what I think. What evidence have you? That's a plain question."

"Will you let me take your fingerprints?"

"My fingerprints," repeated Dick, surprised. "Why? What's the idea? I don't think so. No. Why should I? I suppose you mean you've found them in Mrs Crayfoot's drawing-room? Well, why not? I was there the other day. You know that."

"Oh, yes," Bobby agreed. "But there's a portrait there, the one I mentioned to you, the one that has a sort of resemblance to Miss Floyd. When I saw it first, it was hanging straight. Now it's crooked. Someone has been so interested in it as to take it down to look at it nearer the light. There are fingerprints on it. I think they are yours. And I don't think it's likely they have remained there since your visit the other day. I imagine Mrs Crayfoot has her drawing-room dusted more often than that."

"Didn't give me the idea of a room much used," retorted Dick. "I expect the household routine isn't too awfully regular just now either. If you have found any fingerprints on the thing, why should you say they are mine?"

"They correspond," Bobby explained. "When we were talking in the hut in the forest, I showed you some old rather torn and dirty books I found lying on the floor. You handled them, if you remember, and you left very clear dabs. The pages were dirty and rather damp and in first-class condition to take impressions."

Dick looked as furious as he felt and that was in a high degree.

"A dirty trick," he fumed. "You had no right, laying traps. I'll . . . I'll—"

But as he had no idea what he could do he stopped there, subsiding into a somewhat ineffective but still exceedingly angry glare.

"It wasn't a trap," Bobby assured him earnestly.

"What do you call it, then?" Dick demanded, still very angry. Then a new idea struck him. "How can you tell which are mine?" he demanded. "There were thumb marks all over, I noticed that myself."

"Oh, yes," Bobby agreed, "but there were fresh ones on a page where you quoted from the verses when Horace gives up the hope of having any more luck in love. You read a line or two aloud and remarked it couldn't be put into English. You remember?"

"Know Latin, too, do you?" demanded Dick sulkily.

"Oh, I learnt 'mensa, a table,' isn't it? when I was a kid," Bobby answered. "Forgotten it all now. Wonder if they still teach 'mensa'—and how they pronounce it. As a matter of fact I was once given that poem to write out fifty times for an imposition. Day I ought to have played first time for our house eleven, too. So it's no wonder I recognized it. Sort of branded in. I hadn't any idea of getting dabs at the moment. But afterwards—well, I wasn't satisfied. I began to get a feeling there was something wrong somewhere. Also I had a faint suspicion you weren't—well, being as helpful as you might have been."

"Do you suppose I murdered the old man and then uncle tonight?" demanded Dick, still furious.

"There is no evidence the old man has been murdered," Bobby answered, "and I hope your uncle hasn't been, either. It seems most likely he will get better. But I do think there's the evidence of these dabs to suggest that you were in the Crayfoots' drawing-room sometime to-night."

"Oh, very well, so I was," Dick admitted, more sulky now than angry and a little scared as well. "It's that portrait. I wanted to have another look at it. I know it sounds damn silly and I don't suppose you'll believe it."

"Oh, I don't know," Bobby answered. "I take it you didn't get any answer when you knocked, so you went round to the back to see if you could make anyone hear. You couldn't, but you saw the drawing-room window was open and you climbed in. While you were looking at the portrait you heard a knock at the front door. That scared you, so you put the portrait back in a hurry—crooked—and cleared out."

"You seem to know all about it," Dick grumbled.

"Putting two and two together, that's all," Bobby answered. "Did you guess it was your uncle knocking? Did you tell him you meant to have another look at the portrait?"

"I think I said something," Dick admitted. "I don't remember exactly. I never thought it was him knocking. I thought it was Mrs Crayfoot returning. Or someone who might come round to the back. I didn't want to have to explain, so I did a bunk."

"Do you think it possible," Bobby asked, "that your uncle suspected that you didn't so much want to have another look at the portrait as to find out if the El Grecos were there in the Crayfoot house? And do you think that in that case he may have thought it as well to come along himself, if only to see what was happening? As I understand it, with the El Grecos, it will be very much a case of possession being nine-tenths of the law—or even more."

Dick made no answer but looked sulkier than ever. It was plain he found the suggestion plausible, unpleasant, and disturbing. He mumbled something about having no idea what his uncle had been up to and Bobby had better find out for himself what he wanted to know. Nothing he, Dick, could say. For his own part, he repeated, he had merely gone to have another look at the portrait. He knew it sounded damn silly and he didn't expect to be believed. Only it was the strangest coincidence that such a likeness should exist and he supposed it was why when he saw Miss Floyd he felt as if he had seen her before, as if he had always known her.

"History repeating itself?" Bobby suggested.

Dick flushed.

"That's what uncle was trying to be funny about, isn't it?" he said resentfully. "Uncle was just rotting. Good lord, you don't suppose I've fallen in love with a girl I've only seen once? It was just the likeness that worried me. That's all. If it hadn't been for that, I should never have noticed her. Good lord, why should I? A little thin slip of a girl. A country cottage girl, a smut on her nose, too. I remember that. She was cooking or something when I got there. That's all. Uncle's a jolly sight too fond of trying to be funny."

Bobby made no comment. These were waters he had no need to try to navigate. Dick was showing himself flushed and indignant. He stared at Bobby as if daring him to contradiction. Bobby had a feeling that probably so Dick looked when one of his fits of 'seeing red' was approaching.

"The likeness is plain enough," Dick grumbled. "Anyone would spot it at once. Nothing out of the way in that, is there?"

"Oh, no, I noticed it myself," Bobby agreed; and won for himself a fresh and even more angry glare, as much as to say that if he had done so, it was like his impudence.

He took his departure then, leaving Dick sitting there in pyjamas and dressing-gown and looking very angry and tousled and disturbed. He was on the whole inclined to accept Dick's story and yet there was no support for it, except Dick's own word and the evidence of Dick's unbruised face. But that did not prove that Dick's complicity might not have gone very far indeed. Whoever it was who had been engaged in the fight with Sir Alfred and had shot him, might easily be an accomplice or an agent of Dick's. Nothing to show. All the same, even if all that were true, not much light seemed to be thrown on the disappearance of Mr Crayfoot or, for that matter, on that of the old hermit.

"And why," Bobby asked himself as he drove slowly home through the blackout to his belated bed, "why was there no hatchet or axe in the old man's hut and why was there blood on the floor?"

CHAPTER XXIII

BUSINESS TALK

FROM A DEEP sleep that had lasted, Bobby supposed, rather less than a minute and a half, he woke next morning to the sound of the alarm he had been careful to set before tumbling into bed. By his side stood Olive, looking at him severely.

"I suppose," she said, her voice as severe as her looks, "you won't have any time for breakfast? So I needn't waste my time getting it ready."

Bobby, who realized that the neglected, forgotten, uneaten dinner of the previous night still rankled, answered meekly that he thought he might find time for a cup of tea and even possibly to eat a bite of anything that might happen to be going.

Only very slightly placated, Olive observed that no doubt it had been merely a further waste of time to get his bath ready for him, and then retired to spread throughout the house an appetising odour of bacon frying. Presently Bobby, his eyes a trifle red, but otherwise looking very fit, and much the better for bath and shave, arrived to do porridge, bacon, tomatoes, toast, the justice they deserved. As he ate he told Olive something of the previous day's happenings.

"Instead of getting any further," he complained, "all I do is get a fresh problem to worry over. Who chucked that half brick at me? And why? Who shot Sir Alfred? What was he doing there? Is Dick Rawdon all right? Am I right in feeling sure he was there first? What's behind all that long story they told me, diabolic candelabra and all? Talking for talking's sake? Red herring-ing, so to speak? Or some definite purpose? Is that lawyer bloke an accessory, a principal, or just accidental? One thing," Bobby added thoughtfully, looking with some surprise at a toast rack entirely empty and wondering how it had become so, "one thing pretty plain is that Mr Dick Rawdon isn't in love with the Floyd young woman. His uncle evidently half thought he might be and didn't much like the idea either, if you ask me."

"Why do you think he isn't in love with her?" asked Olive.

"Well, I told you," Bobby reminded her. "Talked about there being a smut on her nose. You don't say that about the girl you're in love with, do you?"

Olive looked at him pityingly.

"Men are dense," she said. "If Mr Dick wasn't half way to being in love with Miss Floyd, do you think he would have noticed that smut? Or remembered it?—or thought it worth mentioning?"

"Oh, well, now then," said Bobby.

"Anyone but a man," said Olive, shaking a dispirited head, "would see at once that it was a case of reflex defensive action."

"A—how much?" asked Bobby, slightly awe-stricken, even though he knew that Olive had recently attended a lecture on the new psychology.

"Not," added Olive, though secretly much pleased by the effect she had produced, "that it needed any stuffy old psychologist to tell any woman when a boy's fighting hard against it, but he knows it's no good, because he's already half way, and when a boy's half way, well, he's there, isn't he? And all over but the asking."

Bobby rubbed the end of his nose thoughtfully, and, reaching automatically for the toast rack, once more looked surprised and pained to find it empty.

"If you wouldn't mind saying that all over again in words of one syllable," he suggested meekly; but Olive looked at the clock and said she hadn't time to explain and he had better be off as all the clocks, including the alarm clock, were an hour slow, having been put back an hour by her the night before, since, in her considered opinion, it was better for Bobby to have an hour's extra sleep than to break down presently and have to take a week off for want of proper rest.

"I rang up to let them know you would be an hour later than usual," she added.

In the face of this revelation of feminine duplicity and guile, Bobby could only utter a howl of mingled remonstrance and protest as he fled away. Fortunately when he did reach his office he found nothing of any very pressing importance to need his personal attention. The usual crop of documents marked 'Urgent' 'Very Urgent', 'Secret and Confidential' were all purely routine, and could safely be left to subordinates. The rest of the day he felt he would be able to devote almost entirely to the 'Rawdon Case' as he was beginning to call it.

A 'phone call to the Barsley Forest police sergeant told him that there was as yet no sign of the missing hermit's re-appearance. Another put through to the hospital brought the reply that Sir Alfred was still in a very precarious condition. Yet another call to Mr Weston's Tombes address informed him that Mr Weston was in Midwych, at the office of his firm. So Bobby rang him up there, received a promise that he would come round at once to have a chat, as Bobby had put it, over last night's excitement. Before Weston arrived Bobby learnt from yet another 'phone call put through to the Tombes A.R.P. centre, that as Mr Weston was a traveller, and often away on his rounds, he did not undertake regular work but acted as a relief. It had been by his own suggestion that the night before he had taken the place of the warden who would normally have been on duty at that particular time and spot. The warden in question had been very pleased at the time to get an unexpected night off, but now was slightly disgruntled at having missed so much excitement. Tombes A.R.P. centre showed in fact some disposition to discuss the whole sensational affair at length, but Bobby confined himself to expressing his thanks for the information received and then firmly rang off. Then Mr Weston appeared, took the chair Bobby indicated, and remarked breezily that what beat him and Mrs Crayfoot, too, was not only what Sir Alfred was doing there but how he had got in.

"Deuced odd, eh?" remarked Mr Weston. "You got any idea, inspector?"

Bobby agreed that it was deuced odd, and said there were just one or two things he would like to ask Mr Weston about, if Mr Weston had no objection.

"You are a traveller by profession, I understand?" he said. Mr Weston nodded.

"Corsets," he said.

"Eh?" said Bobby.

"Corsets," Mr Weston repeated. "You know. Things women wear," he explained.

"Oh, yes," said Bobby.

"A dying trade," said Mr Weston moodily. "If things go on the way they are, in fifty years women will be wearing nothing at all."

"Too bad," said Bobby.

"Except," conceded Mr Weston, "slacks and a permanent wave."

"Oh, well," said Bobby, a trifle shaken by such a prospect.

"You can't trust women," pronounced Mr Weston as one who knew. "I had a pal whose family did well once on hatpins. Where are they now?"

Bobby wasn't sure whether this referred to the pal's family or the hatpins. As in neither case did he know the answer, he said nothing.

"Not that it hasn't turned out all right for him," Mr Weston admitted. "He's switched from hatpins to pin tables."

"Quite a change," agreed Bobby.

"Profitable," Mr. Weston said with envy in his voice. "Wish I could get into pin tables. Easy money. Always easy money for you when the mugs think it's easy money for them."

Bobby thought that very true and then as Mr Weston seemed to be settling down for a comfortable but not very relevant chat, Bobby said:

"I really asked you here because there's something I thought you might do to help me."

"Delighted, I'm sure," declared Mr Weston. "Anything legal, as they say in the agony column adverts."

He chuckled at his little joke, beamed on Bobby, and waited. Bobby said:

"Would you mind repeating in a rather loud angry sort of voice, 'Take that, you red-headed swine.'"

CHAPTER XXIV
MORE BUSINESS

MR WESTON GASPED, turned pale, stammered, tried to speak and failed, stared at Bobby helplessly.

"I'm pretty sure I recognized your voice while we were chatting, but I should like to be quite sure," Bobby explained when still there was no answer.

"That's why you got me talking, is it?" complained Mr Weston. "I thought . . . thought we were just being matey. A low trick," he said severely.

"You might have killed me," Bobby remarked, by way of bringing the conversation back to actualities.

"You . . . I . . . I mean . . . it wasn't you, was it?" Mr Weston asked.

"Oh, yes, it was," Bobby assured him. "Very much me."

Mr Weston was beginning to recover himself. He said, but rather feebly:

"Well, anyhow, it wasn't me."

"Come, come," said Bobby smilingly. "We both know it was."

Mr Weston gave in.

"How did you know?" he asked.

"Easy enough," Bobby answered. "Your voice, for instance. Part of a policeman's job is to remember and recognize voices."

"You've got it all wrong," protested Mr Weston, trying to recover lost ground, but Bobby shook his head.

"Now, please, Mr Weston," he said, "as a business man, don't let us waste time."

"You can't prove anything," Mr Weston said, trying now to make his voice sound confident and not succeeding very well.

"I might, I think, if I wanted to," Bobby answered, "but I don't know that I do. No great harm done. Attempted assault and all that, of course. No ill feeling either. All trades have their inconveniences and I suppose a policeman's troubles include half a brick occasionally. Nasty things, though, half bricks. It might have been attempted murder. Or even murder outright."

"I only wanted to give the swine a scare," Mr Weston said. "I took care to miss. Very careful I was."

"Care in the blackout?" murmured Bobby.

"I aimed high," Weston protested. "To make sure it didn't hit," and though Bobby remembered how close the thing had passed by his ear, he made no comment. Weston added: "I don't see what made you think of me?"

"Easy exercise in logic," Bobby answered. "You were interested in Miss Floyd's chocolates. Thought there might be money in them. So was someone else, someone who visited both Miss Floyd and the shop that sold the things for her. Both Miss Floyd and the shop girl mentioned the red hair. He was plainly interested in the chocolates, presumably from the same money point of view, and he was a stranger in the district. So probably he had heard about them from a resident. You are a resident. And you knew about the red hair, witness your remark that accompanied that half brick of yours. Proof it was the same man and someone you knew. You were on the spot as an air raid warden but at your own suggestion, not doing a regular tour of duty."

"That's all just guess-work," grumbled Weston. "You couldn't prove a thing."

"I daresay I could swear to your voice," Bobby answered. "I wouldn't mind betting I could pick out your voice from fifty others. We needn't discuss that, though. At least, I hope not. If you'll just answer a few questions. I gather from the half brick incident and the accompanying remark that you aren't friends any longer. I shouldn't wonder if he hadn't tried to do you down."

Weston nodded gloomily.

"That's right," he said.

"What's his name?" Bobby asked. "And his address?"

"Sammy Stone, 'Sammy to you,' he says before you've known him two minutes—pally. Pally with everyone to see what he can get. I don't know where he lives. Somewhere near London."

"Do you know where he is staying in Midwych?"

Weston shook his head.

"What does he do?"

"He calls himself a financial agent. His real job is buying up retail businesses cheap, nursing them a year or two, and then finding a sucker to sell to at a profit. You can always boost a business for a time if you spend a bit. What you spend on the boosting doesn't go through the books and so there's a big and growing profit to show."

"Have you known him long?"

"Met him at the Brightwell Hotel, you know, opposite the Central station. Everyone on the road knows the Brightwell. Very well run. Cheap, too. All the boys stop there when they're in Midwych. I drop in now and then for a chat and hear the news. Stone has been on the road, too, and knows a lot of the boys. He's a great lad for standing drinks, and 'Sammy to you' and all that. That's how he hears of his bargains—retailers who have died and the widow might be ready to sell out cheap. That sort of thing. He heard me telling some of the boys about the chocolates Walters was selling like hot cakes at seven and six a pound, and calculating what the profit must be. Afterwards he stood me a drink and we got talking. I didn't tumble to it at the time but then I began to think he had asked a good many questions. One of the boys told me he was in Midwych about a picture dealer and framer's business he had bought up and was trying to boost. I thought I would like another talk so I went round and found him there. Welcomed me like a long lost brother, he did. Played me for a sucker all right—me," said Mr Weston bitterly, "that's been on the road where they don't grow suckers ever since I was a kid. What he said was he had been thinking over our talk and we might do a deal. Stood me another drink at the local and it was all settled up I was to get Miss Floyd to tell us what she put in her chocolates to make 'em taste the way they did. Then we would put them on the market."

"Where was Miss Floyd to come in?" asked Bobby.

"Her?" asked Mr Weston, slightly surprised. "Oh, we would have paid her for the recipe, of course—a fiver, perhaps. She could never have handled it herself, you know, not in a big way. Just a girl," he explained, waving her aside, as it were. "Business this was," he added.

"Quite so," said Bobby, reflecting that business resembles charity in that it covers a multitude of sins.

"Not a job for amateurs, marketing a new product," Mr Weston went on. "Well, what do you think? Sam said not to press the girl. Not to hurry. Wait for him to explore the ground. I was to get samples and he would take them round to the big firms and get a contract and then we could get an advance from the bank. He said he never put up his own money, always the bank's. All the bank has to do, you see, is to make an entry against your name, and there's your capital in a stroke of the pen. Glad and ready to do it, too."

"Can't say I've noticed any gladness and readiness myself," Bobby murmured, a little dazed by these revelations of high finance.

"Ah, you aren't in business, got to be a business man to understand it," explained Weston tolerantly. "Why, Sammy Stone told me once he had credits from seven banks going all at once, using one to keep t'other quiet, if you see what I mean. Lord, if he can put it across me that knows the road from A to Z and back again, don't you think he can with a bank manager and them with their mouths open for half a chance to use customers' money?"

Bobby could only shake a bewildered head at this picture of bank managers so different from his own impression of those aloof and godlike creatures, incarnate and immortal spirits of the universal negative.

"Well, now then," he said feebly.

"So you can guess," continued Mr Weston, "I felt pretty sick when I found he had been round to see Miss Floyd on his own, got her to give him a sample of her flavourings, had it analyzed, applied for a provisional patent, and," said Mr Weston, his voice quivering with indignation, "when I tackled him, tried to put me off with a fiver."

"Just like Miss Floyd," Bobby murmured.

"Yes, but this was me," said Mr Weston with an innocent sincerity that was perfectly genuine. "It wasn't so much the money. It may not amount to anything after all. The public may not cotton to the flavour, not enough to count. It's a gamble, is public taste. What hurt," said Mr Weston gravely, almost solemnly, "was the insult to me as a business man."

"I see," said Bobby.

"Wouldn't you?" asked Mr Weston earnestly, "have felt like half a brick?"

"At any rate," retorted Bobby, "I'm glad I didn't feel half a brick."

CHAPTER XXV
EL GRECO PRINTS

BOBBY'S INTENTION HAD been to call next on Dr Maskell, but after what Weston had told him, he decided to try to have first a talk with this Mr Sammy Stone, so adroit with bank managers, so interested in the new flavour discovered by the solitary of the forest.

A little nervous at the thought of confronting one so gifted in matters of finance, Bobby was half inclined to leave his wallet behind and empty his pockets, just as a matter of general precaution. However, he decided to risk it. The address given him by Mr Weston was in a street at no great distance and thither he took his way. The shop was in a good position and looked prosperous and well stocked but at the moment was without customers. A man came forward at Bobby's entrance and observed gloomily that if it was drawing pins, they hadn't any and weren't likely to, either, not till the war was over. Bobby explained that it wasn't drawing pins, it was Mr Stone he wished to see. He was told Mr Stone wasn't there. He might be in later, perhaps, or he might not. So Bobby said he would call again, and was business good, and the shopman said still more gloomily that it was neither good nor bad, there just wasn't any to be either the one thing or the other.

"The only things people want," he explained, "are the things you haven't got."

"Too bad," said Bobby, a little absently, for his eye had caught two photogravure reproductions prominently displayed. "Mr Stone hasn't been here long, has he?"

"Took over," said the other, "three weeks before the war. Quite sure there wasn't going to be a war, he was, even though that's why he got it cheap. And now," said the shopman, not without a certain relish, "wishes he hadn't."

"Oh, well, war does upset things, doesn't it?" Bobby observed vaguely, though guessing both from this and from certain signs of dust and neglect he was beginning to notice, that 'boosting' a business, especially a business of this type, a picture framer's and dealer's, was no easy task in days of war. Nor was he much inclined to think that Mr Stone had made himself greatly beloved by his employee. Facts it might be useful to remember, he supposed, and nodding at the two photogravures he had noticed, he said: "What are those? I've seen something like them somewhere—same sort of style."

The depressed looking shopman showed for the first time signs of animation.

"About here?" he asked. "Anywhere in Midwych?"

Then he looked depressed again when Bobby shook his head.

"In a picture gallery abroad, I think," Bobby said. "El Grecos, aren't they?"

"That's right," the shopman answered, evidently surprised at such knowledge.

"Sell well?" Bobby asked.

"Oh, they aren't put there to sell," the shopman explained. "Just as well, too, because if they were, they wouldn't. Not every one's taste, they aren't."

"I suppose not," agreed Bobby. "Only what are you showing them for, if they're not for sale?"

"Gent asked me to," replied the other, and seemed inclined to think that answer sufficient.

"Was the gent," Bobby asked, "a tallish, darkish, youngish man with a big nose? Name of Smith?"

"That's right," the shopman agreed, looking surprised again. "You know him? Aren't hunting 'em, too, are you?"

"Hunting them," Bobby repeated. "Why hunting them?"

"Well, that's what Mr Smith's doing," the shopman explained. "He told me he was the art critic of the *Morning Announcer,* and he's writing a book about El Greco and his pictures he wants to make a complete List of. He says there are two have got lost but he's heard they may be somewhere round here so he's trying to find them, so he can put them in his book. Willing to hand out a pound note or two to any one who can tell him anything about them, and another pound or so if he's let take photos for his book—that is, if they're good specimens in good condition, which he says isn't likely, or they wouldn't have got lost so completely. I expect he's right about that, but you never know. He asked me to show those prints on the chance of someone seeing them and saying they knew of two like them. No one can mistake an El Greco. I thought at first that's what you meant."

And in these last words sounded a faint accent of hope, the shopman evidently still thinking that possibly Bobby really did know something about the lost paintings. In which case some portion at least of the promised pound or two might, the shopman hoped, find its way to his own pocket.

"Very interesting," Bobby murmured. "How do pictures get lost?"

This was an academic question to which he neither expected nor received an answer. He hesitated whether to enter into further explanations or not. He decided it was not necessary. On the face of it, neither the lost El Grecos nor the somewhat mysterious activities of Mr Smith, had any connection either with the disappearance of Mr Crayfoot or with the attack on Sir Alfred Rawdon, the only two matters with which he, as an officer of police, was concerned. Nothing wrong or suspicious in trying to locate lost paintings, not even on the part of a gentleman who washed his hands mysteriously in forest streams and fled at speed on the approach of strangers. All the same, Bobby was not much surprised on returning to his office and ringing up the *Morning Announcer,* which, as a 'national' newspaper had an office in the town, to be informed with some asperity that the art critic of the *Announcer* was not 'Mr Smith,' but, as everyone knew, the celebrated Henry St Kitts, whose real name might possibly not be St Kitts but was certainly not Smith. These were facts, the *Announcer* suggested, known to all, or at least to all no longer in daily attendance at a kindergarten. So Bobby apologised humbly for an ignorance the *Announcer* evidently felt beyond pardon, hung up, and decided that steps would have to be taken to try to get in touch with this illusive Mr Smith who was neither the representative of a Bond Street firm of art dealers nor the art critic of the *Morning Announcer.*

Strange, Bobby thought, as he began to make the necessary arrangements for trying to accomplish this, strange how his attempt to pursue what he was beginning to call the 'chocolates' theme, should have led him back once more, back to this El Greco trail.

"Only," he asked himself, "can it be even possible that they come together in some way to explain the missing Mr Crayfoot, the disappearance of the hermit? If Crayfoot means chocolates, does the hermit mean El Grecos? If you add together the chocolates and the two El Greco pictures—" But then he paused, shaking a puzzled head at the abysmal incongruity of associating two things so utterly diverse. "The 'Diabolic Candelabra,' too," he mused, "and what does it all add up to?"

His thoughts went back to the wrecked hut in the lonely forest the missing hatchet that should have been there and was not, to the bloodstains on the earthen floor, and then he told himself again, as so often before, that it was no good wasting time in vain speculation till he had more facts to build upon.

"Even if I'm right in believing that there's been murder done and that already there's a pretty clear pointer to the guilty person," he mused, "I've got to know a lot more before I can even so much as hint a suspicion."

He left the routine machinery he had set in motion for the identification and production of the mysterious Mr Smith, to do its work, and got out his own small car he generally used now on official errands, since its consumption of petrol was small. For he had a strong idea that Dr Maskell would be anything but willing to come to the police and so the police had better go to him.

CHAPTER XXVI
DR MASKELL'S SUGGESTION

BOBBY WAS LUCKY enough to find Dr Maskell at home, just returned from a morning round of visits. In answer to Bobby's inquiry he said that Sir Alfred was still in a critical condition. It might well be a day or two before it would be possible to feel confident of the issue. Certainly there was little likelihood of it being possible to question him for even a longer period.

"I suppose you haven't found out anything yet?" Maskell asked; managing to convey in his manner how unlikely he thought it that police in general, and Bobby in particular, would ever find out anything.

"Nothing of much value," Bobby admitted. "One can guess there was a burglar in the house and that Sir Alfred interrupted him, but that's about all."

"I suppose Sir Alfred knocked at the front before he went round to the back, if that's what he did," the doctor remarked. "If there really was a burglar in the house, why didn't he clear out when he heard knocking?"

"Knocking might only have meant a visitor," Bobby answered, "someone likely to go away again. It's the sound of the key in the lock scares burglars. Or it might not have been heard, if the burglar chap had his head in one of those cupboards he was searching so carefully, or in one of the packing cases in the attic he was overhauling. Whoever was there wasn't an ordinary burglar, he was looking for something special he was keen on finding."

"What?" the doctor asked sharply, but Bobby only shrugged his shoulders and the doctor gave him a quick and doubtful look. Then he said: "It was Crayfoot's house. Any connection with Crayfoot's being missing?"

"I don't know," Bobby answered. "I wish I did."

"Could it have been Crayfoot himself, do you think?" Maskell asked. "I mean, was it Crayfoot Sir Alfred interrupted?"

"Crayfoot burgling his own house?" Bobby asked. "Why should he? And if it was, why shoot Sir Alfred?"

The doctor laughed uneasily. His manner had less assurance now. He seemed to regret what he had said.

"Oh, I don't know," he said. "I'm not a detective. It was only an idea. Funny business, altogether. Aren't you going to call in Scotland Yard to help? You were there yourself, weren't you, though?"

"I transferred here from the Yard," Bobby agreed. "I don't expect they would be awfully pleased if I asked for assistance just now. They're like the rest of us in war-time—work doubled, staff halved. I expect I shall just have to try to worry it out by myself."

"Well, I suppose you know best," Maskell remarked; an unusual admission for him to make since his general attitude was that no one knew best, except himself.

"By the way," Bobby said, "I believe a Mr Stone asked you to analyze a flavouring for him?"

Dr Maskell favoured Bobby with a hard stare, as if wondering what that had to do with him. Then he said:

"Yes. Well? What about it? Some stuff of that vagabond quack's they call a hermit. Less deadly than most of his brews."

"Did Mr Stone tell you why he wanted it analyzed?"

"No. Some sort of new flavouring, he said. Wanted to be sure it was harmless. He asked me to have lunch with him at the Rawdon Arms to give him the result. I told him it wasn't likely to hurt anyone. He asked a lot of questions about the ingredients and if it made any difference how they were mixed. I told him I didn't know anything about that. I gave him the chemical formula, but I couldn't say what special plants it all came from. Sugars—sucrose—occur in many plants, from trees to grasses."

"It wouldn't necessarily follow," Bobby remarked, "that anyone possessing the formula would be able to get exactly the same result, the same flavour, I mean?"

"Might, might not, how should I know? I'm not a cook," the doctor retorted. "Has this any connection with the Crayfoot affair? I thought Stone's idea was to use the stuff for a new pickle or jam or something of the sort. Not that I cared. I didn't ask. He paid my fee for the analysis, paid for my lunch, too. I knew why. Wanted to ask a lot of questions. Things I couldn't tell him. I'm not a cook. I told him so and he didn't like it. He struck me as a business man with a keen nose for possible profit. Crayfoot's a business man, too. And you had asked me to do an analysis—earth on which blood had been spilt. I couldn't help noticing." He shrugged his shoulders but he was watching Bobby closely. "Then I heard about Mrs Crayfoot being worried over her husband and now there's this affair at Crayfoot's house. At a guess Crayfoot and Stone are both after the same thing."

"It does look like that," Bobby agreed.

"Seen the hermit? Asked him what he knows?"

"We've not been able to find him, either."

"I rather wondered," Maskell said slowly. "One of my patients, Mrs Morris, let out she was expecting him last Saturday and he never arrived. Not unusual in a way, I suppose, erratic, untrustworthy, no one could ever depend on him. Well, it probably saved old Mr

Morris's life. They were dosing him with some of the stuff that old humbug palms off on people. I suspected as much and it came out on Saturday. I tell you, inspector, if anything has happened to that old scoundrel, it means a good many people round here will have a better chance of life and health. Swilling down his filthy concoctions. Mind you, it's quite true the immediate result was often a success—apparently. Suggestion, you know. But the fundamental trouble isn't touched and back it comes worse than ever—seven diseases worse than the first. That man was a public danger. A public danger and nothing you people would do about it. Just let him go on. He was nothing more than a licensed murderer."

"Have you any reason to think any harm has come to him?" Bobby asked.

The doctor glared.

"Think I'm a fool?" he demanded. "Mrs Crayfoot doesn't know what's become of her husband. You say you can't find the hermit. Two business men trying to get from him some sort of fool recipe they believe might be worth money. Blood on the floor of his hut. What's that add up to?"

"What do you think?" Bobby asked.

"Good lord, how should I know? I'm not a policeman. Thank God. But you have Stone and Crayfoot both after the stuff—the recipe. Stone gets it and Crayfoot gets angry and disappointed. Quite likely the old scamp promised it him and sold it to Stone. Crayfoot goes to find out what's happened. There's a quarrel when Crayfoot finds Stone has been beforehand. The hermit tries to chase Crayfoot away. Threatens him with the chopper he uses for cutting wood. He's done that before. Crayfoot tries to take it from him. In the scuffle he succeeds and the hermit tries to get it back and Crayfoot hits out. He doesn't mean to kill. My God, no. It's really self-defence. Defending his own life. But who is to know that? Here's a dead man and—and Crayfoot killed him. He can't get away from that. What else can he do but try to hide the body? He has lost his nerve and he is afraid and there's nothing else to do that he can see." The doctor paused and stared and laughed, an odd, harsh, strangled laugh. "I've never killed a man," he said, "but I expect it's enough to make any man afraid—even if he never meant it, even if it was only self-defence, to save himself."

"It might be like that," Bobby agreed thoughtfully. "A quarrel. A struggle. One man killed. The other panics, hides the body, decides to run for it, returns to his house at night in secret for clothes and money. When he is interrupted he panics again and shoots and escapes."

"You put it very clearly," Maskell muttered, the first time he had seemed willing to admit that Bobby might possibly possess any shreds of intelligence. He got out his handkerchief and wiped his forehead, on which beads of sweat were showing, for the picture he had drawn had evidently moved him deeply. He went to a small cupboard and got out whisky and a syphon of soda. "Have one?" he asked.

"No, thanks," Bobby answered. Then he said: "There were no fingerprints on the window that was forced. Only smudges."

"Gloves," retorted Maskell. "They all do, don't they? Obvious surely," and it was plain that mentally he now withdrew his acknowledgement of the possibility of Bobby possessing any intelligence. He poured himself out a liberal allowance of the spirit and added little soda. "Well, here's how," he said and drank. "Yes, you put it very clearly," he admitted then, more genial now under the influence of the spirit.

"If I did," Bobby said, "it was because you made it all sound so real and dramatic."

"It just struck me perhaps that's how it was," Maskell said. "You can't help guessing, thinking, imagining things. Can you?"

He poured himself out another drink and Bobby wondered if Maskell, who had not much the air of a drinking man, often took spirits so freely so early, for it was not yet quite time for lunch.

"If it was like that," Bobby said, "Crayfoot would be wise to come forward and explain."

"Confess, you mean?" the doctor asked, and gave again that odd, harsh laugh of his that had in it so little of mirth, so much of scorn. "Confession's the last resort of weakness," he said. "Go down with your flag flying if you must, not whining for mercy." He looked again at the whisky bottle, seemed to hesitate, then with sudden firmness picked it up and restored it to the cupboard where it was kept. "Very likely I'm all wrong," he said. "Only guesswork. Very likely when you find Crayfoot you'll find he has a perfectly good explanation." He went across to the window and stared out at the distant mass of the forest that from here, as indeed from almost every other viewpoint near, dominated all the scene. "A dangerous place," he said. "Trees and men are enemies. Primitive man knew that. They're conquered now but they're still there—dark places, hidden places, damp and secret and dangerous, places where you can die and no one ever know. Crayfoot's been in there—how long? Saturday, was it? He may have met with some accident if nothing else."

"We are arranging for a search," Bobby said. "Boy scouts. Home Guards. Police. Everyone we can get hold of."

"Ah, yes," the doctor said. "A thorough search, eh?"

"Of course it would take an army weeks to make a really thorough search," Bobby agreed. "And then you couldn't be sure."

"No," Maskell said and made a gesture towards the forest. "Anyone who had a secret to hide—well, the forest would hide it well," he said.

CHAPTER XXVII
STORY OF A STRANGER

IT WAS IN thoughtful mood that Bobby drove away from Dr Maskell's house. The suggestion he had just listened to was, he had to admit, not unreasonable. It would account for much of what had happened. Dr Maskell, too, in putting it forward, had described the imagined scene with a vividness of insight and emotion, as of a thing actually seen, that had been impressive. One seemed to be aware of the old recluse's sudden burst of anger, of the threatening and flourished hatchet, of the other man's reaction, of the brief, fierce scuffle, of the angry blow struck in the heat of passion and bearing swift death with it, then of the panic-stricken concealment by the survivor of the dead man's body.

Only, if it had been like that, and the doctor's dramatic recital had almost persuaded Bobby to belief, which was the survivor? Who the dead man?

One merit the theory had was that of simplicity. It explained much and explained it credibly and neatly. But there were gaps. It did not account, for instance, for the odd behaviour of the Rawdons, uncle and nephew, or what piece of knowledge or information they were holding back. For that there was something they knew or believed or suspected that they had not told him, Bobby remained convinced.

His next destination was the small local police station where he was told that nothing had recently been seen or heard of the recluse of the forest. Not that there was anything very surprising in that in itself, for he often vanished for long periods at a time. But it was certainly not his custom to wreck the contents of his hut before his departure. There was also the fact that he had not kept his promise to visit the Morris farm. Uncertain as were both his moods and his temper, he had never been known to break a promise. The difficulty had been to get him to give his word, but once given, it was invariably and strictly kept. This was the first time so far as was known, when a clearly made promise of his had remained unfulfilled. 'A point of honour' he had been heard to say.

"Interesting detail," Bobby remarked thoughtfully when Sergeant Turner told him this. "One might draw deductions. Snobbish, though, and not very safe or certain, either."

Turner looked puzzled but Bobby did not explain. Too imaginative an idea, he felt, to appeal to stolid, matter-of-fact police sergeants, drawing near a pensionable age. In fact, he did not know that it appealed very strongly to him himself.

"It's because of this Crayfoot gentleman being missing," the sergeant remarked. "It makes people take notice of no one having seen the old chap lately. Over at the Rawdon Arms there's some as were saying last night as maybe they had done each other in. Pub talk, of course."

"Pub talk is worth listening to sometimes," remarked Bobby, a little startled, though, to find thus repeated the theory Dr Maskell had so recently put forward. "Only if there are corpses lying about the forest, surely we ought to have found one by now?"

"That's what I told them," declared Turner mendaciously, for in point of fact no such difficulty had occurred to him. "If they're both deaders, I said, where are they, I said? But then, they said, how about one being done in and the other done a bunk?"

"Yes, but which?" Bobby asked.

"Ah," said Turner, "there's that. One of 'em, only which?"

"Which do you think?" Bobby asked.

The sergeant pondered, not much used to thinking. For he was of those who prefer that others should perform that tedious and difficult task, communicating to him the result in the shape of orders he had only to obey. Finally, with effort, he came to a decision, and said:

"Well, sir, in my humble opinion, it's either one or the other."

"Eh?" said Bobby, who had been deep in his own thoughts. "What's that? Oh, yes, yes, I daresay you're right. It often is, isn't it?"

"Yes, sir," said the sergeant, greatly pleased by this official approval.

"Only perhaps it isn't," Bobby added. "You can never be sure till you know."

"Very true, sir," agreed the sergeant, greatly impressed by a saying he forthwith adopted as his own and was never tired of repeating feeling indeed that if only he had known it before very likely he would have become an inspector himself.

"Difficult, though," Bobby continued, "when you don't know whether you are after Crayfoot as victim, as murderer, as runaway, or as what. Officially, we have no reason to be interested in your old man of the forest. He may have merely thought he would like a change of residence and smashed up his things before leaving. Or—or anything," he concluded, somewhat weakly.

He subsided into silence then, rubbing the tip of his nose, looking very worried, and presently accepting with alacrity the sergeant's suggestion that he should share the dinner Mrs Turner had managed to let her husband know was ready, in danger of spoiling, and did he, or did he not, intend to waste good food?

Over the meal Bobby learnt of the general belief in the neighbourhood that something very queer was going on. It was an opinion Bobby fully shared. Apparently there were even rumours in circulation that it was Sir Alfred himself who was responsible for Mr Crayfoot's disappearance, since otherwise what was he doing in the missing man's own house and how had he got in? Mrs Turner let it be plainly seen that she disapproved of these stories. One should not, she implied, be too ready to entertain such ideas about a man in Sir Alfred's position. Now if it had been young Mr Rawdon, for instance, young men being young men, and, in the opinion of the sergeant's wife, generally up to no good.

"It is a fact," Sergeant Turner admitted, "that he's been hanging about Coop's cottage a lot, and what's a young gentleman like him keeping company with a bad character like Coop for? Done a spot of burglary in his time, too, if all tales be true, has Coop," added the sergeant, "though given it up since he married, along of Mrs Coop and the girls not standing for it."

"Do you mean Mr Richard Rawdon and Coop have been seen in company?" Bobby asked.

"I saw them together with my own eyes," Mrs Turner declared, and nodded her head twice in confirmation.

Bobby did not pursue the question of how the good lady could have seen all this with anyone else's eyes. But he looked worried and began again to rub the tip of his nose with even more energy than before.

"I didn't report it, sir," the sergeant said, a trifle uneasily. "Not being a police matter."

"No. No. It wasn't, was it?" agreed Bobby absently. He asked: "Has Coop ever been charged with burglary?"

"There's no record," the sergeant answered. "He started the talk himself with his boastings when the beer was in. I wouldn't wonder if it wasn't true though, in spite of him being the liar he is in a general way."

"Mrs Barnes as is Mrs Coop's nearest neighbour," added his wife, "saw Mr. Richard yesterday and mentioned it because of him acting so queer like. Walked right up close to the cottage, he did, and then away again. When she came back he was still there a-roaming."

"Paid for his beer with a pound note that night, Coop did," the sergeant continued the story, "and was remarked on, for it's not so often he has the likes."

"If it's Mary Floyd that he's hanging round after," Mrs Turner said suddenly, "and her as decent, respectable, hardworking a girl as you could wish for, only weak with that queer little sister of hers she lets keep away from school, which I do not hold with, but you know what young gentlemen are and likely to turn any girl's head, which it did ought to be stopped," and she stopped herself to fix each man in turn with a challenging stare.

"Not a police matter," said her husband sternly.

"Well, it did ought to be and why isn't it?" came the prompt and unanswerable retort.

"Was the hermit ever at Coop's cottage?" Bobby asked. "He was rather friendly with them, wasn't he?"

"With Loo Floyd he was pals, like she was with him," the sergeant agreed. "But he never went anywhere and in a general way he didn't like it if anyone came to him."

"He went to visit people sometimes," Mrs Turner said. "If they were ill like Morris's."

"Yes," agreed the sergeant, "but only if you had some of his medicine and he wanted to see how it was acting. There's many think he knew more about herbs and plants and such-like than all the doctors put together, only he would never tell. Said it was all there in the forest for those who like to look, and what was the good of talking to people like doctors with their heads all stuffed so full of what they learned at school and college there was no room for more. Hated doctors he did, just as they hated him."

"Didn't these Morris people," Bobby asked, "expect him to come back? They haven't seen him again, have they?"

"No," answered the sergeant. "Jimmy Marriott, what works over Edgeton way, says he saw a fellow making off in a hurry from the old man's hut and the old man shouting after him and waving a hatchet, like as if he was chasing him off. But that was Wednesday or Thursday, Marriott says, though not sure which, and so could have nothing to do with Mr Crayfoot being missing. And the hermit has been seen since, too, so that's nothing to count. Unless," the sergeant added, a trifle uncomfortably, "the man came back again some time."

"Yes, there's that," agreed Bobby. "Would Marriott know the fellow again?"

"No, sir, said he was a stranger and he only had a glimpse of him as he bolted down the path like a rabbit with a terrier hot on its tail. Fattish he said, and looked like he came from the city."

"Not youngish and darkish with a big nose?" Bobby asked.

The sergeant shook his head.

"Did Marriott say anything about the colour of his hair?" Bobby asked again, and again the sergeant shook his head.

"I think I do remember he said he was a bit bald," he answered. "Marriott noticed that because the chap hadn't any hat," and Bobby supposed that all this meant the stranger was neither Mr Sammy Stone nor yet the elusive Mr Smith.

The sergeant, noticing that Bobby looked worried, searched his memory and added:

"Marriott said the chap cleared out in such a hurry he dropped his cigar he was smoking. Marriott picked it up and finished it."

Bobby remembered the cigar ash he had noticed in the hut. That was now explained apparently. Not much help there though. He wished very much that he knew who was this stranger thus suddenly appearing and whether he played any part in the affair or was merely an accidental and irrelevant intruder.

Important to be sure which, but he did not know how he was to find out.

"I didn't report it, sir," Turner said, a little uneasily, for he feared the inspector might think he should have been told of all this before. "I didn't think much of it, the hermit being like that for chasing 'em off. Nor no complaint received and so not a police matter."

"That's all right," Bobby told him; for Bobby was never inclined to grumble unnecessarily at subordinates, even though he could be severe enough when there was real neglect of duty.

Officially, the hermit, his ways and manners, his disappearance if he had disappeared, all that, was not, as the sergeant put it, 'a police matter'. The only official reason for trying to get in touch with him was to ask, as so many others had been asked, if he knew anything of, or could give any information concerning, the missing Crayfoot.

"The whole thing's like looking at midnight in a dark cellar for a black cat that most likely isn't there," Bobby said dispiritedly. "I don't know whether I'm investigating the murder of the hermit by Crayfoot, or of Crayfoot by the hermit, or of both of them by someone else, or of neither of them by anyone at all."

"In my humble opinion," declared Turner, "Mr Crayfoot's had a row with his missus and gone off to give her a scare like, and scared she is, and Sir Alfred got his from trying to go after a burglar on his own, instead of letting us know," and Bobby was inclined to agree that this was the most reasonable and the most likely explanation.

CHAPTER XXVIII
UNEASY BEES

SOME CONSIDERABLE TIME had next to be devoted to completing the arrangements for the search of the forest to take place the next day. If it were unsuccessful, then another, more thorough and more extensive, would have to be organized for the following Sunday, when more help would be available and more ground could be covered. Yet Bobby could not help feeling, as he remembered the great, far-stretching green wilderness, vast and distant and secret, he had watched from Dr Maskell's window, from the windows of Barsley Abbey, that to find there anything the forest wished to keep concealed was but a hopeless task. The sea guards its secrets well. The forest, too.

He drove away then and came soon to his next place of call, Coop's Cottage. As he drew up and alighted, Mary came out of the cottage, grave and serene and quiet as he remembered her. A little, he thought, like the forest in which she lived, still and silent and withdrawn, both of them, and watchful, too. Nothing, he fancied, would ever be likely to disturb that deep tranquillity to which her spirit and her surroundings seemed alike attuned. So, he guessed, she had looked when locking up her stepfather in the cellar where at one time she had kept him imprisoned; so, he knew, she had looked when facing threats and anger with the counter-threat of a cauldron of boiling soup.

Silent, she stood, waiting his approach. When he was near, she said:

"I thought it was the doctor. I wasn't sure that he would come, but when I heard your car, I thought he had."

"Have you sent for him?" Bobby asked. "I hope your mother isn't worse?"

"It wasn't for mother," Mary answered. "Peter made us promise not to let her have any more doctor's stuff. Peter always said doctors were licensed murderers, and policemen ought to get after them instead of worrying other people."

"Perhaps he and the doctors are both wrong," observed Bobby, smiling as he remembered how vehemently Dr Maskell had expressed his opinion and rather wishing for a chance to tell him the hermit's. But probably Maskell knew it, and in any case had too deep a contempt for any unqualified man's attainments and beliefs to be annoyed by any opinion he might express. "Oh, well," he said, "I suppose you don't feel quite like that or you wouldn't have sent to ask him to come."

"It was mother wanted him for stepfather," Mary explained. "He has been knocked down by a car. He came in looking dreadful, his face all bleeding and he said he thought his ribs were broken and his back, too, and he wasn't likely ever to get over it. Mother was frightened."

"Oh, yes," said Bobby, very interested.

He made no further comment, however, as he followed her into the cottage. Inside, in the kitchen, Dick Rawdon was sitting. He did not look too pleased at seeing Bobby, but made no remark, though he nodded a greeting. He had apparently been talking to Mrs Coop. It seemed that Loo had not been home all night and Dick had been offering to go out and look for her. He thought, he said, that the very early morning before dawn would be the most likely time, when Loo might be expected to begin to move after her night's rest. Mrs Coop was explaining that it would be quite useless. No one could find Loo if she wished to remain hidden. So well she knew the forest she could make herself almost, as it were, a part of it, swallowed up entirely in its immensity.

"Is it so very unusual? Doesn't she now and then spend a day all alone, wandering about in the forest?" Bobby asked, a little surprised at the uneasiness Mrs Coop was displaying. "I thought I remembered your telling me that?" he added to Mary, who did not answer.

"She came back in the night," Mrs Coop said. "She took a loaf of bread and went away again. Why did she do that?"

"How did she get in?" Bobby asked.

"The door wasn't locked," Mary said. "It never is when Loo is out."

"If she was here last night, she was all right then," Bobby said.

"I've been telling them that," Dick said.

Neither Mrs Coop nor Mary said anything. But Bobby felt that for reasons they did not wish to explain this midnight visit had only increased whatever uneasiness they felt.

"It's the bees," Mrs Coop said abruptly. "They know."

"Mother thinks," Mary explained when Bobby looked at her in a puzzled way, "that the bees know something has happened."

"Are you worried, too?" Bobby asked her.

"Yes," Mary answered. She said: "Loo came back in the morning first and there was something she had seen that had made her afraid. I asked her what it was, but she would not tell me. She went back into the forest, but she did not want to. She has never been like that before. It was almost more her home than here, and why should she be afraid of her home? I asked her but she would not say, and then she went back although she was afraid."

"I'm sure there's something," Mrs Coop said. "The bees, too. They expect to be told when there's a death."

"Is there a death?" Bobby asked, startled.

"Coop came back all over blood," Mrs Coop said. "He said a car had knocked him down. He said he wasn't likely to get over it."

"He has said that before," Mary remarked.

"The bees came," Mrs Coop said. "This morning, flying and flying round and round, past my window. Very early it was. All day they've done no work. They know. They always do, but they have to be told as well."

"It may be the weather," Mary said. "Sometimes they all come flying back in a terrible hurry. You can see them trying to get into the hive all at once in such a hurry they block up the entrance. Like a traffic block. They know long before you about the weather. Sometimes there's nothing you notice yourself and then you read in the paper there's been electricity storms."

"This isn't the weather, the weather doesn't frighten Loo," Mrs Coop said obstinately. "There's something Loo's seen and it made her afraid, and the bees know, and they are upset and angry because no one has told them."

"Well, if they know," Dick interposed, looking half amused, half impressed, "what's the good of telling them?"

"They have to be told," Mrs Coop repeated as obstinately as before. "If they're not, they're angry and it brings bad luck. Sometimes they all just fly away and after that you can never keep any any more."

"We can't tell them what we don't know ourselves," Mary observed in her tranquil way.

"They rather went for me," Dick remarked. "I was near the hives and they all came buzzing round."

"I called him in," Mary explained. "When they are so upset they are quite likely to attack any stranger. You never know what bees are thinking. They won't let stepfather come near. Once they chased him nearly half a mile and he had to run as hard as he could all the way. But they let him alone if he doesn't go near. With bees you can never tell."

"Do you ever get stung?" Dick asked her curiously.

"Oh, no," she answered, surprised at the question.

"If they go away because they haven't been told," Mrs Coop said, "there won't be any more honey."

"No," agreed Mary. To the two men she explained: "Their honey helps us to live. It is very good of them," she added gravely.

"Oh, well," said Dick, considering this.

"What I really came to ask you about," Bobby said, "was whether you had seen or heard anything of the man you call the hermit. I don't know his name except Peter."

"No one does," Mary said, "except Loo. He told her once but she promised not to tell. He hasn't been here, but then he never does go anywhere."

"Do you think it is anything to do with him that is keeping Loo away?" Bobby asked. "Is that why she looked frightened?"

Neither Mary nor her mother answered. Bobby felt that that was in fact what was troubling them. He asked:

"If she took a loaf away with her, would it be for herself or for someone else, do you think?"

"She doesn't generally take anything to eat," Mary said. "Sometimes I gave her fruit or honey. She said there was plenty to eat, the forest was full of things to eat. Peter told her about some and some she knew herself. If she took any bread, most likely she gave it all to Henry George or the birds."

"Who is Henry George?" asked Dick.

"A squirrel," Mary explained. "They are friends."

Dick looked bewildered but said nothing. Bobby walked across to the inner door of the kitchen and opened it. A sound of scuffling hurried retreat above told him he had not been mistaken. Mary said to him:

"It was only stepfather listening. He always does when he can."

"Not too bad to get out of bed, then," Bobby remarked. "Did he really look very badly knocked about?"

"His face was dreadfully bruised, he could hardly walk," Mary answered. "He said he didn't suppose he would get over it. He really was bad," she added. "He said the car that hit him threw him into the ditch by the side of the road."

"I see," said Bobby. "Well, you might tell him that if he likes to come and see us, he can. Just as he likes, of course. Only if he wants to come at all, he had better be quick about it. Or he may find it's too late."

"I will tell him if you like," Mary answered, "but I think he heard you and I think you meant him to and that is why you spoke so loudly."

Bobby smiled faintly.

"You are a clever young lady," he said.

"Oh, no," she answered. "But I do like everything to be quite simple and plain and straightforward."

"If everything were, there would be no job for me," Bobby said.

He bade them good-bye then, but when he shook hands with Mrs Coop she held his for a moment and would not leave hold. He guessed she wanted to say something to him and bent down so that she could whisper. Dick had drawn Mary aside and was saying something to her to which she was listening with her habitual gravity. Mrs Coop murmured in a voice only he could catch:

"Why does that young man come here? The night before last he and Coop, they were whispering together—whispering and muttering together and I heard Coop laugh."

Bobby had a feeling that when Coop laughed those who knew him best felt there was probably mischief afoot. He made a few reassuring remarks and then took his leave. That Coop was the burglar interrupted by Sir Alfred and guilty of the shooting, Bobby felt pretty certain. But he had no evidence. It would be difficult to disprove Coop's story of the car that had knocked him down. No evidence as yet on which an arrest could be made, though observation and inquiry might produce something. An attempt could be made, for instance, to find out if he had been seen at the relevant time in the vicinity of the Crayfoot residence. In the meantime the message Bobby had left for him might have results. That the wicked flee when no man pursues is still as true as ever it was, and if they are left to themselves their own sense of guilt often drives wrongdoers to offer excuses and put forward statements that in the end help to provide the necessary evidence against them.

CHAPTER XXIX

THE SEARCH

THE SEARCH THAT was carried out the next day had small success. Whatever secret the forest held, it guarded well. Aloof and unconcerned it seemed, untroubled by the noisy trampling, the loud shouting from one group to another, the intrusion into its most hidden glades where seldom had any penetrated before. Traces of picnics in unexpected places, an ancient motor car years before disposed of by running it over a high bank into dense bush, the remnants of a burntout caravan remembered as an occasion on which careless holiday-makers had barely escaped with their lives, a brown Homburg felt hat of good quality and little worn, an apparently semi-permanent camp for gipsies or tramps, though it showed no signs of recent occupation, the axe that Bobby had missed from the hermit's hut and that a boy scout had now found in the heart of a bramble bush, these made up the total of the day's discoveries. Of the vanished hermit himself, or of the missing Crayfoot, no least trace anywhere.

Bobby took no part in the search. There were too many things he had to attend to that his absorption in the case had forced him to neglect for the time. He spent the day clearing up such matters, and in the evening drove out to Barsley Forest to see Sergeant Turner and to have a look at the objects found. Turner, it seemed, had always known about the deserted camp which at one time had often been used during the summer by gipsies and tramps. Then there had been some sort of quarrel with the hermit, from whose hut the camp was distant but a bare mile or so.

"After that, they all cleared out," Turner explained. "The old man fair put the wind up them. One of the gipsy women came to us. Scared she was. Said there would be murder done. She didn't explain why, but if you ask me some of her lot had got hold of the story that the old man had a store of gold sovereigns hidden, and he caught them poking about his hut, looking for it, and chased 'em off. With that hatchet of his. What the woman said was that some of them were planning to get back at him and she didn't want any trouble. So I went along next day just to warn them like. There was no one there. Not a soul. So I asked the hermit. Sitting outside his hut he was, and when I asked about it, all he said was most likely they were running still. So they were, too, in a manner of speaking. Talked about in the neighbourhood it was, how they had been seen making off fast as they could and never came back neither. What the hermit did, only the good Lord knows. Anyhow, whatever it was they didn't wait for more."

"Formidable old boy apparently," commented Bobby. "He seems to have known a lot and kept it all to himself."

"That's right, sir," agreed the sergeant. "Let no one know a thing and best not meddled with."

"When did this happen?" Bobby asked.

"Last year," the sergeant told him; and Bobby said it wasn't likely there was any connection with recent events, but for additional assurance it would be best to make certain, by a general inquiry, that no strange tramps or gipsies had been reported recently in the neighbourhood.

As they talked they had been busy packing with great care the hatchet recovered from the brambles near the wrecked and deserted hut, in order to send it to Wakefield for expert examination.

"Not that I suppose they'll find much," Bobby remarked as he applied the final seals, "not after such a long time."

"No, sir," the sergeant agreed, "though you never know. Almost anything those experts are liable to find, anything at all."

"So they are, aren't they?" agreed Bobby in his turn, though not quite sure that this wasn't a somewhat double-edged compliment.

"Looked like blood to me, those stains, I mean," the sergeant went on, and added: "I told Jimmy Marriott, the boy that found it, to come round and there would be a shilling or two for him."

"Half-a-crown, I think," Bobby said. "Worth it." He added thoughtfully: "A violent old gentleman, rather too fond of swinging that hatchet of his."

"Inoffensive if left alone," the sergeant said. "Only he couldn't bear visitors, and in especial not doctors or lawyers or journalists. Fair set him raving."

"I know he and doctors disliked each other," Bobby said. "Rivals. Bitter about it, too. But why lawyers specially? Or journalists?"

"One of the papers started putting in pieces about him," the sergeant explained. "Very nice pieces, too, but it set him raving when people came to look and brought their cameras with them. We had to bring him in when he started going for them with that hatchet of his. I warned him. Nothing to get mad about, I said. I said anyone who wanted could come and take pictures of me and I wouldn't turn a hair and why should he, I said. Very nice pictures, too, could be took of me in my garden, as I know, for a nephew of mine done it."

"What did he say to that?" Bobby asked.

"You never knew which way to take him," answered the sergeant, his good-tempered countenance clouding over. "He might have been wanting to go for me with that hatchet of his from the way he glared at first and then he started to laugh, as if all at once he had seen something funny. Not quite right up here," explained the sergeant, touching his head significantly, "seeing there was nothing to laugh at."

"Nothing at all," agreed Bobby.

"No, sir. After that, he always seemed more friendly like. But I had to bring him in because of his taking no notice of a summons over a complaint by some of them he had chased off. He asked very particular and earnest not to be put in a cell, because he said it would drive him mad to be shut up like. I didn't want to make him more balmy than he was so I took a chance and let him sleep out in the tool-shed with the door wide-open. He had a name for always keeping a promise once he made it, though I reckon I chanced my stripes."

"It was a bit of a risk," agreed Bobby, "but better, I think, than risking making him balmier still." He gave the sergeant a friendly smile. "No man deserves his stripes," he said, "unless he is prepared to risk them. Anyhow, it was all right?"

"Yes, sir. Though I had a bit of a shock when I found the shed empty in the morning. But there he was in the garden, grubbing away at a flower-bed where he said he had found something. Told me a lot, he did. There wasn't much he didn't know about plants and herbs and such-like. Surprising things he told me and talked a lot that morning though silent as if dumb with most. It was like he was so used to never talking that once he started he couldn't stop—like turning on a rusty tap you can't turn off again. Told me a lot about cancer."

"Cancer," repeated Bobby, startled.

"Yes, sir. Something he was brewing from roots and flowers and such-like he thought might be a cure once he had it right. That's why he was so excited over whatever it was he found where he was rooting in my flower-bed. Said it was rare and he had only just noticed it, but it might be just what he wanted to finish off his cure."

"What was it?" Bobby asked.

The sergeant shook his head.

"I didn't notice rightly, sir," he said. "I didn't pay much attention."

"I daresay not," remarked Bobby. "Could you show me which of your flower-beds it was?"

"Well, yes, sir," answered the sergeant, "but I dug it all up last year and laid it down in potatoes when they started to tell us to dig for victory. Cleared out everything in it on the rubbish heap. Potatoes did well, too," he added with satisfaction. "As fine a crop as ever you saw."

"Need potatoes all right," agreed Bobby. "Need a cure for cancer, too. I wonder if it was any good?"

"Well, sir," the sergeant said. "They do say there was Mrs Miller died after taking it."

"Not too good," observed Bobby.

"No, sir. Only the doctors had given her up and anyhow she had no pain after she started taking the hermit's stuff. Then there's Aggie Hunt as well to-day as ever she was, though the hospital said she must have an operation or die for certain. But she took what he gave her and didn't; and now the doctors say it was all a mistake and she never had cancer at all. And old Mr Morris sticks to it it's doing him good, but Dr Maskell took on awful and said it was his death he was taking and clear murder, like Harriet Abbott."

"Was that someone who died?"

"Yes. Dr Maskell blamed it on the hermit's stuff, but the hermit said she hadn't been let do what he told her, so no fault of his, seeing she didn't take it proper. So there you are, sir, and hard to tell."

"So it is," agreed Bobby; and wondered if in fact the old man had really hit upon some distillation from herbs and plants that was in some sort a remedy or even a relief in cancer cases. If so, and if the old man could be found and persuaded to give up his secret, he might come to rank among the greatest of human benefactors. An odd thought. One never knew. A pity, he told himself, that doctors weren't trained in detective work. Then they would know that even the smallest clue presenting itself from even the most humble, the most unlikely quarters, ought to be followed up with the utmost diligence.

"That's another grouse he had against the papers," the sergeant added. "He said someone wrote a book to prove cancer came from using gas for cooking and it ought to be stopped. But the papers wouldn't notice it because of losing the gas advertising if they did."

"Did he think so too, that cooking by gas had something to do with cancer?" Bobby asked.

"No, sir. Said it hadn't, but if you thought so, then you were on the right track. He said it could have been followed up and maybe made a success, if only the papers had printed about it instead of being afraid of losing their advertising."

"Food for thought," Bobby remarked. "Do the papers need the advertisers more than the advertisers need the papers? Question for the B.B.C. Brains Trust next week."

"Yes, sir," said the sergeant, "only would they answer it? Handpicked, them questions, if you ask me. I wrote up once to ask why men had nipples, that being a puzzle to me and seemingly not needed. But they never took any notice."

"Probably broke down under the weight of their own blushes," Bobby suggested, and then they were interrupted by the arrival of Master Joe Marriott, a nephew of the man who had reported the swift flight from the hermit's presence of the stranger who in his haste had apparently left behind his hat and abandoned his cigar.

CHAPTER XXX
PICTURE OF A HERMIT

JOE PROVED TO be a bright, intelligent youngster, but had not much to tell. The troop of boy scouts to which he belonged had been allotted a special area to search. This had been divided up between the lads, to each so much, each section carefully marked off by string and stakes, so that not an inch should be missed. The portion allotted to Joe had contained a good many bramble bushes; and in the midst of one of these, so hidden that only sharp eyes would have seen it, he had found the axe. Bobby asked him if he could show them the precise bush. The boy explained that following the instructions of his scout master he had made a circle of stones around it and consequently would be able to point it out as and when required. Bobby arranged to meet him early next morning, soon after dawn, so that school should not be interfered with, and then sent him off with half a crown and a promise of another shilling for the morrow.

The sergeant very plainly thought this would be a waste of time, since surely the exact spot where the hatchet had been hidden was of no importance. But Bobby said you never knew. He said:

"You know I've heard a lot about the hermit and I know his name was Peter, but no one seems to know his other name and you seem to be about the only person he has ever talked to. Except little Loo Floyd. What sort of idea did you get of him?"

The sergeant looked worried. Ideas were not much in his line. Then with relief he remembered a comment his wife had made.

"Well, sir, he did give you the idea that he hadn't had a bath since the one they gave him when he was born. Fair scrape the dirt off the back of his neck with a knife, so you could."

"Well, that's interesting," Bobby observed, though it had hardly been the sort of idea he meant. "Seems to go with his reputation for always keeping his word."

The sergeant blinked, wholly unable to see any connection between the lack of a bath and keeping promises.

"What I meant more," Bobby continued, "was how did he strike you as a man?"

The sergeant perpended.

"Queer like," he pronounced finally.

Bobby decided the going was too difficult and gave it up. The sergeant seemed to feel he was disappointed and made a fresh effort.

"What he said was as flowers and herbs were good and birds and animals did no harm, but men and women were bad in the lump, especially women. Birds and plants and animals never murdered or lied or betrayed each other like men and women did, he said, especially women."

"Bit of a misanthrope and misogynist as well," commented Bobby.

The sergeant shook his head in a non-committal way, thinking, though, how fine it was to be educated and know such nice long rolling words. Then, to be on the safe side with a superior officer, he said:

"That's right. That's him, that is."

"Did you think he talked like an educated man?" Bobby asked.

The sergeant shook this time not so much a non-committal as a doubtful head. He began to look worried. He was so evidently thinking so hard that Bobby waited, hoping something might come of it. Presently he said:

"Now you mention it, sir, maybe it was that worried me and the wife, too. What we thought was it was all along of him being not quite right in the head. But maybe it was because of him being a gentleman."

"Interesting," said Bobby. "Very."

"Once a gentleman, always a gentleman," said the sergeant.

"Something in that," agreed Bobby, much impressed by this aphorism so unexpectedly offered.

"Only why should a gentleman go living like that?" inquired the sergeant and answered his own question by adding thoughtfully: "But there, I reckon the gentry can go dotty just like anyone else."

"Or even more," agreed Bobby; and grew silent, as he tried to put together in his mind the picture there forming of the forest recluse.

A contradictory picture his impressions seemed to present. Passionate, eager, and recklessly impatient, or why these sudden fierce outbursts of anger that seemed to flare up in him so readily? Careful, patient, and gentle, or else how could he have secured this wide, intimate knowledge he seemed to possess of the life of the forest? A fugitive from his fellow men he seemed to condemn and despise, and yet not insensible to human contacts as shown by his friendship with little Loo and by that outburst of chatter to the sergeant in which Bobby found something pathetic, something of humanity breaking through a crust of misanthropy and long-maintained reserve. An educated man, that is one who owed his knowledge and training to books and teaching, and yet one who while still carrying on his studies had cut himself off entirely from all such aids. Living in physical dirt and squalor, and yet apparently preserving a mental refinement which made him regard a promise given as sacred. Possessed of such strange powers as could set a band of gipsies into panic-stricken flight, but yet falling back on the flourishings of an old hatchet wherewith to frighten away unwanted, unwelcome visitors.

As much, Bobby felt he knew now of the strange old man, as he knew of most of those whom he met day by day. But little to show whether he were murderer or victim or gone upon a journey.

Rousing himself from these speculations, Bobby suggested that it was time they had a good look at the Homburg hat brought in by another of the boy scout troop. The sergeant produced it and showed the initials "M.H." on the lining.

"Not much to go on," he said. "'M.H.' might be anyone."

But Bobby remembered at once that these were the initials of Mr Montague Hart, the Rawdon family solicitor, of whose record he knew more than Mr Hart suspected. He wondered if this meant that Mr Hart, too, had been there or thereabouts at the time of the old hermit's disappearance. If so, how had he come to lose his hat and why had he been content to leave it behind?

"Did you say," Bobby asked the sergeant, "the old man didn't like lawyers either?"

"Hated 'em," the sergeant answered. "Doctors he called licensed murderers. Journalists were a pack of Paul Prys. And lawyers just scum, that ought to be killed at sight."

"Killed at sight, eh?" muttered Bobby. "You know, I don't much think the old gentleman was very safe left at large. The killer in thought might provoke killing in fact."

"Yes, sir," said the sergeant, trying to think this out.

"Ever say what he thought of police?" Bobby asked curiously.

"Tools he called us, sir. Just tools. I took no notice though spoken offensive like."

"Oh, well," Bobby said, "it might be worse. Perhaps we are all tools and can be nothing else."

With the sergeant's help he packed the hat, too, for dispatch to Wakefield, there to receive that expert examination whereby, as the sergeant had remarked, almost anything might be discovered. Then Bobby returned to town and put in hand certain inquiries whereof the result was: first, the identification of the hat as resembling those supplied by a leading Midwych hatter to Mr Montague Hart; secondly, the fact that Mr Hart had purchased the previous Monday another he had been careful to ask should resemble as closely as possible the one last bought; and, finally, that he had on the Saturday before bought in Tombes yet another and a cheaper one. He had entered the shop without a hat, explained that he had lost his own while motoring, and he had left wearing the one just bought.

CHAPTER XXXI
BIRDS AFRAID

DAWN NEXT MORNING, or soon after; and Bobby, walking briskly through a forest glade where the dew still lay, where on the bushes spiders' webs sparkled more than did ever precious stones. With him were Sergeant Turner, very sleepy, and little Joe Marriott, very wide awake, for to him it was a great adventure, but to the sergeant just another spot of routine.

These two Bobby had picked up and brought here in his car, now left behind at the nearest spot it had been possible to reach on wheels.

The glade they had just entered, long and narrow in shape, was traversed by that little stream which presently ran at the foot of the slope whereon stood the hermit's hut. At the end where they had entered towered an enormous oak, still magnificent in age, and well-known as a forest landmark under the name of the 'Druid's Oak', though whether that name represented ancient tradition or merely stood for a guess that from its age and its position in an open glade apart from other trees, it might well have been the scene of our ancestors' worship, was an undecided question over which local antiquarians still loved to quarrel.

A magnificent picture it presented now in the slanting rays of the risen sun that framed it as in a glory of the dawn. Not even the urgency of the errand they were on could prevent Bobby from stopping to admire its aged splendour and he even told the sergeant he wished he had brought drawing materials with him. He would have liked to try to make a sketch of it, he said, and the sergeant said, very respectfully, 'Yes, sir', and thought that was the absolute limit and the rummiest remark he had ever heard a policeman make on duty.

"Queer," said Bobby aloud, and the sergeant gave a guilty start, for the moment thinking that here was a case of mind reading and he was being asked to justify his mental disapproval. "Very queer indeed," repeated Bobby, staring upwards and thus happily relieving the sergeant's apprehensions.

"Yes, sir, very queer, sir," he said, looking carefully above and around and wondering greatly what there was in any way curious or 'queer'.

"Those birds, sir?" asked little Joe Marriott. "I saw them do just the same yesterday."

"Did you, though?" asked Bobby. "Queerer still. Let's see if they come back." Seeing how puzzled the sergeant looked, Bobby added: "Did you notice?"

"Well, sir," the sergeant admitted, "I can't just rightly say as I did particularly."

"Birds," Bobby explained, "flying straight for that oak. Looked as if they were going to settle. Then all at once, when they were quite near, they wheeled and flew off."

"Did they, though?" said the sergeant, still puzzled, and much inclined to ask, had he dared, if they were there to do a bird-watching act.

The birds showed no sign of returning. Bobby went towards the oak. When he was quite near, he heard an angry chattering from trees growing at the side of the glade. He turned from the oak towards the spot whence this chattering came. It ceased immediately, but he heard, he thought, a movement, a rustling. He was not sure. In any case trees were growing here far too closely, too thickly, for any chance of successful pursuit or search. Joe was close behind. He said:

"That was a squirrel."

"Yes, I think it was," Bobby agreed.

"It was here yesterday," Joe told him. "Tommy Miles and Matt Train tried to catch it but they couldn't. Matt says he saw a little girl, but we all looked and there wasn't one."

"Did Matt say what she looked like?"

"He said it was a kid girl, that's all. Mr Young, that's our scout master, said it was only Matt imagining things. Mr Young said it wasn't likely there would be a little girl there, and if there was, she couldn't have got away without our seeing her, not with all of us on the look out. Mr Young said Matt must have been dreaming, but I expect it was just a suck."

"Might be," agreed Bobby, but thought that if by any chance it was little Loo Floyd who had been there she would have been fully able to slip away unseen—or, for that matter, to lie snug in safe concealment, had she so pleased.

He was well convinced she knew more of the forest, its life and its ways, than Mr Young and all his troop of boy scouts put together and many times multiplied.

He walked back towards the oak. He wondered what things it had seen in all its long thousand years of life. Perhaps few or none. Perhaps all through the long procession of the centuries this tiny hidden glade had remained in sunshine and rain, in winter and summer, as peaceful and quiet as it showed itself to-day.

Presently they came to the foot of the slope whereon stood the lost hermit's hut, its entrance now boarded up as Bobby had ordered should be done. Following the stream they came to where an arrangement of stones Joe had placed in position indicated the bramble bush they sought. With interest Bobby recognized that this spot was precisely the one where he and Olive, on the occasion of their visit here, had seen, bending over the stream, in the act apparently of washing his hands, that stranger who had departed with such haste on becoming aware of their approach. Odd that so near stood the bramble bush where the hatchet had been found, and Joe showed how it had lodged in the middle of the bush. It had been thrown there, he said, because the twigs and leaves and branches around were neither broken nor bruised, while those above did show such signs.

Joe was given another half-crown, praised for his careful observations, and sent home, pleased with the half-crown and the praise, but disappointed at missing the ride back in the inspector's car to which he had been looking forward. The sergeant waited hopefully for his own dismissal, and then coughed respectfully to remind his superior officer that he was waiting. Bobby roused himself from his thoughts and said:

"I'll get you to wait here for the time, Turner. I am going to have another look at that oak we passed and I think I had better be alone."

The sergeant looked all the dismay and doubt he felt.

"You don't mean you are going to make a picture of it, do you, sir?" he asked anxiously.

"Oh, no," Bobby answered. "Not on duty. Can't go sketching trees on duty. It's those birds. I want to know why they flew away again just as they were going to settle."

"Something frightened them, sir," suggested Turner. "Perhaps it was us."

"Might have been," agreed Bobby. "I would like a look round, though. I may be some time—an hour or so perhaps. I'll get you to wait here."

"Yes, sir," said the sergeant, pale with dismay, for he had come out before breakfast, and now he could almost smell, he could almost hear, the happy frizzling of the contents of the frying-pan wherewith, even at this moment, his wife would be getting busy.

Sadly, moodily, he watched Bobby go striding back the way they had come. Bitterly he asked himself what evil star had presided over his birth that had fated him to become a policeman. How right, how strangely right, had been the astrologer in his favourite Sunday paper in foretelling that this day would be a day of disaster for those born when he had been born.

CHAPTER XXXII
DISCOVERY

WHEN BOBBY REACHED again the glade they had passed through before, it seemed as peaceful, the ancient oak as untroubled and quiet in the still morning air, as on his previous visit. The dew had gone and the jewelled drops that had sparkled on the spiders' webs; and now, with the sun higher in the sky, the oak had lost a little of that glory in which before it had been bathed. Under it, old gnarled roots rose above the ground, forming in one place a kind of rough seat. Bobby seated himself there, rested his elbows on his knees, his chin in his cupped hands, fixed his gaze on the ground, and waited. Lost he seemed in profound and melancholy meditation, but in reality attentive and watchful in every nerve and fibre of his body.

Half an hour passed. Another, and so an hour had gone. Bobby hardly moved all the time, scarcely as much indeed as did the branches and the leaves above when now and then a soft breath of wind blew down the glade. A detective learns patience, needs patience more almost than any other quality. Not even when Bobby became aware of faint movement in some bushes on his right did he stir. A squirrel came scrambling out and then ran back again, exactly like a scout reconnoitring. It was the first sign of life that he had seen since his return, the first movement that had broken the almost unearthly quietude and stillness reigning here. Even the birds that flew by seemed to avoid the direct passage overhead, or, if they found themselves there, to increase the speed of their flight away. All grew still again and Bobby himself had hardly so much as moved a muscle. Even when he heard what seemed a suggestion of soft footsteps behind, he was careful not to look round. He had a feeling that if he did so he would see nothing or at any rate no more than trodden grass re-straightening itself or leaves and branches quivering back into their previous position. Even when presently a low and careful, hesitating voice said softly from the other side of the oak, "Why are you sitting there?" he took no notice, made no attempt to reply.

"Why are you sitting there?" the same small voice repeated.

This time he lifted his head momentarily, gave a casual, indifferent glance backwards, and then resumed his former attitude, his chin cupped in his hands, his gaze on the ground. A trifle more loudly, the small voice repeated once again:

"What are you sitting there for? Why don't you speak when you are spoken to?"

This last phrase, Bobby guessed, was a repetition of a reproach the speaker had often heard addressed to herself. He looked round. Loo had ventured forward now but remained poised on her toes, ready to vanish at speed. On her shoulder sat a squirrel. Henry George, Bobby supposed, though he certainly could not tell one squirrel from another. It was watching him intently from its small, sharp, beady eyes, and Bobby could not help feeling that it knew and understood all that was passing. Absurd, of course. When he still did not speak, Loo remarked, not so much to him but as if dropping the observation at random for the benefit of any it might interest:

"Mary says it's very rude not to answer when you're spoken to, and it doesn't matter if you are thinking thinks to yourself."

"Oh, is that, you, Loo?" Bobby said, as if suddenly noticing her. "How is Henry George?"

"Very well, thank you," Loo answered; and Henry George himself chattered excitedly as if he heard and understood the reference and thought it rather a liberty. Loo said once more: "What are you sitting there for?"

"I am waiting for Peter," Bobby answered. "Perhaps if I wait here long enough he will come."

Loo shook her head doubtfully.

"When I call him he won't answer," she said.

"Is that what makes you afraid?" Bobby asked.

The child nodded.

"So it does Henry George," she said, and once more the squirrel chattered, as if in confirmation.

"Is that why you haven't been home?" Bobby asked again.

Once more she nodded.

"When he wakes up," she said, "he might like me and Henry George to be there."

"Is he asleep?" Bobby asked, but she only answered:

"He won't speak to me when I call him."

"Will you take me to where he is so that I can call him, too?" Bobby asked.

But at that she shook her head vigorously.

"I promised I never would, never," she said, "and it's ever so important, not just an ordinary promise, but a big promise."

"Did Peter tell you why it was such a big promise?"

"He just said you must never break a promise, never. He said he learnt that when he was small like me. He said it was the only thing he was ever told that was truly true."

"It's a funny thing, Loo," Bobby observed thoughtfully, "but very often when you have forgotten everything else there's just one thing you remember. Why is that, do you think?"

Loo, whose confidence had now been completely won, sat down to consider this. Henry George alighted from her shoulder and scampered off. A few yards away he sat up and made a queer little calling noise as if wanting Loo to follow him. She shook her head, but he went on calling. Evidently he was uneasy and restless. Loo remained in deep thought. Bobby said:

"Suppose something happened and you had to go right away. I don't mean because you were made to but because of something right deep down inside that made you."

"Is that what happened to Peter?" she asked.

"I think so," he answered.

"Like when you've gone to bed and the leaves rustle and the branches and everything out there in the forest whispers and whispers till you know you must get up and go," Loo said. "I told Peter once and he said it was like that with him, but how did you know?"

"I think I guessed," he said.

"Don't you ever feel like it, too?" she asked.

"I mustn't," he explained gravely. "You see, I'm a policeman and policemen aren't allowed."

"It must be funny being a policeman," she remarked.

"Oh, it is," he assured her. "But suppose it was like that and you had to go and live somewhere, in the moon perhaps?"

"I should like that," she told him thoughtfully. "I like to dance in the moonlight and all the rabbits and the fairies and everyone all come out to watch. Peter came, too, sometimes."

"Are there fairies?" Bobby asked.

"Oh, yes," she answered confidently. "Lots and lots and lots. You can see them ever so plainly, but they won't let you touch them, not like rabbits and birds and squirrels. Peter says they are touchable but fairies aren't, because they are imaginable. Peter says that's because they are more real than being real, but I don't see how they can be, do you?"

"I think I can guess what he meant," Bobby answered. "Did he see fairies, too?"

"He said he was too old; he said when you are old you can't, not even with spectacles. He said when I was old I wouldn't either. It's different when you are old, he said."

"That's quite true," Bobby said, "and nothing we can do about it, either. Loo, when Peter said you weren't to tell where he was, are you sure he meant always?"

"Always and always," she answered promptly. "He said it again after the man came, that I wasn't ever, ever, ever to tell anyone."

"Oh, yes, well," Bobby said. "What man?" he asked lazily.

"Peter said it was the man who sends Mary money for her chocolates."

"Oh, yes," Bobby said again, careful to show no sign of excitement that might startle the child into withdrawing the confidence he hoped he was beginning to establish.

But here was apparent confirmation that Crayfoot had in fact been at the hermit's hut as the finding of his card there had suggested.

It was only after a minute or two of silence that Bobby went on:

"Was the bear at Peter's hut you told us about, there before the man or afterwards? Or did they come together?"

But Loo did not answer and looked so afraid and startled, so much on the point of vanishing into the hidden safety of the forest, that Bobby was more than ever convinced that there was something she had seen, something of importance if only he could win her confidence and persuade her to tell him what it was. But this, he felt, was not the moment, and leaving the theme of the bear for the time and returning to that of the chocolates, he said:

"Well, if the man wanted to ask Mary about her chocolates, why didn't he come and talk to Mary instead of to Peter?"

"It wasn't about chocolates, Peter said," explained Loo gravely. "Peter said he wanted to find out where Peter lived when he didn't live where he was. So Peter told me again I was never to tell."

Bobby gave no sign that now he had succeeded in obtaining confirmation of what he had so long suspected—that somewhere in the forest, near or far, the old man had a second habitation, a secret and a hidden refuge he had allowed none other to know of. Except this child on whom he had so strongly impressed it that she must never tell her knowledge.

"Is this other home of his where Peter is now?" he asked, trying to make his voice sound careless and indifferent.

Loo shook her head and as she did so gave a quick upward glance towards the huge, wide-spreading, overhanging branches above. It was a look that again brought confirmation—this time of an idea that had been forming itself in his mind ever since he had noticed how birds apparently intending to settle on the oak so swiftly and so abruptly turned away, as though overcome by sudden fear.

"Peter is up there, isn't he?" he asked.

"Right deep down in a great hole in the tree," she answered, "and he won't speak to me or answer when I call and he never moves either. Why doesn't he?"

"I think," Bobby replied, "he doesn't answer because he doesn't hear. I think he never moves because he can't."

"Is that what it means being dead?" Loo asked.

CHAPTER XXXIII

QUESTION OF IDENTITY

It was not until late in the afternoon that Bobby was able to get away from what may be called the routine work always consequent on such a discovery. Once that, however, was well in train he drove to Coop's Cottage, and was not greatly surprised to find Dick Rawdon there before him.

"I was hoping I might run across you," he told Dick. "I rang up the factory and they told me you had left early."

"I wanted to ask if Loo had turned up all right," Dick explained somewhat hastily; and Bobby thought that was very likely true, but probably not all, or even the greater part, of the truth.

"Loo came back this morning," Mary said. "She told us about Peter. I got her to go to bed. She has been asleep all day."

"I suppose you've heard?" Bobby asked Dick.

"It's all over the place," Dick answered. "I went along there, but your men shooed me off."

"I expect they would," Bobby said. "They didn't tell me. Probably they didn't know who you were. Just another snooper to them. Would you be willing to see the body in case you can identify it?"

"How can I identify a man I've never seen?" demanded Dick, though with a certain note of uneasiness in his voice, or so Bobby thought.

Before he answered Dick's remark, Bobby said:

"There are some things I know and some I merely guess at. It's those I want to ask you about. I think you may be able to help if you will. I am sure you agree the police have a right to expect every help anyone can give them. All the same, no one is bound to answer questions. And of course you have a right to the presence of a lawyer. Mr Montague Hart, for example."

"If you have half the brains I expect," Dick retorted, "you know jolly well I'm not likely to want Hart. Uncle hangs on to him because his firm knows all about the estate and debts and so on. I think he's a dud. I've never known him do a thing except cadge my cigars."

"Oh, he does that, does he?" Bobby said, interested.

"Smokes one and puts another in his pocket if he gets the chance," Dick growled. "What about it? Mean anything to you?"

"Everything always means something, doesn't it?" Bobby suggested, evading a direct answer. "Question always is, what? About the questions I would like to ask you?"

"Fire away," Dick told him. "I'll try to answer. I don't want the poor old chap's murderer to get away with it."

"Shall we have our chat here?" Bobby asked. "My car's outside, if you would rather go anywhere else. Just as you like."

"Here as far as I'm concerned," Dick answered. "You must ask Miss Floyd, though, I think. Her show."

"Oh, yes, sorry," agreed Bobby. He turned, not, however, to Mary, who did not to him, as she did to Dick, represent the only person in the world really worth considering, but to Mrs Coop. "Do you mind?" he asked. "It would save time."

"Oh, please, please go on," Mrs Coop answered, plainly anxious not to miss anything.

"I would prefer it," Dick said. "I would like Mary to hear anything you have to say."

"Now poor Peter's dead," Mrs Coop said, "I shan't get any more lotion for my back."

"I expect stepfather will be listening," Mary put in, glancing towards the inner door of the kitchen. "He generally is," she added, as one stating an ordinary and recognized fact.

"I don't know that it matters," Bobby remarked. He walked across to the inner door which opened on the small lobby whence rose the stairs to the upper floor. He called up them: "Would you like to come down, Coop? I expect there will be some questions I shall want to ask you, too, presently."

"I can't hardly move, I'm that bad," wailed a voice from above. "Crippled for life most likely, the doctor says, and life not likely to be long either."

"Well, that's good hearing," said Bobby cheerfully. "Anyhow, it won't stop you answering my questions."

He went back into the kitchen and closed the door. Mary said:

"You aren't going to arrest him, are you?"

"I don't know," Bobby answered. "It depends. On what help he is ready to give us, for one thing."

"What for?" Dick asked. "Arrest him what for, I mean? You don't think he killed Peter, surely?"

"Well, at any rate he is not entirely free from suspicion," Bobby answered. "Of course, there are others too—several others." To Mrs. Coop he said: "I'm sorry, but there it is. I don't suppose it's much of a surprise."

"Coop wouldn't murder anyone," Mrs Coop said. "There's things he might do, but not murder. I'm sure of that."

"Are you?" Bobby said to Mary.

"He wouldn't plan to do it," Mary answered. "He wouldn't mean to, but he might. In a fright. To be safe. To get away. Something like that. But I don't think he killed Peter."

"Well, then," Dick said, rather as if any opinion Mary expressed settled the matter at once and finally.

"You see," Bobby explained, "it's pretty certain he shot Sir Alfred and Sir Alfred's not out of danger yet. At the hospital they seem to think his chances are good, but they won't let us see him yet."

"No, I know, they told me that," Dick said. "What makes you think it was Coop?"

"His face is badly bruised and his story about being knocked down by a car isn't exactly convincing," Bobby answered.

"You were going to run me in if I had shown a black eye or two, weren't you?" observed Dick. "Circumstantial evidence, I suppose."

"Yes," agreed Bobby. "You haven't told me yet if you would be willing to view the body. It's a question of family resemblance. I would like your opinion."

"Oh, you've got on to that, have you?" Dick muttered.

"I think it possible he may be your great-uncle you told me about," Bobby answered. "The one in love with a girl who married someone else and he took it so much to heart he left home and started to wander about the country like any tramp or gipsy."

"We thought it possible," Dick admitted. "There was no very conclusive proof great-uncle had really died. There was the possibility that if anyone had actually died and been buried out in France, that it might be his footman pal—Crayfoot's grandfather. Nothing much known about either of them after the girl turned great-uncle down. Not her fault perhaps, but it does seem to have broken him up. It was only an idea. We didn't think it very likely. But it was going to be jolly awkward if it did turn out like that. That's why we wanted it kept quiet till we knew. You see, under the entail, if great-uncle were living, then Uncle Alfred wasn't Sir Alfred at all, never had been, never had any right to the property. Make a hell of a mess of things. Legally, I mean. Especially with that cousin of ours on the pounce. I mean the cousin who wants to keep the entail going and prevent the sale of the pictures because he hopes to get hold of the whole lot for himself some day. Uncle says if he does, then he'll want to break the entail all right himself and sell out at a big profit or some other dirty trick like that. Uncle doesn't like him. No more do I for that matter. Now this has happened it won't matter so much, I suppose. No doubt now about Uncle Alfred being Sir Alfred. I don't see how the question can come up now the poor old chap's dead."

"I expect the coroner will want his identity established at the inquest," Bobby said, and Dick looked disturbed.

"I never thought of that," he said. "I don't see how you are going to prove anything," he added. "I don't see how family likeness could count for much. You haven't got anything to show, have you? Or do you want to keep it quiet?"

"No reason to," Bobby answered. "My own idea is he probably was your great-uncle. I think if he hadn't been, there would have been more heard about the disappearance of the two El Grecos and the Diabolic Candelabra—especially the last. I think it is because it was known your great-uncle had taken them that it was more or less kept quiet about their loss. Then there was the permission given him to put up his hut on the Rawdon estate land without apparently any record being kept either of the request or the consent. It suggests to me he did it off his own bat, so to speak, knowing no objection would be raised. Another small point is the emphasis he seems to have laid on keeping his word once it was given. Working-class people are just as scrupulous in act but they don't so often talk about it or call it a point of honour. It's a phrase that very much struck me when I heard he used it. A working man would talk about letting you down or sticking to what he said or something like that, not about points of honour. Another thing is that he seems to have gone exceptionally squalid in his person and his ways of life. I've noticed that before. When well-brought-up people let themselves go, they go all the way."

"Are you going to bring all that up at the inquest?" Dick asked, not appearing much to relish the prospect.

"Oh, no," Bobby answered. "All that comes under the general heading of what the soldier says not being evidence. I only meant to show you why I think as I do. After all, I'm not so much interested in who he was as in who killed him. Of course, the two do seem as if they might be fairly closely tied up."

Mrs Coop had been listening with eyes opening wider and wider. She burst out now:

"Well, I never. Peter . . . a Rawdon . . . Sir Peter . . . only then Peter wasn't his real name . . . ?"

She subsided into silent bewilderment and Mary said:

"Whoever he was, he has been wickedly murdered."

"I don't forget that," Bobby said gravely.

"You've no idea who it was?" Dick asked.

"Ideas, yes," Bobby answered. "Proof, no. We may get some when we've been able to make more inquiries. There's been some talk of cutting down the oak so as to be able to examine it more carefully."

"Fingerprints?" Dick asked.

"Well, one would hardly expect to find dabs on a tree," Bobby answered. "Surface much too rough. But there may be something. Murderers do sometimes leave clues on the scene. There was the Vera Page murder in London some years ago. The murderer left a finger stall near the body. Other cases, too. The doctrine of exchange. Nothing you can do without leaving some trace, receiving some trace yourself."

"Crayfoot's missing," Dick said. "Doesn't that look as if he did it and then bolted?"

"His disappearance has got to be explained, of course," Bobby agreed.

"I don't see how you are ever going to be certain," Dick said slowly. "I don't see that it matters very much now. What worried us was whether Uncle Alfred was really Sir Alfred with a legal right to the property."

"There are still the two supposed El Grecos and the 'Diabolic Candelabra'," Bobby remarked. "Worth a goodish bit. Where do they come into the story?"

"Well, do they?" Dick asked.

"Money values have always to be remembered," Bobby reminded him, "and El Grecos would have it all right—if they are genuine and in good condition."

"A toss-up if they are," Dick retorted. "Nothing to show. Of course, there's the Cellini stuff. Cellini's name counts and there would be a curiosity value as well. I suppose there might be enough to put the property straight again. Only where are the blessed things? I should say it was odds on they've been lost or destroyed or something long ago.

"Supposing the old man had them, whether he was actually a Rawdon great-uncle or a Crayfoot grandfather, have you any idea where they could be? Not in his hut or someone would have seen them. So where?"

"No idea," Dick answered. "I don't see how he can possibly have had them. Do you? I suppose other people did visit that hut of his sometimes. I never heard anyone ever said anything about having seen oil paintings or silver candlesticks there, and they aren't things you can overlook very easily. Especially when the paintings are El Grecos and the candlesticks by Cellini. Of course, the old man may have kept them hidden somewhere. Some place like that hollow oak where you found the poor old boy's body. Good God," exclaimed Dick excitedly, as a sudden idea occurred to him, "do you think the things were actually hidden there? I mean, in the hollow oak? And whoever killed him knew somehow and was trying to get them, but the old man interfered, and got killed as a result?"

"It's a possible theory," Bobby agreed. "No sign of any struggle near the oak, though. The body had apparently been hauled up by a rope round a branch and then pushed down into the hollow in the tree. Means an exceptionally strong man, unless there were two on the job. All the same your idea is quite possible."

"Might mean the murderer was Crayfoot," Dick remarked, more taken up with his own idea than with Bobby's comment. "He was trying to get hold of the things, he was caught in the act, and that ended in the killing."

"It would fit all right," Bobby agreed again, "but no more with Crayfoot than with others—with Mr Coop, for instance. Change Crayfoot to Coop, and the theory is just as sound."

CHAPTER XXXIV
COOP'S THEORY

WHEN HE HAD said this, Bobby looked at Mrs Coop and at Mary, wondering what they would think of the suggestion. Neither of them made any protest, nor could he see that they appeared much surprised. He had the clear impression that not for the first time had the possibility occurred to them. The door opened and Coop himself appeared.

"Just like a cop," he said bitterly, "taking away a respectable man's character. I'll have the law on you for that. Slander, it is, that's what it is—slander and evil speaking." He paused and then pointed a finger at Dick. "What do you want to pick on me for?" he demanded. "Why couldn't it be him? Or her?" Now he was pointing at Mary. "She had the best chance to know what he had tucked away, hadn't she? Loo would know and as like as not told her. The only one Loo would tell." He swung round on Bobby. He spoke earnestly, feelingly: "You would think she was just a girl like any other girl, wouldn't you?" he asked. "All boys and giggles. Well, take it from me, there isn't anything she's not up to, for all she looks like butter wouldn't melt in her mouth or a thought in her head beyond what ought to be, scrubbing the floor or cooking the dinner and such-like. You can't trust any woman, and her less than any. Why, you seen her yourself ready to throw a pot of boiling soup over me, all for nothing. You forgotten that?"

"Oh, no," said Bobby. "I remember it very well."

"Well, then," said Coop triumphantly.

"Look here," began Dick, rising in wrath, but Bobby checked him.

"That's all right," he said; and as Dick spluttered indignantly and incoherently, Bobby added to Coop: "You had better go back to bed and stay there till you look a bit more respectable. Sir Alfred got in some jolly good work. Mistake, though, after he had floored you, not to make sure you weren't armed. I expect he never thought of that."

"He never would have floored me only for—" began Coop indignantly and then paused and hurriedly corrected himself. "Mean to say," he said, "he never would have floored me if we ever had had a fight, which, of course, we never did, never having occasion, and him a gentleman and all."

"You can thank your lucky stars it isn't a case of murder," Bobby said. "Bad enough as it is—attempted murder. I'm only waiting till Sir Alfred is able to tell his story. And I may as well tell you I've got a man on guard to see nothing happens to him. Of course, you can tell your own story first if you like. Oh, and then there's Mr Smith. I want to hear what Mr Smith has to say, too."

Coop stared and gasped and went as pale as his discoloured and bruised face permitted.

"You mean that chap who came to the Abbey to see uncle?" interposed Dick. "Is he in it, too?"

"I'm inclined to think," Bobby answered, "he started it all. Anyhow, I want to hear what he has to say. Just as I want to hear what Coop has to say. Sir Alfred, too. I don't mind which story I get first."

"Meaning you want me to talk," snarled Coop. "Well, I'm not. See?"

"Just as you like," Bobby answered amiably, and Coop scowled at him and went towards the door.

He opened it and then turned back.

"If you ask me," he said, "the bloke who did the old hermit in is Mr blooming Sir Alfred Rawdon. You take my tip. That's my theory."

With that he gave Bobby a significant nod, repeated, evidently a little proud of the expression, that that was his "theory", and went out, banging the door behind him. They watched him walk away and Dick said angrily:

"Cheeky brute. Why don't you run him in? Isn't that face of his good enough proof?"

"Well, for one thing," Bobby answered, "I haven't heard yet what Sir Alfred has to say. Just possible he won't be able to identify him. Or even that he may not want to."

Dick looked slightly disconcerted at this last suggestion and then said:

"I don't see why you think Smith started what's been happening? I don't see what he has to do with it."

"Well, he started everyone thinking and talking about the missing El Grecos, didn't he?"

"We've always known about them," Dick said. "There was always an idea they might turn up somewhere."

"Did anyone else know the story or at any rate think of it as anything more than an old story?" Bobby asked. "Smith set everyone talking by the way he has been nosing around. He made inquiries in likely shops in Midwych. He called on you. He called on Dr Maskell to ask if he knew of anything like them in the house of any patient he visited. He talked about them at the 'Rawdon Arms' too, and very probably made other inquiries I haven't heard about. People know old paintings are valuable. Have exaggerated ideas, very often. And it did look as if these El Grecos were just there for anyone who could pick them up—a small fortune for the finding, and not so small either. You agreed—didn't you?—that if they were found, it wouldn't be too easy for you to prove your title against a possessor. Smith certainly knew something about the hermit, for he visited the hut. He may even have got hold of something to show who the old man really was—either your great-uncle or Crayfoot's grandfather."

"I suppose he's on your list of suspects, then?" Dick asked.

"Oh, yes," Bobby agreed. "No more than others, though." He turned to Mary: "There's another thing I want to ask you," he said. "Do you think it likely Peter had a sort of second habitation in the forest where he could go when he wasn't at the hut—a secret home, so to say? I feel fairly certain he had. He used to buy oil. At the hut he had an outside fireplace and an old stove indoors. He used wood for fuel—picked it up free under the trees. No sign of an oil stove or anything of the sort. So I expect he had some other place somewhere he went to sometimes and that there he used oil for heating and lighting. An oil stove wouldn't show, whereas a fire could be seen at night and its smoke by day. Or perhaps he used candles for light and that's why he wanted the Diabolic Candelabra."

As he spoke he was watching Dick more closely than he watched Mary but Dick's expression showed nothing beyond surprise and a lively interest.

"That's an idea," he said, and added, half reluctantly: "You do spot things, don't you? I knew about the buying oil, but I never thought what it meant. If he has another hut somewhere no one knew about, then that is where the El Grecos may be and the candelabra?"

"It seems possible," Bobby agreed. "What do you think?" he asked Mary.

"Loo told me once," she answered, "that he had somewhere else to go besides the hut."

"Did she tell you where it was?"

Mary shook her head.

"Do you think you can get her to tell you now?"

"I'll ask her," Mary answered, "but she said she had promised she never would."

"But he is dead now," Dick said. "A promise doesn't matter now."

Mary looked doubtful but said nothing.

"Well, if you'll ask her," Bobby said. "Oh, you might ask her at the same time why she took that loaf of bread you told me about."

"I've wondered about that," Mary said and now with a touch of unease in her generally tranquil manner.

"She took some potatoes, too," Mrs Coop remarked. "At least, I think she did."

"Well, the kid would want something to eat, wouldn't she?" Dick asked.

"Oh, no, not in the forest," Mary answered. "She always says the forest is full of things to eat."

"Oh, well, now then," Dick said, looking very puzzled.

Bobby got to his feet.

"I think that's all I had to ask," he said. "I'll be going now. Plenty to see about."

"Look here," Dick said. "I suppose you won't take any notice of what Coop said—I mean, about it's being uncle. I take it he was just talking for the sake of talking?"

"I don't know," Bobby answered, and Dick looked at him uneasily.

"You might as well start suspecting me," he said, and when Bobby gave him a quick glance, he exclaimed, a sudden shrill note in his voice: "By God, I believe you do."

Bobby said nothing, and Mary came across and stood by Dick's side. Silent as ever, she did not speak, yet there was something confident and trustful in her very presence as she stood there. But Bobby as he went away was reminding himself how often women had put an utter faith in men in no way worthy. He found himself wondering if it could be like that this time.

CHAPTER XXXV

"SAMMY TO YOU"

THE INQUEST WAS held the next day. It was purely formal, an adjournment being at once granted 'to enable the police to complete their inquiries'.

'If they can,' was Bobby's unspoken comment as he left the court; and when he got back to his office he heard that Mr Samuel Stone was waiting to see him.

"That swine Weston been saying things about me, hasn't he?" Mr Stone asked angrily; and Bobby learnt that Mr Weston had been dropping hints in various bars concerning the probable complicity of Mr Stone in recent events. "I'll sue him for damages," declared Mr Stone. "Defamation of character. What did he tell you?"

Bobby smiled and pointed out that communications made to the police were confidential. Besides, he felt that the more uneasy Mr Stone remained, the more likely he would be to come forward with statements that might be true, in which case they would be exceedingly useful, and might be false, in which case they would be more useful still. It is a paradox, and one useful to remember, that a liar is often a better guide to the truth than is the honest witness. Nor was Bobby much impressed by Mr Stone's bluster and he began indeed to wonder whether it was not a case of 'he doth protest too much'. Not that that was proof of guilt. People bluster when they are scared as well as when they are guilty. On the whole, he found the story Mr Stone was telling agreed fairly well with what Weston had said, except that in Mr Stone's version Weston's part diminished almost to vanishing point. According to Mr Stone ('Sammy to you,' he said once or twice, beaming on Bobby) Weston had done no more than remark in the presence of Mr Stone and many others, in a public bar, on the unusual flavour of some chocolates recently purchased by his wife.

"I don't go about with my eyes shut," declared Mr Stone, "and I happen to know the big confectionery firms are keen on finding new flavours. So I thought I would look into it. Weston hadn't said where his missus got the things. But it didn't take me long to find out they came from Walters's, near where he lives. So I went along and bought a box and tried 'em out. Not bad at all. Might catch on, I thought. And believe it or not, on the back of the box there was a pencil note giving the address where they came from—Miss M. Floyd, Coop's Cottage."

Having been given his choice, Bobby decided not to believe it. Much more likely, he thought, that the address had been provided by Weston whose part in the affair Stone evidently wished to minimize as much as possible. Not that that mattered much, as far as could be told at present.

"Mr Stone—" Bobby began.

"Sammy to you," interrupted that gentleman and offered a cigar which was gently and firmly declined.

"Your business relations with Mr Weston," Bobby continued, "don't seem to concern us. I believe you visited Coop's Cottage and Miss Floyd tells me—"

"That's right," interrupted Mr Stone hastily, evidently anxious to cut short whatever Mary might have said. "Gave her a pound note for a bottle of her flavouring. My word, was she pleased? Not so often a windfall like that comes her way. Take it from me," said Mr Stone, chuckling richly, "I could have had a kiss or two into the bargain if I had felt like it. Married man, though," and he concluded with a wink that made Bobby long to throw a paper-weight at his head.

"Miss Floyd informs me," Bobby said coldly, "that you took the bottle of flavouring without her consent and against her wishes."

"You surprise me," declared Mr Stone, but not as though his astonishment were great. "Aren't girls just the world's champion liars? The little hussy. And after the way she thanked me for that pound note! Well, well, well!"

He shook his head sadly and was still shaking it as Bobby went on:

"Mrs Coop confirms Miss Floyd's story."

"Oh, she would," protested Mr Stone. "Mamma backs up her little girl. Never mentioned that pound note, I'll be bound. Or did I leave it just for fun?"

Without answering this, Bobby continued:

"I believe you gave the bottle to Dr Maskell for an analysis?"

"That's right," agreed Mr Stone. "First thing any firm would do. And not too good for any chance of any more biz. with them if they spotted anything harmful in the stuff's make-up. Can't be too careful."

"I think you asked Dr Maskell to lunch at the 'Rawdon Arms'," Bobby went on, "and asked him about mixing the ingredients and so on?"

"That's right," agreed Mr Stone again. "Paid him a whacking big fee and the price of a slap-up lunch as well and wanted value. Didn't get it, though. Close-mouthed bloke, that doctor. If you ask me, knows more than he says. Not a man to trust," said Mr Stone, shaking his head sadly, and obviously implying that was not the case with Mr Samuel Stone. "Keep an eye on him if I were you. Eh?"

Bobby ignored this counsel. He said:

"I think you know a Mr Smith?"

Stone regarded Bobby warily.

"Lots of Smiths," he said. "Which one did you mean?"

"I mean the one who has been at your shop in Midwych making inquiries about El Greco paintings?"

Mr Stone hesitated, and Bobby knew perfectly well that he was considering whether to admit or deny knowledge. Deciding finally that admission would be safer since the extent and the nature of Bobby's information were alike uncertain, he said:

"Oh, yes, couldn't think for the moment. Smith, he calls himself, does he? Asked us to show prints of some old Greek paintings, didn't he? Give you three to one in half-crowns Smith isn't his real name."

Bobby ignored this sporting offer, though inwardly he paid a tribute to Mr Stone's persistent ingenuity in trying to turn the conversation. He said:

"Can you tell me anything about him or about the paintings he is trying to find?"

"Not a thing," declared Mr Stone. "He may be on a good thing or he may not. Some of these old pictures are worth a pile. I picked up one by an old bloke they made a film about—Rem. something or another. Trade name apparently, not his own. Gave ten bob for it, took it to Christie's. They said the frame might be worth a bob or two, after deducting what it cost to chop it up for firewood. I've got it still. You never know. Looks just the same to me as the ones in art galleries. I went special to have a look-see. No difference."

"Did Mr Smith say anything about their probable value?" Bobby asked.

"Not likely. If you're on a good thing, you don't broadcast it, do you? May be a good thing all right. You can't tell. All a toss-up." Bobby was watching him closely as he talked. It seemed fairly certain Mr Stone did believe very thoroughly in the 'good thing', and even more certain that Mr Stone had an exceptionally keen nose for 'good things'. Any suggestion of a 'good thing' would automatically set him scheming and planning for a share—or all. Another certainty was that Mr Stone meant to say as little as possible. The way he sat and beamed and his flow of chatter was sufficient evidence. Bobby decided to try a different line of questioning.

"Why did you choose the 'Rawdon Arms' for your lunch with Dr Maskell?" he asked.

"Oh, come, I say, Inspector, now then," protested Mr Stone. "Had to go somewhere, hadn't we?"

"Was it because you knew Smith had been there, making inquiries, and you didn't want to lose any chance of hearing what was going on?"

"Lord, no," protested Mr Stone. "Those pictures are Smith's pigeon, not mine. And a wild goose-chase, if you ask me."

Bobby paused for a moment to admire this happy mixture of ornithological metaphor. Mr Stone filled in the gap by muttering in reminiscent indignation:

"Frame worth a bob or two for firewood."

"Did you expect to see Mr Weston at the 'Rawdon Arms'?"

For the first time Mr Stone looked a trifle disconcerted.

"Not much you miss," he grumbled. "No, I didn't."

"Do you think he had followed you or Mr Crayfoot?"

"Now that's a thing," answered Mr Stone candidly, "that's been worrying me a lot."

Bobby went on quickly, for already he had decided to risk a guess at how a man of Stone's character would be likely to act in such circumstances:

"Weston went after Crayfoot into the forest and you followed them both. What happened?"

"Oh, well, well, now then," muttered Mr Stone, and this time looked very disconcerted indeed, hovered on the brink of denial, then decided denial would not be safe. He burst out abruptly: "How the devil do you know what I did?"

Bobby only answered by a faint smile and a vague wave of the hand designed to suggest a general omniscience.

"Well, I did," Mr Stone admitted. "I saw him following Crayfoot and I guessed they might be up to something together—trying to do me down like as not. Weston's that sort. You can't trust men like Weston. A snake in the grass," said Mr Stone regretfully, "a snake in the grass. That's Weston and sorry I am to say it. Why, I slipped him a fiver for the hint he gave me without knowing it about those chocolates. Not so bad for saying something he hadn't an idea in the world meant anything. What do you think, Inspector?"

"I think," said Bobby firmly, "that what I want to know is what happened when you followed those two into the forest?"

"Precious little," answered Stone, thus again brought back to the point he was so continually trying to wriggle away from—as under examination do all those with consciences not quite at ease. "I lost Weston almost at once. I'm no boy scout. Then I lost myself. Thought I was going to have to spend the night there. Then I caught sight of Crayfoot. At least, I think it was Crayfoot, but I couldn't be sure. He was a good distance away. Anyhow it wasn't Weston. Not his figure. Whoever it was, he was in a deuce of a hurry. He was almost running along a path that goes up alongside an old quarry."

"Interesting," said Bobby, remembering how he and Olive had looked down over the unfenced edge of that quarry into its dark and tangled depths where the trees and the bushes grew in such close profusion. "Did you follow him?"

"No. But it gave me an idea where I was. I went back the way he had come. I thought I might run across Weston. No sign of him, though."

"Did you go as far as the hermit's hut?"

"No. At least I don't think so. I don't know rightly where it is. I gave up after a time and went back to where I had seen Crayfoot—if it was him. I guessed the path would go somewhere and what I wanted was to find my way out of the wood."

"You saw nothing of the hermit, nothing of Weston?" and when Stone shook his head, Bobby went on: "Apparently you are the last person to have seen Crayfoot. Doesn't it strike you you ought to have come forward with that information before?"

Mr Stone looked more or less innocently surprised.

"I thought it was known he was last seen in the forest," he protested. "Nothing more I could say. Even if I had been sure, which I wasn't. You don't think he did the murder, do you? Doesn't make sense to me —not a respectable tradesman like Crayfoot. What's happened to him is he's running round the big firms, trying to wipe my eye, trying to get an offer for the new flavouring. That's O.K. by me. When he's done the work, he'll find out I've got a provisional patent and then I'll get my cut." He chuckled richly. He said confidentially: "Easy meat, these big firms, if you've got anything of a case, and a provisional patent's more than good. They know what law costs are, and they know, win or lose, they pay. So they pay sooner rather than later. See?"

Bobby began to wonder why Mr Stone was not a millionaire, he seemed to know so well how to transfer money from other people's pockets to his own. Utterly without scruple, Bobby thought, and wondered how far that lack of scruple would take him. Mr Stone went on:

"I'll give you a tip. If it's anyone, what about Weston? He had picked up my idea that the new flavour was worth money—Weston," explained Mr Stone, virtuous with indignation, "is a sort of picker-up of other people's ideas. Suppose he tried to pump the old hermit who by all accounts had the devil of a temper. Result—a row with the hermit bloke reaching for his axe and Weston laying him out with it. Self-defence in a way, but murder, all the same. Eh? How's that?"

"It may have happened like that," Bobby agreed, "but nothing to show it was Weston rather than anyone else."

"Who else?" demanded Stone. "It must have been someone on the spot and I don't believe it was Crayfoot, not him, and it wasn't me—I take it you don't suspect me?" He paused, stared, caught a quick glance from Bobby, his voice grew suddenly loud and shrill, "Almighty God," he almost screamed, "you don't mean you do?"

"I haven't said so," Bobby answered quietly; and Mr Stone lost all his flamboyance, seemed to shrink visibly as he sat there, showed plainly the terror that possessed him, though whether that terror was born of conscious guilt or of innocence suddenly aware of peril, Bobby felt he could as yet form no idea.

Mr Stone began to stammer protests. Why should he do such a thing? Violence was not in his line. He had never even seen the hermit. Bobby cut short the flow of words.

"Motive is secondary to fact," he said sententiously, having often noticed that the sententious is also the impressive.

"Oh, well," said Mr Stone moodily.

A constable came in with a message. Bobby read it and said he would be disengaged in a moment and would the caller please wait. To Mr Stone, he said:

"I won't keep you any longer. If you do happen to think of anything likely to help, let us know at once."

"You can depend on me," said Mr Stone earnestly, much relieved at being thus dismissed. "Anything, Inspector, anything. Weston—he's your man. That's my tip. Good day, Inspector."

"Good day, Mr Stone," Bobby said; and as he went out Mr Stone murmured mechanically:

"Sammy to you."

CHAPTER XXXVI
SMITH, FINN AND FINCH

FOR A MOMENT or two Bobby sat in thoughtful mood. Was there anything significant, he wondered, in this tale of the missing man seen apparently for the last time by living eyes making his way up and round by the old quarry path to the higher ground Bobby himself, and Olive with him, had followed on the occasion of their Sunday holiday picnic in the forest?

Stone had not at first told all he knew. Even now, had he told everything or were there other facts that he was keeping back?

Rousing himself from these thoughts, Bobby touched the bell on his desk. Ushered in by the constable on duty, there appeared a tall, dark, youngish man, a long, prominent nose his most noticeable feature. He was smartly, a little too smartly, dressed, and Bobby had no difficulty in recognizing him. Bobby wondered if recognition were mutual, but the other gave no sign. Bobby said:

"Oh, very good of you to come along. I expect you know what it's about. There's just a possibility you might be able to help us. Lindley Finn is the name, I think. You've given it as Smith recently, though, haven't you? And wasn't it Louis Finch before that?"

The newcomer showed no surprise but looked very sulky.

"A man's got a right to change his name, hasn't he?" he retorted. "I put an advert in the papers all proper and according to law, on solicitor's advice. If it's about this murder in the papers you've dragged me here, there's nothing I know about it. Nothing to do with me. Don't think it was me did it, do you?"

He spoke with evident uneasiness, but that, Bobby felt, was not unnatural in the circumstances.

"So far as that goes," Bobby explained, "I always like to collect facts before I start thinking. Had you any special reason for passing under the name of Smith?"

"No crime in that, is there?" demanded the other truculently.

"Oh, no," Bobby agreed. "Let me see. You carry on a small picture-framer's business in London, don't you? Not very prosperous.

Debts. So on. Things bad all round just at present, I know. Lots of people hit by the war. Besides your picture-framing business, you've done a good many jobs of one sort or another for the big West End dealers—helping prepare catalogues, introducing likely customers, keeping an eye on sales in case anything good was likely to come up, getting commissions to bid, all that sort of thing. 'Runner' is the term they use in the trade, isn't it? One or two of the West End men have been a bit sticky recently about giving you jobs. Prejudiced. You were questioned a year or two ago at Scotland Yard over a burglary in Bond Street at an art dealer's. Some pictures were stolen and a night-watchman rather badly knocked about. Hit over the head and left unconscious. He got better but it was a near thing. Murder if he had died. You remember? It was after that you changed your name to Lindley Finn."

"Had to," Mr Finn declared. "Once the busies been on you, you're a marked man. But it didn't take them long to see there was nothing they could fix on me. They tried hard enough. A washout. That's busies all over. What do they care so long as they get someone sent up?"

Without replying to this, Bobby went on:

"I'm told you were at a big sale once when a dealer spotted a Van Cuyp no one else noticed. Bought it for a guinea or two and sold it for four figures. Bit of good luck for him and bad luck for you that you hadn't spotted it yourself."

"You seem to know it all," growled Finn. "I suppose," he complained sarcastically, "you know what I had for breakfast this day last year?"

"Well, hardly that," Bobby answered, "but we do make a few inquiries. You see, you are quite well known. The moment we began asking questions of art dealers, we got a perfect flood of information. Libellous, some of it, most likely. That doesn't matter. Nothing to do with us, nothing to do with the present inquiry. That little story about the Van Cuyp does rather suggest, though, that you might be specially keen on looking out for a similar windfall if any hint of one came your way. Something of the sort brought you up here, didn't it?"

"If you must know," Finn answered with a great appearance of candour, "I'm up here for Victors, the big Bond Street dealers. They had a tip the Rawdon collection was likely to come on the market, and they wanted me to check up on any chance of their getting their offer in first. That's why I gave my name as Smith. If other dealers heard Lindley Finn was hanging round Barsley Abbey, they might rumble something was on. So Smith it had to be for the duration—the duration of the job."

"I see," said Bobby.

He asked himself how best to continue. All this had been only preliminary skirmishing. He had shown Finn that a good deal was known about him and he hoped that would suggest to him that the knowledge of the police was even more complete. Such a belief might tend to make him cautious in denial, readier to tell what he did know. And that, Bobby felt, was possibly a good deal. He decided on a more direct attack. He said:

"What were you doing near the hermit's hut that Sunday afternoon I saw you there?"

"I thought that was you, I thought that was coming up," Finn grumbled. "No harm anyway. I had heard a lot about the old bloke and I thought I would like to have a look. Wasn't a sign of him anywhere."

"What made you clear out in such a hurry when you saw us?"

"Didn't want a lot of questions, that's all."

"Sure that was all?" Bobby asked. "I can't see why that should make you run in such a hurry. Almost as if you were—afraid."

Mr Finn was beginning to perspire gently.

"I wasn't. What for? I mean, why should I? Victors' instructions were to keep as quiet as I could, keep away from strangers, they said. Confidential job, that's all."

"Even too much," Bobby retorted, "because my information is you have been talking rather freely in pubs and other places. I remember an attaché case you had with you came open and what looked very much like an El Greco print fell out. Never mind that just now, though. You were washing your hands in a pool of the stream when we saw you, weren't you?"

"No. Yes. Well, why not? I got some dirt on them, that's all."

"What sort of dirt?" Bobby asked gently.

"Just dirt. Dirt. I don't know what you mean."

"Don't you?" Bobby asked. "Not far away a hatchet was found. Among some bushes. As if it had been thrown there. We think it had belonged to the hermit. One he used for chopping firewood. I sent it to Wakefield for examination. You know about Wakefield? Place where they identify fingerprints and all that sort of thing. You know. Microscopes. Infra red photographs. The whole bag of tricks."

"My dabs aren't on record," retorted Finn quickly. "At least, they didn't ought to be. It's a dirty trick if they are. I let the busies take them over that Bond Street affair, just to show it wasn't mine they found and they promised me faithful to destroy them. They let me see them doing it. Do you mean they switched them? Of all the dirty tricks—"

Mr Finn was on his feet now, gesticulating, flushed, boiling with that righteous indignation none feel more quickly, more genuinely, more deeply, than do those who are themselves among the unrighteous. Bobby motioned to him to sit down.

"I didn't say anything of the kind," he told him. "I'm not going to tell you what Wakefield reported, whether they did or did not find dabs. You'll probably know about that later on. But if you were promised your dabs would be destroyed, destroyed they were. Scotland Yard wouldn't switch them. That's certain. Besides, you must know dabs are perfectly easy to get. I daresay you've touched something or another since you came into this building we could develop dabs from if we wanted to. I don't say we have. I merely remind you that I saw you near the hermit's hut, that you ran the moment you saw someone approaching, that the hermit's hatchet was found not far off as if it had been thrown away in a panic, that when I saw you you were washing your hands."

"Well, why not, why shouldn't a bloke wash his hands?"

"There was blood on the hatchet," Bobby said. "You may as well know Wakefield does say that. And blood is sticky stuff though it can be washed off—most easily in cold running water."

"You can't fix anything on me," Finn muttered, now very pale. "I never touched the old man, I never saw him. You can't prove anything because there isn't anything I did."

"We'll leave that for the time," Bobby said. "And I wish you would believe we don't want to fix anything on anybody who isn't guilty. If a man is innocent all he has to do is to tell the truth. We test it, and if it hangs together—because that's how truth is tested: truth hangs together and lies don't—well, that ends it. I take it you didn't want to see the hermit, merely out of curiosity. It was about the lost El Greco paintings. Do you mind telling me how you came to hear about them?"

"No secret," Finn answered, looking now a trifle relieved but still plainly both subdued and uncomfortable. "Everyone knew. It's in all the reference books. *The Kensington Universal* lists all known El Grecos. It says two paintings by him are thought to have been in the Rawdon collection at Barsley Abbey but if so they have been lost sight of."

"Does it give any details?"

"It says one may have been the 'Enthronement of a Bishop in Seville Cathedral', which is said to have vanished from the cathedral when some of the vergers or beadles or whatever you call them were making a bit on the side. Only a guess though. Nothing known about the other."

"I didn't mean that," Bobby explained. "I meant about how they came to be lost sight of."

"There's nothing about that," Finn answered. "There wouldn't be. Not the *Universal* line."

"What I want to get at," Bobby explained, "is why it's all come up again now. The *Universal's* not a new publication. If everyone has always known the paintings were missing, why this sudden interest in them?"

Finn did not reply at once. He was evidently thinking hard. Bobby watched him closely. He had recovered to some degree from his earlier panic when Bobby had spoken of his presence near the hut and of the discovery of the hatchet, but his customary self-possession remained shaken. Bobby could almost hear him asking himself how much was really known, how safe it would be to lie, whether it might not be wiser to tell the truth for once. Not much doubt, Bobby felt, that he would have lied without hesitation had he not been so shaken by that previous questioning. He gave Bobby a quick, sudden, searching glance, and then looked away again. Bobby waited. He knew by much experience that it was wiser to make no attempt to press or hurry those under questioning. If they were willing to be helpful they would do their best anyhow. The others, under pressure, would be apt to take refuge in silence or blank denial, whereas, left to themselves, they were equally apt to feel a necessity to talk. Now it evidently occurred to Finn that he was arousing suspicion by so long a hesitation. He said:

"I'm trying to remember."

"Oh, yes," said Bobby encouragingly, making it, so to say, common ground that this was an admirable effort and one sure soon to give results.

"Oh, well," Finn declared, coming to a decision at last and putting on a great air of candour, "it wasn't that exactly, either. I was never one to give another bloke away. I'm no nark. I've never been a cop's contact man. I don't know what your game is."

"My game," Bobby said simply, sudden sternness in his voice, "is to try to bring to justice the murderer of an inoffensive old man."

CHAPTER XXXVII
MR FINN EXPLAINS

THAT SUDDEN HARD note in Bobby's voice broke through Finn's defences, seemed, as it were, to remind him how grave the question was they were discussing, to remind him, too, that his own position was not without its dangers.

"Look here," he said abruptly and rather hurriedly, "I'll tell you the whole thing. I mean about that hatchet. When I got there the old bloke's hut was all smashed up. I thought either he had been mad drunk or there had been a fight. I didn't know which. I had a look round and I saw the hatchet. It was lying near the door. Like a fool, I picked it up. I didn't rumble at first. Just thought it was paint or something. I picked some of it off with my thumb nail. All at once I rumbled. Blood it was. Gave me a shock. I flung the thing away as far as I could. Then I thought what a fool trick that was with my dabs on it most likely. I tried to find it again. I hadn't noticed where I chucked it and I couldn't see it anywhere. Put the wind up me. I started to wash my hands to get the stuff off and then you turned up and that put the wind up me more than ever. I didn't like the idea of being seen hanging round if anything was wrong and I didn't stop to think. I just cleared. That's gospel truth."

He paused, watching Bobby anxiously to see if he were believed. Of belief or disbelief Bobby gave no sign. He had indeed not yet formed an opinion. The tale was plausible, but Finn was certainly both a plausible and a ready liar. This time he might or might not be telling the truth. Nothing to show, one way or the other. Bobby said:

"What were you doing there, at the hut I mean? And you haven't told me yet what started you off making these inquiries?"

"I was never one to get another bloke into trouble," Finn repeated and went on: "If you must know, it was something told me by a bloke called Stone, Sammy Stone."

Bobby did his best not to show his interest. For now at last he thought had come together those two threads in the investigation which hitherto had seemed so far separate that they could not be connected—the clue of the new flavouring, the clue of the lost El Greco paintings.

"How does Stone come into it?" Bobby asked.

"He's the sort of wide-awake bloke who doesn't miss much," Finn explained with a touch of admiration in his voice, giving what was probably the highest praise he knew. "He was taking over a picture-framer's business in town two or three years back and he heard of me as knowing as much of the trade as any man—which I do—and he got me to check up on what the stock was worth. I gave him a good honest estimate. No reason not to. Afterwards I heard he had worked the business up and sold it for a good figure and then it flopped. Puffed it up more than it could stand, he had. Very smart work. After a time he turned up again at my shop. He knew I had treated him honest, given him a worth-while opinion, that's the way to get a connection, get a good name. See?"

"Pity to have to change it when you've got it," murmured Bobby, just to let Mr Finn know his observations were not necessarily going to be taken at face value, and the thrust was acknowledged by a scowl, half resentful, half admitting that the attempt to make a good impression had failed. "What did Stone want that time?" Bobby added.

"It was this way," Finn continued, quite willing to tell a tale that displayed his own cleverness. "Stone picked up somewhere what he thought was a Rembrandt—a Rembrandt, mind you. He took it to Christie's and they had a good laugh, told him the frame might be worth its weight in—firewood. So he trotted it along to me for confirmation. I told him that was right. Rubbish it was, same as they told him. But I kept on looking at it, telling him all the time it was just rubbish and then I offered him a fiver for it."

"Why, if it wasn't worth anything?" Bobby asked, in spite of all his experience puzzled to see where the swindle came in.

"Well," Finn explained, grinning broadly, "if you offer a man a fiver for something you've just told him isn't worth anything, he begins to wonder. If Stone had said 'Done' I should have wriggled out somehow. Not much chance of that. He started asking questions instead, and so I let out at last I thought there was an off-chance that though the top painting was no good, there might be something good underneath. I told him of a case when a top painting had been removed and there was a genuine Raphael underneath, and how there was a Raphael in the National Gallery might bring anything up to half a million if it was put on the market now. It has happened you know. Over-painting, I mean. I never came across a case, but I've heard of them. Some fool of an amateur, hard up for canvas, over-paints good stuff. You tell your bloke a tale or two like that and when you've got him receptive you offer to clean the top off to see, for as much as you think you can sting him for. Sammy's smart, so I only let him in for half a guinea."

"Clear profit though, I suppose," Bobby remarked.

"Well, I spent twenty minutes and a spot of turpentine just to show," Finn answered unblushingly. "Sammy was a bit let down but he didn't rumble, and I had rubbed it in good and hard how it was all a gamble. Anyhow, after that he took me for an expert. Which I am," added Finn simply.

"Yes, indeed," agreed Bobby warmly; though thinking to himself that it was in ways that are dark and tricks that are vain that Finn was a real expert.

"Sammy came up here from town," Finn continued, "over another business he took over before the war and wasn't doing so well, and one night when he was in a pub he heard a bloke by the name of Weston telling of a half-cracked old bloke who lived all alone and made a living selling lotions and flavourings and such-like he made up himself and how one of them was pretty good—Sammy was on that in quick sticks—and how most likely the old bloke had some hold on the Rawdon family or why did they let him squat on their land and never ask any rent? Sammy asked the bloke he had put in to run the shop for him about the Rawdons, Sammy never having heard of the family or the Rawdon collection either. The bloke told him how valuable the paintings were and how the Rawdon family was hard up but couldn't sell because of the entail. That made Sammy think. Me being an expert in pictures as he knew, he came along to get an idea what sort of a hold the old fellow could have and could it be about the pictures and the entail? Because Sammy had heard of pictures that couldn't be sold being copied, and then the copies being hung and the originals sold instead. He reckoned if there was anything like that the old bloke knew, it might be worth while to know it, too. The idea was we might claim a reward for getting the stuff back. See?"

"Yes," said Bobby, without comment but with meaning.

Finn looked at him and grinned.

"Not much you miss, is there?" he said. He added virtuously: "It did strike me maybe it was a spot of blackmail, from seller or from buyer —or from both—Sammy had in mind. So I told him nothing doing if it was that and he said he hadn't ever thought of such a thing. I didn't see there was anything we could do about it, and then just by chance I came across a book in the public library that was a sort of history of Wychwood Forest and neighbourhood and that made me remember the story of the two El Greco paintings that were supposed to be lost. I thought I would see if there was anything in it about that, so I took the book home, and sure enough there was a chapter all about the Rawdons and their history and their famous gallery of old masters, and it said how one of the family at the end of the last century had disappeared for a gipsy and what a pity it was because he was an amateur artist of great talent. Man and pictures both vanishing about the same time, I'm no blasted busy, but I can put two and two together."

"I'm sure you can," Bobby agreed heartily, and Finn looked very pleased; he might have blushed indeed, so pleased he was, had he but known how. He went on:

"It was no sure thing, but I thought there was a chance that's what had become of the El Grecos. I put it to Victors, the big Bond Street dealers. I half expected them to turn it down, but they didn't. In the picture trade you can never tell, and never any telling what happens to these old paintings that don't look much unless you know. They promised to finance me up to twenty pounds, me to have a third share if I struck lucky. And they gave me some rather good El

Greco prints to show round as specimens of what the missing stuff was like."

"Find out anything?" Bobby asked.

"Not a thing," Finn answered. "No one knew anything unless it was Dr Maskell, and if he did, he rumbled, and closed down tight."

"Maskell?" repeated Bobby, once more startled but trying not to show it. "What makes you think he knew anything?"

"Not what he said," retorted Finn, "because he didn't. But you could see he was interested. Asked questions. Showed he didn't fall for my yarn about me writing a book. I made up my mind I would keep an eye on him. Not so easy when it's a doctor running round after his patients. But I soon found that he and the old hermit bloke hated each other like poison and yet he was trying to see him—and what for? Because it wasn't because he was sick."

"How do you know he was trying to see him?"

"Because I was myself. I never did. The old bloke was never there. But once I saw Maskell driving away, and another time I saw his car standing empty not far off."

"Are you sure?"

"Oh, yes. I knew the number."

"Did you see Maskell himself?"

"No," admitted Finn. "I got lost. Sounds silly, I know. Give me London. You can tell where you are when it's street. Streets are all different. But those blessed trees are all the same, so once you've turned round, you don't know which way to head. Worse than any fog. It was nearly dark before I got to a road and back to Midwych. What I say is, what was Maskell doing there if he hadn't the same idea as me and wasn't trying to get in first with the El Grecos?"

Bobby refrained from expressing an opinion. But the suggestion that Maskell had been one of the dead man's visitors was both interesting and disturbing.

"If you ask me," continued Mr Finn, as one who knew his opinion was of value, "either it was Maskell did in the old bloke or it was no one. Maskell rumbled he had those El Greco paintings tucked away somewhere, had a try for them, the old man wouldn't part, there was a scrap, the old man got the worst of it, Maskell shoved his body where you found it and went off with the paintings. Eh? What do you say?"

"Possible," agreed Bobby, "only not much evidence, is there?"

"Get a search warrant," advised Mr Finn, now deftly assuming the part of valued counsellor and assistant, "and have a look. I'll lay you ten to one Maskell's got those pictures, and if you look you'll find them."

Ignoring this suggestion, Bobby said:

"When you were making your inquiries, did you hear anything about its being possible the hermit was a man who had at one time been a gipsy, then been employed as a footman at Barsley Abbey and then gone back to a gipsy life? He is supposed to have been Mr Crayfoot's grandfather according to the tale I heard."

Finn looked blank, almost too blank, Bobby thought.

"Well, that's a rum tale," he said, "that's a new one to me. This thing gets rummier and rummier all the time, don't it?"

"Do you know a man named Coop?" Bobby asked; and when Finn shook his head and this time looked really puzzled, he went on: "He's a frequent visitor to pubs. Spends most of his evenings in one or other."

"I might know him if I saw him," Finn said. "What about him?"

"There was a burglary at Mr Crayfoot's," Bobby explained. "I expect you've heard Sir Alfred Rawdon was shot. The house was ransacked. Nothing much taken so far as we know. I think Coop was the burglar. I am wondering if in default of a search warrant, he had been sent to see if the El Greco paintings were in Crayfoot's possession."

"If it was anyone it was Maskell," declared Finn very emphatically. "If Coop's been trying to fix it on me, he's just another liar. I don't say I've never seen the bloke, because I may have, but not that I know of. Never had anything to do with him. Maskell's your man."

"Either Maskell or another," agreed Bobby, and so brought the interview to a close.

CHAPTER XXXVIII
DR MASKELL'S SYMPATHIES

LATE AS IT had now become, Bobby decided it was necessary, blackout or no blackout, to have immediately another talk with Dr Maskell. The story about his car having been seen near the hermit's hut rested only on the unsupported evidence of a not too trustworthy witness, but the doctor ought to be informed promptly and offered an opportunity for any comment he might wish to make. So Bobby started off at once and was lucky enough to find Maskell at home, though not in any very amiable mood—but then Bobby knew already that with Dr Maskell amiable moods were rare—and much disposed to answer all questions with a brief and emphatic negative.

This negative was especially emphatic in reply to Mr Finn's allegation that his car had been seen standing empty near the hermit's hut. Finn's story was dismissed as a stupid lie, probably told to divert suspicion from himself. Quite possibly Finn had seen Maskell driving along one of the roads in the neighbourhood. Why not? No doubt, admitted the doctor, he could draw up from his record of professional visits a more or less accurate itinerary for the last few weeks, or years for that matter, but he had no intention of doing anything of the sort. He would, he explained, see the whole police force in general, and Inspector Bobby Owen in particular, at the bottom of the sea before wasting his time on so futile a job. The police were welcome to believe what they liked and think what they wished, assuming always that they were, in fact, capable of thought. Their beliefs and disbeliefs left him completely cold, as cold as did the fate of the murdered man. A mischievous old humbug well out of the way, in his opinion, and the only wonder was that it hadn't happened before. Probably, the doctor suggested, whoever was guilty, if guilty was the right word, was somebody one of whose relatives had been poisoned by the old scoundrel's filthy messes.

"His dying," declared Dr Maskell, "means others living, his death, life for others. I could give you a list of those who would be alive and well to-day if they hadn't been bamboozled into taking his poisons. Don't ask me to waste any sympathy on him."

"I won't," Bobby promised. "Did you ever hear any gossip about his identity?"

"What do you mean, his identity?" the doctor demanded. "He was well enough known, part of the stock in trade of all quacks is to get known. Anyhow, I don't waste my time gossiping," he added grimly, and indeed did not give the impression of one likely to yield to that amiable if deplorable weakness.

More closely pressed, he answered snappily that he had never heard anything about the old man's origins. Or, alternatively, as the lawyers say, if he had heard anything of the kind, it had passed entirely from his mind.

Bobby passed to another subject.

"Recently," he said, "this man Finn came to see you. He told you his name was Smith and said he was making inquiries about two El Greco paintings."

The doctor nodded acquiescence.

"Travelling salesman, I should think," he remarked, "from the way he talked. I remember he showed me an engraving. Said it was like two he was trying to trace. Something about a book he said he was writing. Where does he come into the business?"

"I wish I knew," Bobby admitted. "Were you able to tell him anything?"

"I'm not an art critic," snorted the doctor, rather as if saying 'I'm not scum'. "I told him I went to see patients, not their pictures." He gave again that grim smile of his. "I did tell him if I had ever seen a nightmare like the thing he showed me, I should certainly have remembered it."

"Did he say anything about their having a big cash value?"

"Not that I remember," answered the doctor carelessly. "Have they any? I understood he only wanted to know their whereabouts for this book he said he was writing. Most likely, considering the interest people about here take in art, they've been burnt or destroyed long ago."

"I wonder if you ever heard anyone mention the Diabolic Candelabra?" Bobby asked.

"What's that?" the doctor asked. "Sounds interesting. I don't mind telling you I thought Mr Finn, if that's his name, a bit of a wrong 'un. Do you mean you suspect him of being mixed up in the murder?"

"I suspect so many," Bobby admitted sadly, "it makes me feel dizzy merely to try to remember them all."

Maskell laughed; at least the sound he produced was evidently meant for laughter, though unaccustomed muscles of merriment creaked rather badly when thus abruptly called into action.

"I suppose you are sure it was murder, not suicide?" he asked, more amiability in his tone now, "I haven't seen the injuries, but I have known a man try to kill himself by banging his head against a wall. Hurt himself badly, too. I should think it would be possible to inflict very serious wounds on yourself with an axe and then throw the thing away. Quite feasible."

"I think it must be taken as a case of murder," Bobby answered, thinking to himself that at any rate it was hardly feasible for a dead man to tie a rope round himself and haul himself into a tree in order to deposit himself in its hollow interior.

"Only a suggestion," Maskell said carelessly. "My sympathies are with the murderer." He paused and gave Bobby a hard, challenging stare, as much as to ask him what he thought of that. When Bobby made no comment Maskell went on: "If you can call it murder and not a public service. What about Crayfoot? Has he turned up yet?" and when Bobby answered by a shake of the head, the doctor added: "Queer business. A murder and Crayfoot bolts. See any connection?"

"I see the possibility of a connection," Bobby answered cautiously. "But only a possibility. I don't know what kind of connection, and I have no proof."

"I take it proof always is a difficulty, isn't it?" the doctor commented with something like a sneer. "You may guess and you may suspect, but when it comes to proof—stumped, eh?"

"Sometimes," admitted Bobby. "Sometimes the proof turns up in time. One never knows. Finn says he saw Crayfoot climbing a path that goes up by the side of an old forest quarry—Boggart's Hole, where the monks got the stone they built Barsley Abbey with. I expect you know it. The last anyone saw of Crayfoot apparently. So the puzzle is, what was he doing there and what did he want?"

"Boggart's Hole?" repeated Maskell. "Yes, I know it," he said thoughtfully. "There have been accidents there. I suppose you've had it searched?"

Bobby assured him it had been searched thoroughly, and therewith took his leave, not dissatisfied.

CHAPTER XXXIV
SUSPECTS

BY NOW IT was too late for any further action that day, so Bobby drove back home; told Olive he would be sitting up late to try to reach some conclusion on the facts as he knew them; overbore her prompt and passionate protest by advancing the odious platitude that duty is duty; accepted her offer, put forward with bitterness, of a jug of black coffee strong enough to keep Morpheus himself awake for a week;

accepted also, and again with gratitude, her further offer to sit up and listen to his various theories.

"I won't criticize," she promised earnestly. "I'll just listen."

"Grand," said Bobby with hearty approval.

"Of course," said Olive humbly, "now and then I may just have to ask you to explain."

"We will not," said Bobby coldly, "split hairs about where explanations end and criticism begins. But I don't like that humble tone of yours."

"Oh, why?" asked Olive surprised.

"Because," explained Bobby, "the wife's humility goes before the husband's fall."

"Marriage maxim No. 1," Olive remarked thoughtfully, "Marriage maxim No. 2 being 'Serves him right'."

Not dissatisfied with this retort to which Bobby was unable to produce an adequate reply, Olive retired to the kitchen to brew that Morpheus-defeating beverage she had promised. She returned with it of the strength of an R.A.F. bomb and of a blackness to satisfy even an Air Raid Warden on his nightly prowl.

"Now then," she said, settling herself.

"Take alibis to begin with," Bobby began. "Alibis are always important—the senior Mr Weller was quite right about that. If you can show you were somewhere else when it happened, obviously it wasn't you."

"Delayed action," interjected Olive.

"A hatchet applied to the head isn't delayed action," Bobby pointed out. "The thing is, there's nothing to show the exact time of the murder. Before we saw Lindley Finn on Sunday, but how long before? The blood on the hatchet was dry enough for him to pick at it with his thumb. But how dry? Then it had apparently been lying in the grass. That would delay drying. What happened may have been only an hour or two before, or it may have been much longer."

Olive took a piece of paper and wrote:

"Alibis out."

Then she said:

"Not much help."

"Then there's motive," Bobby said. "Who benefits? is a sound question. But here there's a complex of possible motives. The new flavouring."

"You can't think a new flavour for chocolates could lead to murder," Olive declared.

"Anything can lead to murder," Bobby answered. "When Wainwright was asked why he poisoned his sister-in-law, he said it was because her ankles were so thick."

"Good gracious," said Olive, giving a hurried glance at her own and a trifle relieved to observe that they were as slim as ankles should be.

"A new flavour might mean money," Bobby continued. "I rang up one of the big confectionery people this morning and they said they might give quite a fair sum for one, if it was really good."

"This was," said Olive with conviction. "Like going to heaven in a band box."

"Then there are those El Greco paintings and the candelabra," Bobby went on. "A small fortune there and not so small either. Or a quarrel. Or the question of the old man's identity. Or revenge."

Slowly Olive wrote down: "Flavouring, Pictures. Identity. Quarrel. Revenge." Then she shook her head:

"They need sorting out," she said. "Identity. I don't see why it mattered so much who he was."

"If he was actually the Rawdon who left home to turn gipsy and didn't die anywhere in France, it would matter a good deal," Bobby retorted. "Make all sorts of complications. Or he may have been Crayfoot's grandfather, the ex-footman. Or neither perhaps."

"How are you going to find out?" Olive asked.

"I don't know," answered Bobby, relieved to be able to give a plain answer to a plain question. "Let's go over the whole list of suspects one by one and see what we get."

"How many suspects as you call them, are there?" Olive asked.

Bobby began to give the list, checking them off on his fingers.

"First," he said, "there's the present baronet, if baronet he is, Sir Alfred Rawdon."

"Oh, but that's silly," protested Olive, "when he's been murdered himself as near as can be."

"Doesn't prevent him," retorted Bobby, "from having murdered someone else first, does it?"

"Oh, well," said Olive and wrote down the name.

"The nephew, Dick Rawdon," Bobby continued.

"Oh, but that is really silly this time," declared Olive. "Why, he's head over heels in love with Mary Floyd."

"Can't murderers be head over heels in love?" asked Bobby. "Sometimes that's why they are murderers."

"Oh, well," said Olive again, and put down Dick's name below his uncle's.

"Mary Floyd," Bobby continued.

Indignantly Olive laid down pencil and paper.

"That's worse than silly," she declared. "Why, she's ever so sweet."

"She may be, but she is capable of keeping a man in a cellar for a week," Bobby pointed out, "and I don't suppose 'sweet' was the word he used. You saw her yourself that Sunday. Touch and go whether Coop didn't get a whole dollop of boiling soup over him. Justifiable homicide perhaps, but homicide all the same and that's not so far from murder."

"Well, it would have served him right," said Olive, and, under protest as it were, put down Mary's name.

"Crayfoot next," said Bobby.

"Bobby! Really!" Olive exclaimed, looking quite bewildered. "Why, we've been getting our bread from him almost ever since we came."

"Not a reason," pronounced Bobby, and Olive shrugged her shoulders and set down that name too.

"Dr Maskell," said Bobby next.

"Oh, well," agreed Olive, "I could believe anything of him. I think he's perfectly horrid and awfully rude as well," and she hurried to add his name to the growing list before Bobby could change his mind.

"Sammy Stone," Bobby continued.

Olive smiled with a certain contempt.

"Soft and fat," she commented. "Cheat, yes. Murder, no."

"Cheating sometimes leads to murder when the cheat's afraid of being found out," Bobby reminded her, and so down went his name.

"Mr Weston," Bobby said next, and once more Olive's pencil hung suspended in protest.

"Bobby," she said, "that nice little man. Why, I had tea with Mrs Weston in town the other day and she was telling me where you could buy as many tomatoes as you liked—only," added Olive sadly, "a policeman's wife has to be so careful—so beastly careful." The pencil came down to the paper but still did not write. "You can't mean," she argued, "that perhaps I've had tea with the wife of a murderer?"

"Might happen to practically anyone," Bobby told her. He added thoughtfully: "Weston had a violent quarrel with Crayfoot. Might mean a lot or nothing, but it's got to be remembered"; and so yet another name was entered on the growing list.

"Is that all now?" Olive asked, and Bobby shook his head and said: "Lindley Finn next."

So then it was Olive's turn to shake her head.

"Financial shark," she pointed out. "Not the murderer type, just a shark."

"Sharks are killers," Bobby said. "What is the murderer type?"

"Big and brutal and jaws sticking out," said Olive, "and—oh, well, you know."

"I don't," Bobby declared emphatically. "The murderer type is you and me and the next man. Murderers aren't always the worst criminals, though murder is the worst crime. Curious. Contradictory, too. But then so is the world—curious and contradictory, I mean. I think pretty nearly anyone might commit murder—given circumstance and provocation and opportunity. And motive."

Olive said nothing, but wrote down Lindley Finn's name.

"Montague Hart," said Bobby next.

"Who is he?" asked Olive. "Oh, the lawyer. Well—a lawyer," she admitted.

"There's a certain amount of evidence," Bobby observed. "His hat. Nothing much in that. Easy explanation. Blown off while he was taking a walk in the forest and so he had to buy a new one. I expect he's the man Marriott saw the old hermit chasing away. But Marriott can't identify him. Dick Rawdon says he smoked cigars—generally Dick's, apparently—and someone smoked a cigar at the hut. It looks to me as if Hart visited the hut, found the place empty, decided to wait, smoked his cigar while doing so. That may have put the old man's back up—he didn't smoke himself, apparently. At any rate, nothing's been said about his buying tobacco. Touchy old boy, too.

Perhaps that's what started him persuading his visitor to retire. Theory again, but it fits."

"Yes, but had he any motive?" Olive asked, as she added his name to her still growing list.

"The El Grecos," Bobby answered. "They're the standard motive. Big cash value and possession proof of ownership." He went on: "Next, that Coop chap."

Olive looked contemptuous, but made no protest till she had written the name. Then she said with authority:

"It's not Coop. If he had done it, he would have been hiding in a panic, not bullying his wife and fighting Mary."

"Is that psychology?" Bobby asked.

"Common sense," retorted Olive.

She looked at her long list of names and shook her head disapprovingly.

"You've made me put down everyone you can think of just at random," she complained, and ignoring Bobby's interjected "Oh, no," she added: "Well, anyhow, it's everyone you know ever went near the poor old man or had anything to do with him—except Mrs Coop and little Loo."

"I was coming to them," Bobby said. "We had better have them on the list as well—both of them."

Too astonished to protest, Olive obeyed. Then she blinked at the two names as if she didn't believe it and said "Well", and it was a 'Well' that in one syllabic said as much as whole dictionaries could have conveyed.

"I've no proof," Bobby explained, "that Mrs Coop is really a helpless invalid, and Loo is so strange a child that with her one can be sure of nothing. Remember how she left that unlucky school inspector woman to lose herself in the forest? One can get lost and die of cold and exposure even in an English forest. Remember those Derbyshire hikers some years ago? Remember, too, it was Loo who knew where the old man's body had been hidden, and I've a very strong idea she knows even now a good deal more than she has told us. Or why did she spend those nights in the forest and why did she take food from the cottage?"

CHAPTER XL

TWELVE NAMES

BOBBY LEANED OVER Olive's shoulder, reading absently that long list of names she had written down and letting his mind dwell upon each one in turn.

"There's always the chance," he said presently, "of its turning out to be someone we've never even heard of—some tramp or another. There seems to have been a lot of gossip going on about a hoard of sovereigns he was supposed to have hidden somewhere."

"You don't think so, though," Olive asserted. She added: "I don't."

"It all points to one of those names," he agreed; and this time ran his finger down the list and then brought it back and let it rest, pointing to one name.

"Bobby," Olive breathed, and she had gone a little pale. "Bobby, do you mean—you know?"

"No good thinking that you know," he answered, "till you can show the evidence—and I can't. Not yet."

"There are two little incidents you've told me of," she reminded him thoughtfully.

"Yes, but any clever counsel would simply enjoy himself sweeping them into the dustbin."

"If that's the one who is guilty," Olive said uneasily, "it means there's a trap waiting."

"I suppose so," Bobby agreed. "I didn't mean it at the time, but it struck me at once it was like that—I mean, it meant the trap was there for anyone to walk into who wanted. Probably no one will. They might."

"There's still nothing to show," Olive mused, "who the old hermit really was—and nothing to show whether Mr Crayfoot has gone away on his own affairs, or run away in a panic, or whether he's still out there somewhere in the forest."

"I think he's there still," Bobby said. "One thing we've got to remember is that the old man, whoever he was, whatever his identity, and to us it doesn't matter whether he was a Rawdon and rightful holder of the title and the property, or whether he was the ex-footman, or whether he was neither the one nor the other, he still had a violent temper and was inclined to chase off visitors with that axe of his."

"Doesn't that suggest," Olive put in, "that if he found one of his tramp friends in his hut trying to get the money he was supposed to have hidden, it might have meant a fight or something, and the poor old man getting killed, and nothing to do with any of these people?"

"I feel pretty sure myself," Bobby said, "that he knew enough about the sort of people he met on the road to have taken precautions. Very likely that sort of thing happened all right, more than once perhaps, but I think we may be certain he had prepared. It is one of the reasons why I feel so certain he had a second abiding place somewhere in the forest. You remember he bought oil he can only have wanted for cooking and heating, but there was no sign of lamp or oil stove at the hut. All cooking done outside apparently and firewood used for fuel. An oil stove would be much less likely to give him away than any fire. A fire would show light by night and smoke by day, whereas an oil stove would give neither. That may be why he wanted the Diabolic Candelabra the Rawdons talked about. He may have used candles sometimes or kept them in reserve in case the oil ran out."

"I suppose there is that," Olive agreed. "An oil stove would be much more secret. Only why did he want to be so very secret?"

"Genuine hermit impulse," Bobby suggested. "Some people love solitude. At the hut he was always on tap, so to speak, and if he wasn't there, it could be thought he had gone wandering or was just out for the time. Whereas really he was snug in his second refuge. Also it seems likely he had possessions he didn't want known or talked about. If he took the Diabolic Candelabra for convenience, he may have taken the El Grecos to remind him of the life he had left. Or because they appealed to him in a way they did to no one else. You know, I can imagine anyone getting an almost mystical passion for an El Greco. As they used to say in the advertisements, El Grecos have something others haven't got. I know the first time I saw an El Greco it seemed to get up and hit me in the eye."

"I don't care," observed Olive thoughtfully, "for pictures that do that. I like one, like 'The Shrimp Girl', you can sit and look at and feel lovely and peaceful, not hit about."

"Question of taste," Bobby observed. "Anyhow, we aren't discussing art. What I'm getting at is, I think he needed some secret place where he could go and be sure of being alone and where he could keep things he didn't want seen or known about. And yet he had to have another place as well everyone could know of. Otherwise people might have got wondering and started to hunt him up. Some of the lot he hobnobbed with on his tramps would certainly be curious. Especially at first there would be lots of talk about him. Tramps and gipsies and vagabonds generally soon get to know as much about each other as you do in any other closed professional society. They are as curious as monkeys and as thievish as monkeys and I'm sure they were soon trying to find out all they could about him. It wouldn't be long before they were paying him visits and having a look round his hut when he wasn't there. All his possessions of any value he would need to keep somewhere else or they would soon have been stolen. And he would be specially anxious to keep them hidden if in any way they suggested his past he had tried to cut loose from."

"It's the El Greco paintings you are thinking of?" Olive said.

"The Diabolic Candelabra as well," Bobby answered. "Silver and more obviously valuable. The El Grecos might mean nothing to some people. Bits of coloured canvas. But silver is always silver."

"If he has them," Olive said, "that means he really is a Rawdon and a baronet—or was, rather, the poor old thing, living all alone like that."

"His own choice," Bobby said. "Possibly it suited him better—possibly he wanted to be let alone, not tied up with titles and property and all that. One way of life and he chose it. He seems to have kept himself busy with herbs and things. Discovering a new flavour mayn't count for much."

"Oh, but," Olive interrupted, "it was so—so Nice."

"So it was," admitted Bobby. "There's the cancer cure, too. You can't be sure it was really worth while, in spite of any success it had, because sometimes cancer vanishes of its own accord. But even if he were merely on the track of something good—well, it would have made it all worth while, all his life, I mean."

"Yes, I suppose so," Olive agreed, "and it's all lost now."

"A few blows with a hatchet to let out knowledge that might have meant so much to all the world," Bobby said. "I suppose we shall never know." After a long pause, he added: "It's one reason why the second hideout has got to be found. You see, it's just possible he may have kept some of his cancer cure there and, if so, it could be analysed."

"If the El Grecos are there, too," Olive said, "that will prove—I suppose it won't though," she added doubtfully; "he might still be either the baronet or the footman."

"I don't suppose we ever shall know," Bobby remarked. "I suppose in a sense it doesn't matter. What I've got to do is to see a murder doesn't go unpunished—and find out what's happened to Crayfoot. Quite possibly he is the murderer and quite as likely he is the murderer's second victim if by bad luck he chanced to see what was going on—and the murderer knew it."

"Poor Mrs Crayfoot," Olive said softly, "it must be awful—not knowing."

"Can't be sure," Bobby repeated, "till he's found—or his body. Anyhow, there's the set-up, beginning from Mrs Weston's liking for chocolates that started as tangled a story of death and disappearance and hidden treasures as anyone could wish for."

"I shall never," declared Olive firmly, "want to taste chocolates ever again."

"One thing leads to another," Bobby said. "If Mrs Weston hadn't enjoyed her chocolates so much, Weston wouldn't have talked about them to his pals in the pub. Then Stone would never have heard of the old hermit or spoken to Finn, and Finn would never have looked up the Rawdon family, and Sir Alfred wouldn't have known inquiries were being made about the lost El Grecos involving a hint that his title wasn't secure. And then he wouldn't have consulted his lawyer, and Dick Rawdon wouldn't have been called in as heir, and wouldn't have gone off to question Crayfoot and start him wondering in his turn who the hermit really was. Nor would Dick have visited Coop's cottage and most likely set Coop guessing as well. It all hangs together, everything leading on from one thing to another, the perfect blue print of a crime."

"You've forgotten Dr Maskell," Olive said.

"No," Bobby said. "No. He is not a man to forget. Finn visited him, too. Certainly his quarrel with the hermit was old enough."

He began to pace the length of the room again and then paused to stare once more at the long list of names that Olive had set down, one below the other. He read aloud;

"Sir Alfred Rawdon.

"Dick Rawdon.

"Dr Maskell.

"Mr Crayfoot.

"Mr Weston.

"Sammy Stone.

"Lindley Finn.

"Montague Hart.

"Coop.

"Mrs Coop.

"Mary Floyd.

"Loo."

He paused, began to make cryptic marks against each name, and then threw down his pencil with an impatient gesture.

"Twelve names," he said, "and which one is the right one? Of twelve, one, and nothing to show which. It might quite well be Sir Alfred himself. He had a pretty strong motive. He had to face the possibility of becoming a pauper, liable to a strict accounting for every penny spent during all the time he had been in possession. There's the El Greco motive, too. If he could have got hold of them he could have sold them right away and most likely they would have brought enough to pull him clear from his financial difficulties. Not much chance of recovering them either except by violence or something like that. Legal proof of ownership was almost impossible."

"Do you think Mr Crayfoot had them all the time?"

"It's on the cards," Bobby said musingly. "No proof again. Perhaps he had and perhaps he hadn't. But anyone on their track might think it a good idea to try to find out. Coop, for instance. Dick Rawdon claims it was the Floyd portrait he went there to look at. Perhaps it was really the El Grecos he was after. He stood to lose his position as next heir and he admits he needed money for his factory development. He was getting advances from the bank, or so he says—of course, that can be checked if necessary—but, anyhow, they would have to be paid back, and a few thousands extra capital no doubt he could turn to very good use. Getting hold of the El Grecos would have given him a very useful lump of fresh capital, and there never was a business yet couldn't do with that. Motive and opportunity. Both Rawdons had it, uncle and nephew, too. Also they don't seem to trust each other too much. Rightly or wrongly, I'm pretty sure uncle suspected nephew of trying to get ahead of him with those El Grecos.

Or why did Sir Alfred go hot foot after nephew Dick to the Crayfoots' place the night he got shot?"

"I don't see that they had more motive or more opportunity than anyone else," Olive commented.

"Oh, they hadn't," Bobby agreed. "All the same, they had it. So had others, certainly. There's Crayfoot's card I found at the hermit's hut. Suggests he had been there. Good evidence though not conclusive. Someone else might have got hold of a card of his and left it there to incriminate him. Not likely but possible. Again, the evidence he was seen near Boggart's Hole isn't conclusive—witness not too trustworthy. Lindley Finn we saw ourselves—and who can tell if the blood on his hands was old and dry as he says or fresh and new? He admits he handled the axe, so fingerprints are no use. Stone's evidence that he saw Weston following Crayfoot may be accepted as he admits he followed Weston. How do we know which of them got there first or what happened when they did? For what it's worth there's Finn's statement that he saw Dr Maskell's car standing near by, but Maskell denies it, and who is to decide? Maskell admits he thinks getting rid of the old man rather praiseworthy than otherwise—the day's good deed. But people are always saying things like that."

"Not the murderer of his victim, surely?" Olive interposed.

"Maskell's not an ordinary type," Bobby answered. "You can never tell. Then there's the lawyer and the story of his hat, but the explanation he gives is—well, acceptable. I don't happen to believe it, but I can't prove anything. The cigar business is suggestive, but again proves nothing. My own idea is that he was trying to find out on his own who the old man really was—ex-footman or rightful baronet. Meant to play his own hand if he could make sure. Most likely with a twitching nose for the El Grecos as well. A small fortune waiting to be picked up, those El Grecos—and either footman or baronet might have them. Coop was certainly the burglar that night at the Crayfoots'. He heard the nephew come and lay low. Then he heard him go and tried to get away himself, but ran straight into uncle's arms. Which suggests he had some idea of what was going on and an eye on the paintings for himself. Or he may have been hired by someone else. But until we can get a statement from Sir Alfred there's not much we can do. The attack Coop made shows he is ready enough to kill, though probably only when worked up to it by panic. What we do know is that he and Dick Rawdon have been seen talking and we don't know what about. Maybe Dick was hiring him for a job—burglary. Come next to Mary Floyd—"

"I simply won't believe—" interrupted Olive with some heat, but Bobby shook his head at her.

"It doesn't matter what you or I believe," he said. "We've got to know, not believe. And it's no good saying she's a girl and girls don't kill people, because sometimes they do. Remember Lizzie Borden."

"She was acquitted," Olive retorted.

"Yes, I forgot that," admitted Bobby. "And I don't know that it matters. Acquittal doesn't always mean innocence. Look at—but I had better keep off slander. Anyhow, if you remember, we both heard Mary and her mother say there was only one way to save Loo, only one way to stop the old man's encouragement of Loo's craze for wandering in the forest. Perhaps there was only one way and perhaps they took it."

"Oh, Bobby, don't," Olive said. "It's not possible," she said and looked deeply troubled.

"Then there's Loo," Bobby went on. "She's quite incalculable, but it is a fact that she alone knew where the old man's body was hidden. How did she know it?"

Olive did not answer and Bobby went on:

"What I said about Mary applies to her mother as well." He paused, and after a long silence Olive made no attempt to interrupt, he said slowly: "One has to think of everything, consider everything. Nothing is impossible when you are dealing with men and women."

CHAPTER XLI
BOGGART'S HOLE

OLIVE LOOKED AT the clock.

"It's nearly three," she said. "We had better get to bed."

"I must go out instead," Bobby answered; and when Olive looked a question, but did not speak: "To Boggart's Hole," he said.

"To watch the trap close?" she asked. "Oh, must you?" He did not answer, for he knew she knew already the reply. She said: "Not alone? Bobby, if you're right, not alone. You'll take some of the men with you?"

"I'll knock up Sergeant Turner and take him along," Bobby promised. "Poor chap. He won't like it. Resign on the spot most likely if he could."

Olive went to make him a small packet of sandwiches and to fill a thermos flask. Years before, when he had been a raw beginner, a senior man had warned Bobby that a good detective never forgot his sandwiches, advice Bobby had always remembered for himself and had on occasion passed on to others. He provided himself, too, with a revolver. But though he put some cartridges in his pocket he did not load the weapon. A policeman's business is not to kill, but to bring before the Law those it is the affair of the Law to judge, either to condemn or to set free. Then he started off and, according to his promise, stopped at Sergeant Turner's house, where he found that worthy, not only in bed, as was natural at that hour, but also with a temperature and something more than a threat of approaching influenza.

So it was alone that Bobby drove through the night, slowly and with caution, for blackout regulations had to be observed and indeed once he heard a 'plane overhead. It might be an enemy 'plane, he supposed, and he remembered how old John Bright had cried out during the Crimean war that almost could be heard above the land the beating of the wings of the angel of death. Well, that phrase had justified itself now in unexpected ways. He was too far away to hear the sirens if they went, but there were no searchlights jumping to and fro about the sky, no flares floating down, no distant clamour of the guns. So he continued on his way and coming presently to a convenient spot, he left his car and alighted.

Switching on now and then the strong electric torch he carried he made sure as best he could that he was on the right path. Presently he thought that he was at or near the spot where he and Olive had paused that Sunday for a while by the unprotected edge of the old, deserted quarry. He wondered if he could assure himself of his position by finding that tree on which he remembered showing Olive bruises caused by what seemed the pressure of a rope.

A hopeless task in the dark, he decided; and he drew aside under bushes that gave some shelter, but not much, against the heavy, falling dew. He had brought a rug with him from his car, as Olive had instructed him to be sure to do, but he did not find it much protection. Indeed its clammy folds seemed only to serve to collect tiny pools of dew and to intensify the chill dampness of this black hour before daybreak.

He had had no sleep. No wonder that he dozed in spite of chill and damp and his own high-keyed expectations. He woke, startled into consciousness by an approaching sound, that of cautious steps nearby. It was still dark, but in the east a faint hint was showing of a promise of the light to come. He strained his eyes to see whose were the footsteps that had roused him. He could distinguish nothing save vague shadows near that were those of trees. A tiny scratching sound came, a tiny light sprang up, magnified so by contrast with the surrounding darkness that it flamed like a torch, and by that struck match he saw clearly the face of Mary Floyd. The next moment the light had vanished again, and she also into darkness into which it was hopeless to attempt to follow her. He wondered if she had seen or guessed his presence. Impossible to tell and yet he did not think she had, for the circle of light made by her match had been but small, and for himself he did not think he had made any movement. Anyhow, now she had gone; and nothing for him to do but to renew his patient vigil.

Again he strained his eyes, his ears. The light was stronger now, or, rather, the darkness was less intense. The trees nearby were beginning to appear as trees, and not merely as splashes of deeper shadow in the night. Not but that beneath them the night still lay as blackly as ever. He thought he heard a noise behind, a tiny noise, some creature of the forest returning to its lair or about to start out upon its daily search for food. A low, quickly ended chattering told him it was a squirrel and made him think of Loo. When he looked again towards the quarry, he was just able to distinguish a figure, whether of man or woman he could not tell, outlined there by the edge of the quarry against the eastern sky where rays of the sun were beginning to dart upwards, like fingers searching to release the earth from the dominion of the night.

He got to his feet and began to move forward, slowly, cautiously. In that dim half light with the day not yet come and the night still lingering, one incautious step, one stride too far forward, one unlucky slip, and a fall of fifty feet clear was waiting. His attention was on where he trod and when he paused to look again that figure he had seen, or thought he saw, by the quarry's very brink, was no longer there. Vanished completely and without sound, so that he was half inclined to think he had been tricked by his own imagination. Difficult to be sure with trees and shadows all around all indistinguishable. He found he was standing now on the very edge of the quarry. Below him lay a pit of unimaginable blackness, as though he stared down into the very heart of the night. Behind him a breath of wind that had sprung up with the coming of the dawn moved almost imperceptibly through the bushes and the trees. In front the light of the coming day grew stronger. For prudence sake, since here the ground sloped to the quarry's edge and was crumbly and unsafe, Bobby lay down and wriggled forward on his face and belly, so that he could look over the brink of the quarry into that tremendous pit of night.

Half-way down the sheer descent he could distinguish, as he had half-expected, a small faint light, less than a light, the reflected glow perhaps of a reflected glow. Perceptible but no more. Strange to see that tiny glow there, half-way down the face of a precipice. He took his torch from his pocket and threw the beam on the bare cliff-like wall of naked stone that stretched for a sheer fifty feet up and down without so much as a crack or a crevice or patch of moss to afford foothold or handhold save for one thin ledge on which a few lost shrubs and a stunted tree had somehow managed to find sustenance for growth.

Impossible to reach that ledge though, without at least some aid of rope or ladder whereof his torch showed no sign.

Though he was not sure he thought he could distinguish what seemed a faint, distant, muffled sound of voices. Another and a nearer sound made him look round. Loo was at his side, Henry George on her shoulder, his small beady eyes fixed malignantly on Bobby. Loo said:

"They are down there. I think we ought to leave them there, don't you?"

CHAPTER XLII
HIDDEN LADDER

BOBBY KNEW WELL what care was needed in talking to Loo if her confidence were to be won, if she were not to slip away into those recesses of the forest she knew so thoroughly, where she seemed as much at home as any spirit of the forest and the trees, any faun or dryad of ancient tale and legend. So he gave her merely a casual glance, made no answer beyond a careless, uninterested 'Hullo, Loo' and then resumed his contemplation of the pit below as if forgetting she was there. After a time she said:

"Peter said I must never tell, never."

"Tell what?" Bobby asked. "How's Henry George?"

"Very well indeed. Thank you so much for asking," replied Loo primly; and Henry George, who always seemed to know when his name was mentioned, chattered what was very clearly meant as 'Mind your own business'.

"I don't think Henry George likes me," Bobby observed, and Henry George endorsed this opinion by more chatter of evidently deliberate and intentional insult.

"Be quiet," Loo rebuked him; whereupon he jumped down from her shoulder and ran up a nearby tree, wherefrom, perched on a branch, he watched them from small, malignant eyes. "I'm sorry he is so rude," Loo apologized, "and I try to teach him to be better, but it's very difficult. He always hates everyone except me, because he thinks they want to put him back in a trap. He was caught in one when I found him and took him out."

"Is it you," Bobby asked, remembering something, "who sets off the rabbit traps?"

"When I find them, I do," she answered. "Wouldn't you?"

Bobby did not attempt to reply to this searching question. Instead he said:

"Down there, over the edge, is where Peter used to go sometimes, isn't it?"

"He said I wasn't ever to tell," Loo answered. "He said I was to promise I never would and a promise was 'poinonour', so everyone always had to keep it."

"I wish they always did," Bobby remarked. "'Poinonour'—point of honour," he translated. "Well, what's that?"

"It's awfully, tremendous important," Loo told him, rather evading the point, however.

"There's someone down there now, I think," Bobby observed, "but how did they manage to get down I mean? Even Henry George couldn't by himself. Much too steep."

"Peter had a ladder," Loo explained. "He climbed down and then he took it inside with him. I saw a man climb down just now. He had a ladder, too. I took it away. Peter said I must and then tell him. But I can't now, can I? Now he's gone to be dead in the tree."

"How did you know he was there?" Bobby asked.

"That was Henry George," she answered. "He told me."

"Well, who told him?" Bobby said, but this time got no answer and Loo only looked puzzled.

Then she said:

"I expect it was fairies."

This, however, was so clearly an effort of the imagination that Bobby did not attempt to pursue the subject. Instead he asked:

"Who was the man you saw this morning?" And when Loo did not answer, he added: "Was it Mr Dick?"

But Loo was still silent and he guessed she did not wish to answer. Useless to try to press her and he had no time to coax. He said instead: "What did you do with the ladder when you took it away? Did you hide it somewhere? What was it made of? Rope? Will you show me where you put it?"

"No," said Loo.

It was uncompromising and left Bobby wondering what to do next.

"I don't think that's very nice of you," he protested. "If I hid anything anywhere, I would always show you."

But even this moving appeal failed, though Loo did so far relax as to answer:

"Peter said I wasn't to, not ever."

"Well, I've got to get down there somehow," Bobby explained, and Loo's uninterested expression showed clearly that this was his affair and nothing to do with her.

They were both silent then for a time. Loo's attention plainly wandered. Bobby found himself wondering what was going on there beneath their feet, in this secret cave that had for so long been the old hermit's second dwelling. At any rate no one could leave it now without his knowledge. Henry George descended from his branch and sat at the foot of the tree, evidently prepared to welcome any attempt at appeasement. Bobby said presently:

"Have you seen Mary? I have."

Loo gave a low laugh, a laugh so natural, so happy, so childlike, that Bobby was startled, for he had come to think of Loo more as a wanderer from some remote spirit world of her own than as human child.

"She's trying to find me," Loo gurgled, "but she never can, no one can, not unless I want them to."

Evidently she had no intention of being found just now. Abruptly she vanished from his side. The moment before she had been sitting quietly there and now in a moment she had flashed away, and Henry George with her. Perhaps she had gone to find Mary herself or perhaps she wanted to be sure of not being found. Bobby returned to the problem of what to do next. It was clearly impossible to reach the mouth of the cave without a ladder or rope of some kind. Precautions would have to be taken, too, since the vanished Loo might be somewhere in the vicinity, still on the look out and ready to play again her old trick of removing any such rope or ladder. Thanks to the sergeant's inopportune attack of influenza—thanks also to his own impatience and too great self-confidence as he now ruefully admitted—Bobby was alone. No one he could leave on guard when he made the descent he contemplated. He supposed he ought to have rung up headquarters to send help, but at the time it had seemed desirable to avoid delay. Nor had he wished to risk a premature alarm by summoning men to whom he would have had no opportunity of giving the necessary instructions and explaining the need for care and concealment.

The sun was up now, the light stronger. Peering down over the precipitous edge of the quarry, Bobby could see plainly the narrow ledge of rock on which at one end grew a few bushes and a stunted tree. Without satisfaction, he observed that a rope, dropped from where he lay, from the only spot available since only here grew a tree strong enough to hold securely rope or ladder made fast to it, would fall on that end of the ledge where it jutted first from the quarry face and was scarce wide enough to afford foothold.

"If the old boy alighted there—and he must have done—and wriggled along that narrow edge of rock, he had Blondin beaten at his own game," Bobby told himself uncomfortably; and then told himself again that perhaps the ledge was wider than it looked and at any rate, if an old man had been able to use it, then so could he.

At the farther and wider end of the ledge there grew the few bushes and the stunted tree that veiled, he supposed, the entrance to the secret cave whose existence he felt was now certain. The drop from the ledge to the floor of the quarry was something under twenty feet. An active man, under the spur of necessity, could risk that, especially as the fall would be broken by undergrowth coming close up to the foot of the cliff. A torn shirt or belt or something of the sort tied round the stunted tree on the ledge would further diminish the distance of the drop, and Bobby wondered why Loo's trick of the removal of the means used in the descent should seem so effective. Not difficult, Bobby thought, for anyone so trapped in the cave to effect an escape.

Presumably the hermit had preserved the secret of this hidden habitation of his by using for access some sort of ladder-like contrivance he made fast to the tree up here and could at will disengage from below. Then he could use the same means for effecting a descent to the quarry floor, disengaging it afterwards in the same way, and observing simple precautions to avoid making any noticeable track or path.

Bobby rubbed the tip of his nose a little ruefully as he remembered that when he originally noticed the bruised tree, his not very intelligent comment had been 'Not bird's-nesting', and then had promptly forgotten all about it. At the time, certainly, there had been no reason for him to be on the watch for any suspicious signs, but he felt the incident need not have passed as completely as it had done from his recollection.

"Not," he rebuked himself, "not at all in the best lynx eye and twig the meaning at a glance tradition."

He had made up his mind by now. At the quick run growing daylight now permitted, he returned to the spot where he had left his car, took from it a coil of one-inch Manila rope he had brought with him, and dashed back again at top speed. Very bad luck indeed, he felt, if anything had happened during so brief an absence, but one had to take a chance at times.

CHAPTER XLIII

THE CAVE

A MOMENT OR two he took to recover his breath and for a cautious look around. Then he looped his rope about the tree that had already so often, he was sure, served the same purpose. Doubled thus, it was still long enough to reach the ledge beneath, but only just. To be more precise, its loose ends dangled about a yard and a half or so above the ledge. But that should enable him, he thought, to secure a footing. Whether he would be able to edge his way along without toppling over backwards was, he also thought, much more doubtful. But the attempt had to be made. The feat had been accomplished pretty regularly, he supposed, and so should not be beyond his powers. Once safely, if insecurely, on the ledge, then, by loosening his hold on one end of the doubled rope and pulling on the other, he would be able to recover possession. He had no intention of leaving it in position for Loo to play tricks with. He felt fairly sure that these activities of his had not escaped her watchful and attentive eyes.

Cautiously he swung himself over the edge, collecting more than one bruise against the rough surface of the rock as he began and continued his descent. It was a relief when at last he got his feet firmly on the ledge below, even though that ledge seemed now still more narrow and unsafe than it had appeared from above. For the moment he almost despaired of being able to accomplish such a tightrope performance as an attempt to edge along it must be, and then to his considerable relief he saw that handholds had been cut in the stone. By the aid of these it was comparatively easy to keep a balance as first he loosened his grip on one end of the rope, hauled it down, coiled it over one shoulder and then began to make his way along the shelf. With the handholds, like narrow cups, to help him, he found the task not difficult, and safely he shuffled along for three or four yards till the shelf broadened out at the end where stood the stunted tree and the bushes visible from above. They formed, as he had guessed they would, a natural screen to the cave entrance and beyond them the shelf ended abruptly. It all had an entirely natural air, but now that he was closer, he was inclined to guess that the work of nature had been much improved on, and he remembered that old half forgotten story of how, during the storms of the Reformation period, the monks of Barsley Abbey had fled to a secret refuge in the forest but had been followed, their hiding place discovered, and all of them massacred.

The cave entrance was so narrow and low that Bobby, a big man with big bones and broad shoulders, had some trouble in getting through. Within, however, the passage widened and he could stand upright. So little daylight penetrated through that narrow opening, screened, too, as it was by tree and bush, that he had to get out his electric torch before he could distinguish his surroundings. He saw then that the passage made almost at once a sharp turn to the left and that at this left turn a strong door had been fitted, though one that now stood open and carefully held back by a wooden wedge.

Had this door been locked or fastened until now, he wondered. If so, was that why any inmate of the cave had been unable to escape or to make his presence known by displaying a signal of distress? Any such prisoner, too, would have remained unaware of the search that had examined so carefully the floor of the quarry, but had failed to pay attention to the bare, open face of the cliff, offering in appearance no possible concealment.

Cautiously Bobby moved forward. He felt broken glass beneath his feet. Throwing downward the ray of his torch he discovered that the passage on this side of the door was covered with fragments of broken bottles. Someone had apparently been engaged in an orgy of bottle smashing. One of the larger pieces Bobby picked up. A very curious pungent penetrating smell clung to it, not exactly disagreeable and yet not pleasant either. It made Bobby think of the flavour of the chocolate Olive had once given him to taste. Not that there was any resemblance between that taste and this smell, except in that both were novel, and, so to say, characteristic, unlike anything he had ever come across before.

"One of the old man's new flavours or medicines or lotions," Bobby said to himself; and, throwing the ray of his torch here and there, saw near the door, still on this side, a heap of burnt material. He turned it over with his toe, detaching a large piece that was only scorched. It was canvas, it showed a fragment of a painting, a portion of a sky in which clouds gathered terribly and yet with a glowing light behind, as though they were clouds that hid both the glory and the wrath of God.

Bobby stood and stared. He could hardly believe the conclusion his eyes and mind suggested. He went down on his knees and began to scrabble with his hands in that heap of ash and cinder. He found one long strip on which showed a stretched forth arm, suggesting somehow rather immeasurable length than merely human arm. More and more certain he became that here lay all that remained of the two El Greco pictures, that here someone for some reason or for none had made a bonfire of them.

He got to his feet, mechanically brushed from his hands the ashes of two of what he felt might well have been world masterpieces. He looked again at the large fragment he had found first. Charred and torn and burnt as it was, it still seemed to convey its thundrous message of eternal things behind the poor mask of time.

Bobby laid it down with reverence, wondering who had destroyed it thus and why. He turned his attention to the door and soon saw that it was provided with a strong spring lock and hung in such a way that unless controlled it would swing to instantly. He tried the experiment, removing the wedge, but putting his handkerchief in the lock to make sure it should not fasten. Easy to see that anyone opening the door from without and passing through without taking the necessary precautions would almost certainly find it closed and fastened behind him, cutting off all retreat. Bobby noticed, too, that the inside of the door was covered with iron plating, making the door heavier and more difficult to break through—impossible indeed to break through without tools. He saw also that there was a small space, due apparently to irregularity in the stone above, between the roof and the door. He guessed that the broken bottles he had found had been pushed through this opening to smash on the stone outside in the hope the noise they made might attract attention. Probably, too, the El Greco paintings had been set on fire and pushed through in the same way and with the same object.

A strange end, Bobby reflected, for paintings whereof the recovery would have been a world-wide sensation, even in war time. How great delight and more than delight, had not humanity thus lost. For that matter, how much mere money value had not gone up here in smoke and flame, burning away in this obscure rocky passage in so futile, so useless a bonfire.

So absorbed had he been by these discoveries and thoughts that he had almost forgotten what errand had brought him here. But now, after once again taking precautions to make sure that the door should not be closed upon him, either by accident or design—he broke the blade of his penknife inside the lock in such a way that only by a good deal of trouble could the lock be put in working order again—he made his way on along the passage that the door had guarded. The air grew fresher, the light stronger, as he advanced, and then a new sharp turn taken by the passage gave him a clear view of a great chamber hewn, for it was too regular to be wholly the work of nature, in the very heart of the rock. Air, and some degree of light, penetrated from narrow shafts sloping upwards through three or four yards of solid rock to the quarry face, where, when they issued, they had only the appearance of cracks or crevices in the stone. Though the light thus provided was not strong it was abundantly sufficient for Bobby, emerging from the obscurity of the passages along which he had groped his way, to distinguish the details of the scene.

A first glance showed him two men facing each other in the centre of the cave and showed him, too, that it had been roughly furnished. There was a heavily made table, across which these two men faced each other. There were two or three chairs. In the wall opposite was a kind of alcove in which was piled a heap of rugs and blankets to form a bed. In one corner stood an oil stove for cooking and there was an oil heating stove as well. Near the cooking stove was a rough wooden bench running nearly the whole length of the wall and covered with utensils that Bobby thought at first were simply pots and pans for cooking, but that later investigation proved to be flasks, retorts, and so on that had evidently been used for experimenting with various herbal products. It was here no doubt that the different lotions and medicines the old man had produced, including the new flavouring, had been concocted.

In addition to the light that entered, though scantily, by the ventilating shafts, further light was provided by two great silver candelabra that hung upon the inner wall, the wall on Bobby's left as he stood in the mouth of this passage that led into the main portion of the cave. There was no difficulty in recognizing the Diabolic Candelabra. Each branch was carved in the likeness of a human face twisted into every variety of hate and malice and all ill will. In each branch a lighted candle stood, and in the flickering light they gave, for there was a breath of air that ran about the cave from the ventilating shafts, one could well have imagined that each of those carven heads was alive and each animated by the same delight in wickedness. The evil in the hand that wrought had well translated itself into those carven images.

Yet of all this Bobby was at the moment hardly more than dimly aware, so much was his attention and amazement held by yet another spectacle that same wall of the cave presented, framed between the two candelabra. It happened that through one of the air shafts, one a trifle larger than the others and less steeply sloped, a ray of sunlight fell clear upon this portion of the wall. The clear and golden ray, like an angelic spear of light, passed over the heads of the two men by the table, and struck the very centre of a pattern that now he could distinguish there, a pattern in gleaming white outline, a pattern formed of many human bones, of skulls and ribs, thigh bones and bones of arms, all arranged with careful and as it seemed almost with loving care to fit into some strange and hidden harmony of line and form.

Bobby had always been sensitive to form. From form, from pattern, from design and proportion of curve and line, he had at times received that hint of other things that other people can receive from the harmonies of sound in great music or the harmonies of colour in nature or in painting. In past days he had been stirred in ways he did not understand by his first glimpse of the harmonies still perceptible in the noble ruins of Tintern Abbey, or again by the pattern in a picture he afterwards knew to be the work of one of the great artists of the world. So now there was something in this pattern traced by dead men's bones upon the wall of a hidden cave that seemed to convey to him a message, though a message of which he knew not the meaning.

Oblivious utterly for the moment of his surroundings, he stood and stared, trying to trace there the significance that somehow he was certain it had been intended to convey. Fascinated, he stood before that arabesque of dead men's bones, trying to grasp it as a whole, trying to follow each line and curve so subtly and so strangely traced, and feeling himself utterly baffled and defeated. A rhythm of movement was in it, a suggestion of upward urge that yet returned continually upon itself, as if ever defeated and yet ever striving, persuading him still that if only he could distinguish the prevailing motive, then he would understand. He remembered the enigmatic smile Leonardo da Vinci lent to his 'Mona Lisa'. Yet that he felt had a meaning both small and shallow compared to the intention hidden here. He felt an impulse to go forward and trace with careful finger each curve, each line, each circling loop or sudden start. A queer excitement seemed to tell him that if he did so with care and reverence he would come at last to understand the hidden secret.

Yet of the nature of that secret there came to him no hint.

Then he saw another thing. Apart from this great central pattern, low down, on the right as one faced it, four sentences had been formed, and these were made of the smaller human bones, the bones of the hand and the foot, that had apparently been unsuitable for incorporation in the main design. They had the air of having been added recently. They even spoiled to some extent the majestic symmetry of the central pattern. In modern English capital letters they formed the words of four phrases, one below the other, in this order:

> 'The blood is the life.
> The blood is ill and cancer comes.
> Cure the blood and cure the cancer.'

The lowest fourth and final sentence consisted of but the one word:

> 'Eureka'.

Fascinated, wondering, asking himself how many hours of patient work was here represented, asking himself again and again what meaning lay hidden here, what was the relationship between those four sentences and the pattern above, asking himself if significance and relationship were there in fact, or but the product of his own excited, startled imagination, Bobby still stood and stared. Again the memory came back to him of the old story of how the abbot and monks of Barsley Abbey had sought refuge in the forest, in a secret hiding-place, and never more been heard of. He supposed that here perhaps were relics of their fate and proof of an ancient massacre of long ago, and in his absorption he forgot entirely the presence of those two others by the table, who, for their part, absorbed in their own emotions, remained equally ignorant of his presence and arrival there. But now one of them spoke, his voice slow and hollow in that heavy air, and as he heard Bobby could have sworn that each one of those carven, devilish faces under the flickering light of the candles above, grinned approval. For what Bobby heard to rouse him from his fancies was a startled, incredulous scream:

"You mean you'll murder me; you can't."

And the answer came:

"Why not? Looks like I've got to, don't it?"

CHAPTER XLIV
FORGED CONFESSION

STARTLED FROM HIS absorption in this bizarre and grisly decorative effect, with its strange, haunting hint of a secret underlying significance, Bobby turned quickly. The two men by the table were still unaware of his presence, so utterly was the regard of each concentrated on the other. He might have made ten times the noise he had done without breaking in upon their desperate, fixed attention. One of the men had his back to Bobby. It was impossible to recognize him in the dim light prevailing, that entering through the ventilating shafts, that given by the candles in the Diabolic Candelabra, both together only serving feebly to illumine this huge grim rock cavity. The second man on the farther side of the table, of whom therefore Bobby had a clearer view, was a small, elderly man, with a grey wisp of a moustache. Crayfoot, the missing baker, Bobby guessed. Dirty, unshaven, afraid, he leaned across the table, both trembling, shaking hands upon it as though for needed support, and even from where he stood Bobby could see how those hands, the man's whole body indeed, quivered, trembled, shook, till the very table itself, solid as it was, seemed to shake in sympathy. High pitched and shrill his voice came again:

"You couldn't . . . wouldn't . . . you can't . . . why, it would be murder."

"Well, it's what you done your own self," the other retorted, "what you done to the old hermit bloke, so why not the same for you also?"

"I'll give you anything you like, I'll give you my cheque, I'll—" Crayfoot began, and the other cut him short with a threatening gesture that made Crayfoot shrink tremblingly away.

"Aw, shut it," he said, and in the hand he lifted Bobby made out now that he held a revolver of heavy calibre, probably an old service weapon. "What's the good of cheques and promises and such-like?" he demanded. "Like as not off you would go to the cops soon as ever you was out of here, and then where would I be?"

Crayfoot began to splutter eager, quick protests that never would he do such a thing, never, never. He could be trusted absolutely, he shrilled, and again he was silenced by a threatening lifted movement of the revolver.

"You can't murder me," he wailed, huddling down as he spoke into a curious, crouching attitude, as though in an effort to protect himself from the bullet he was dreading. "You wouldn't do murder?" he cried again. "Not murder. You can't."

"Why can't I?" retorted the other. "It's what you did, ain't it? And don't you go for to deny it, either, seeing as I know what I know. A good thing for you, too, or else you would have starved and rotted here and no one ever known a thing about it, not till kingdom come. And serve you right."

"I never, never . . . I never even knew old Peter had been killed—" Crayfoot protested, and again was cut short by a wave of that menacing pistol.

"Aw, shut it," its holder said. "Shut it and let me think or I'll put a bullet through you as'll make you hold that tongue of yours for keeps."

Crayfoot fell silent, mopping his perspiring forehead with a handkerchief that was black with dirt. Bobby moved softly back, farther into the shadows where the passage entered the cave. He had once or twice been on the point of interfering, but now he decided that danger was not imminent. Killing might come, but not yet. There was quite clearly something Crayfoot was required to do or say, and until then his life at least was safe. Those who mean to kill, kill without talk. Crayfoot, waiting his fate, had collapsed now into one of the chairs near by. Very plainly he had neither the will, the courage, nor indeed the strength to do anything but await passively the other's decision.

"It's not as if I wanted to do you in, only I've got to look after myself, ain't I?" this other man now continued. "Why, I wouldn't hurt you nor no one no more than a babe unborn except for having to. You did in the old hermit bloke and don't you go for to deny it, either, because I know, see? Not that I care what you done, but I got to think of myself, and there's a blasted cop knocking around, Mr Blooming Inspector Bobby Owen, what if I had him where I've got you I wouldn't be just talking like I am, not by a hell of a way I wouldn't. Only seeing it's you, I'm trying to think of a way out, which is more than most would, it being safe and simple and easy like to pop you off and done with it—aw, shut it."

This last was the result of a feeble cry of protest Crayfoot uttered, and, while doing so, nearly fell from his chair in the extremity of his fear.

"I didn't say I would," the other went on, "I only said how safe it would be, no one knowing this place except Loo what I can settle."

He paused again; and the reference to Loo, and a glimpse he now gave of his features as he turned for a moment sideways, enabled Bobby to recognize Coop. Coop went on:

"Very safe and private like down here which no one knows of and for certain sure not that there Mr Blighted Inspector Bobby Owen, poking his nose in other people's business all the time like the busy he is, but a cut above his brains to find this place, see?"

"Yes, I know, of course, he never could," acquiesced Crayfoot as nervously as before.

"Makes me laugh," declared Coop, who seemed to be gradually talking himself into a more genial mood, "to think of him a-chasing and a-hunting all over everywhere; and all the time me and you tucked away here, snug as a bug in a rug, us having our little chat together where no one won't ever know what's happened. See?"

"No, they won't, will they?" stammered the wretched Crayfoot. "Oh, my God," he murmured under his breath.

"Aw, shut it, you make me sick," Coop told him. "You weren't 'My Goding' any when you outed the old bloke, were you?"

"No," agreed Crayfoot, "no," and under his breath he said again: "God help me."

"Well, He won't," snapped Coop irritably, "no one will, especial not Mr Bleeding Inspector Bobby Owen. Now, you listen to me. You wouldn't have nothing to complain of if I done the same to you as you done to old Peter, and I don't know as I didn't ought to, and lucky for you I ain't that sort of chap, ain't it?"

"Yes," stammered Crayfoot. "Yes—God have mercy."

"You and your God," complained Coop. "Aw, shut it, can't you? Putting the old cove through it and thinking you was getting away with it, too, sneaking here the way you did after them silver things and the pictures, which seemingly you've burnt like the silly fool you are, and didn't ought to have, them being worth money."

"It was to get help," Crayfoot protested. "I thought someone might see and afterwards I had no more matches."

"Does in a bloke for to get his pictures," commented Mr Coop disgustedly, "and then goes and gets caught in as neat a trap as ever was and burns them same pictures. Makes me laugh to think of the old bloke catching you in his trap same as he did after him being dead, and there you would be for ever more most like only for me, and no one ever known a thing."

"Someone knew," Crayfoot said. "Someone pushed bread and potatoes and a bottle-full of water on the end of a string through the opening over the door. So someone knew or else I think I should have gone quite mad."

"That was Loo most like," Coop answered carelessly. "Not much she don't know, but I know what to do with her." His voice had an uglier note than ever as he said this, and Bobby promised himself to take good care Mr Coop never had any opportunity of putting into effect any such intentions he might cherish. "Bit of luck for you," Mr Coop insisted, "as how, not being a fat-headed cop, I had brains enough to find out where you was. Lucky for you, eh?"

"Yes," quavered Crayfoot, but without conviction.

"Lucky for you, too," Coop continued, "you couldn't burn them candlesticks or else I would have gone and lost me temper. Why, those painted pictures you done me out of, I reckon I might have got as much as ten or twenty pound each for." He paused, evidently not wishing to make claims that might seem too absurdly exaggerated. "Or thereabouts, and not worth nothing now, along of you, which you couldn't wonder, could you, if I drilled you with a bullet out of disappointment and vexation like. Now could you?"

"No," agreed the wretched Crayfoot as meekly as before, "not at all, I'm sure."

"Aw, shut it," said Coop, quite mechanically. "Now, you listen to me. If a bloke with brains—what's me—wants to think things out, then he'll find a way. It all depends on brains. See?"

"Yes," said Mr Crayfoot, meek as ever.

"Brains," repeated Coop with satisfaction. "Some works for their living. Some has brains and don't. That's me. Brains. Thinking. Put 'em together and what do you get?"

Mr Crayfoot awaited enlightenment and Mr Coop said impressively:

"You get to see. See?"

"Yes," agreed Mr Crayfoot, almost hopefully.

"Which here it is," continued Coop. "You did in the old hermit, didn't you?"

"I never—" began Crayfoot and changed his intended denial to a terrified squeal of agreement as Coop swung up his revolver. "I mean Yes. Yes. I only meant I didn't know you knew."

"Saw it all," affirmed Coop, "and didn't know you had the guts, so I didn't. So now you write out a confession, saying as how it was you, and how you tried to get him to tell you where them great valuable pictures were, and he wouldn't, and took his chopper to chase you out, but you got it from him, which is more than was to be expected from such as you, and laid him out, but not before first you made him tell you about this place, and so you came along and got yourself trapped, not knowing how the old bloke had fixed the door to swing back sharp after anyone went through, and you not having sense enough to see for yourself."

"It was open when I came," Crayfoot protested, stung to defend himself against this charge of stupidity. "I only knew it was there when I tripped on the wire holding it back."

"That was the old bloke's trap, that was," Coop explained, "and very cunning and smart, too. Now you write down what I told you. See? Then you give it me and I let you go because if you try any tricks I send it straight to that there Mr Blasted Inspector Bobby Owen. See?"

Mr Crayfoot had evidently made up his mind to obey. No alternative that he could see, since otherwise he supposed he would be shot on the spot. Or else perhaps left to remain, an even worse fate, once again imprisoned here. He produced a fountain pen and a note-book and began to write. Coop watched him with satisfaction. Bobby, from his unseen position in the shadows of the passage, decided to wait till the confession was completed. He felt he would like to secure it when it was finished. Coop strolled over to the inside wall of the cavern and stood looking first at one of the two candelabra and then at the other.

"Silver ain't what it was," he admitted regretfully, "but they'll fetch a bit all right; and a good thing I brought candles along to stick in 'em, so as we can see what we are doing. I don't reckon even as I'll have to melt 'em, seeing there's no one can identify 'em, though such a lot of ugly mugs I never saw before in all my life. Like they was alive and watching you. Enough to scare anyone, wondering what they are waiting for. Might be Mr Inspector Blooming, Blasted, Blighted, Bleeding Bobby Owen from the way they look as they was saying: Just you wait till we've got you. Only it's me that's got them, see?" He put up a hesitating and almost reluctant finger and touched one of the faces, choosing what was certainly the most hideous, the most repulsive of those devilish features where their creator had so well expressed all that was most evil, most malignant. "The very dead spit image of that Owen bloke," he announced. "But you ain't got me yet, not yet you ain't. See?"

Bobby wished very much to protest. He was certain that grinning carven face in no way resembled his own. He felt quite hurt about it indeed, and considered it was an impression as mistaken as was Coop's final remark. Crayfoot looked up from the table at which he had been writing. He said:

"Will this do?"

Bobby moved forward, for now was the moment he had been waiting for. Coop heard and turned. Crayfoot jumped to his feet with a cry. Coop stammered:

"It's him."

"So it is," agreed Bobby, keeping a wary eye on Coop's big revolver which, however, Coop made no effort to use.

Instead he pointed with his other hand to Crayfoot.

"That's him, Mr Owen, sir, that's him what done in the poor old gentleman. I've just made him write a confession and all so as to let you know."

"Very good of you," Bobby answered, "but are you quite sure it is not you yourself who should have signed it?"

"That's it, is it?" Coop snarled and swung forward his pistol.

Before either of them could make another movement light flying steps sounded, and swift as a ray of passing light Loo's small form sped down the passage into the cave, across it, and at a bound into the alcove and down amidst the blankets and the rugs heaped there. A moment later she thrust out her head.

"He's killed Henry George and Mary and everyone and now he's coming to kill me," she told them and vanished again, down amidst the rugs and blankets that she drew over her head for safety's sake.

"'Ere, now then," said Mr Coop, waving his big revolver to and fro in a helpless way that confirmed the suspicions Bobby had entertained from the first that the thing was unloaded and probably un-fireable.

Abruptly Mr Crayfoot screamed. Not a pleasant sound. Loo's irruption, this new threat, had been too much for what was left of his self-control. It was the cry of a trapped rabbit. Bobby, who had reached the centre of the cave, near the table, was watching the passage. Heavy, running steps were hurrying down it. A man grew visible at the passage mouth, but stayed there, hidden in the shadows. He could see them in the comparative light of the cave, but they could only distinguish him as a vague, menacing form, motionless and silent. There passed an interval that for all any of them knew might have been half a day, might have been a split second. Motionless they remained, like clockwork figures waiting the touching of the spring that would set them all in motion.

Then from the brooding shadow at the entrance to the passage, a movement, a flash, the roar of the report of a pistol that sounded in that confined space like a clap of monstrous thunder.

CHAPTER XLV
THE FIGHT

TWICE MORE THAT loud report rang out; and through the reverberating echoes that went thundering to and fro in each corner of the great cavern, sounded a loud scream, a loud and dreadful scream, mingled with a heavy clattering sound as one of the candelabra, struck by a bullet that had flown too high, came smashing to the ground.

Some of the candles were extinguished by the fall, some flared up in a high greasy unsteady flame, Bobby saw Coop swing round upon himself, so that now his back was to the entry to the passage that before he had faced. He held both hands to his chest, pressing against it as if to hold something there, and then he began to cough.

Bobby sprang back to the table and dropped to the ground behind it, at the same time tilting it to one side so that it formed some sort of temporary protection or shield. Crayfoot had vanished, but Bobby had no time to wonder what had become of him, was not consciously aware of his disappearance. Another bullet smashed against the side of the uptilted table, boring its way very neatly right down the centre of one of its stout projecting legs. Bobby had his unloaded revolver in one hand now and was groping in his pocket with the other for the ammunition he had brought with him. He was thinking to himself in a calm, detached so to say impersonal manner, that he had been inconceivably foolish to neglect loading the weapon. Self-confidence, a stupid self-confidence and reliance on his official authority, had again betrayed him. Coop he had never been inclined to take too seriously. Coop might shoot, as he had done before in a panic-stricken effort to escape, but would never dare defy police. Indeed Bobby had always felt over him a complete and somewhat contemptuous mastery. This was different, this was an uttermost extremity of peril, and before he had begun to thrust his cartridges into the cylinder of his revolver, fierce eyes were glaring down at him over the table edge, a pistol barrel was thrust into his face, a harsh voice said:

"Drop it."

Nothing to do but to obey. No need to ask either to what the 'it' referred he was to drop. He let revolver and cartridges fall. The harsh voice said:

"Hands up. Stand up. Turn round."

Bobby obeyed. He felt something hard thrust into the small of his back. He had no need to wonder what it was. He knew his life hung now upon the crooking of a finger; and not his life alone, but also that of the child, Loo, hiding under the blankets and rugs in the alcove. He remembered clearly, vividly, with what an accent of terror Crayfoot had pleaded with Coop, with Coop who had had himself no chance at all to plead. With that same note of panic in his voice Bobby let his voice rise to the roof of the cavern as, in a kind of stuttering scream, he cried:

"Don't shoot, don't shoot. Oh, please, please."

The answer was an increased pressure of the hard pistol muzzle against the small of Bobby's back, and then in that same harsh voice that was more like the snarl of a beast than human speech, he heard:

"Where are the El Grecos? Where are the pictures? Quick now."

"Oh, my God, don't shoot," Bobby cried again and made all his body quiver as with an agony of apprehension. "I'll show you, they're here, Coop hid them, only don't kill me."

"Show me, show me where they are," his captor ordered, and then: "Where's Loo?"

"Oh, oh," Bobby moaned again, "oh, promise you won't kill me. She's under there, that bench, by the wall, the pictures, too, only they're hidden. Coop hid them. You won't hurt Loo, will you?"

"Of course I won't," was the answer; and with it came a low and horrid chuckle that told with scarce a pretence of concealment what were the speaker's real intentions. "Show me. Show me the pictures. Only Loo first. She says she saw me. Hurry up. No tricks mind. Or you'll have a bullet smash your spine before you know it."

Bobby sent upwards to the cavern roof yet another cry of utter inarticulate terror and appeal. His captor heard it with satisfaction. Well may a man feel secure when he is holding a loaded pistol in the small of another's back walking before him with hands held high above his head. What else can that other do but 'accept the logic of the situation'? Obey or die. What else? No wonder that from the one man cries of terror and appeal were coming. No wonder that the second man was supremely confident. Bobby's hands were still held high, his last hysterical cry of despair was still echoing under the cavern roof as he swung round sharply to the left, at the same time in one simultaneous co-ordinated movement bringing down his open left hand like a chopper on the wrist of his captor's hand that held the pistol, and bringing up his right knee into the other's stomach.

The sudden unexpected attack, coming as it did from one who had seemed so overwhelmed with terror, was successful, but not entirely so, for Bobby's opponent was wary and strong. The sudden sharp chopper-like blow on his wrist knocked the pistol from his grasp; but the upward thrust of Bobby's knee that should have incapacitated him was delivered just the least possible fraction of a second too late; and he was able to avoid its full force.

The next instant they had grappled in an embrace as close as ever lovers knew, breast to breast, almost mouth to mouth, an embrace both well understood meant for the one sweet life as for the other inevitable death. To and fro they stamped, straining every nerve and muscle, and even in that moment Bobby could see how his enemy's eyes glared into his with a strange and bestial fury, how on his lips were flecks of foam, flecks of foam that were tinged with red. Another glimpse he had over the other's shoulder was of Loo's small, frightened face peering out at them from under the piled-up blankets and rugs in the alcove. He wanted to call to her to run away while there was still time, but he had neither breath nor chance. The strength of his opponent seemed as the strength of ten; not, God knows, because his heart was pure but because of the fury of his hate, the rage of his despair. Against that, formidable as it was, Bobby called up all he had, and more, much more, for in his need there came to him those deep hidden reserves with which in the ultimate moment the strange human spirit can inspire the machine of flesh and blood and bone wherein it is enclosed.

Tremendous, huge beyond all normal possibility, were the efforts that each made, each to get free from the other's desperate grasp, each to fasten his own grip upon his adversary, each to break the other's resistance and force him to the ground. How it happened Bobby could never have told, but suddenly they were separate, apart, glaring and breathless. Bobby was aware of the warm salt taste of blood in his mouth from a cut lip. In one hand he held the other's collar and tie that had torn away in his grasp, deceiving the hold he had hoped to make fast. Between them, but farther from Bobby and nearer his enemy, lay the revolver Bobby had knocked from the other's hand. For either to secure possession of it would mean for him swift victory, for the other death inevitable. Both of them saw it at the same time, both sprang to seize it, and since his adversary was nearer and reached it first and was already screaming hoarsely his triumph as his hand began to close upon it, so Bobby with a flying kick sent it spinning away along the floor. Then turning to resume the struggle he saw his adversary still grinning at him with a continued certitude of victory. Disappointed of the recovery of his pistol, he had taken advantage of the brief pause and freedom from the immediate struggle to draw a sheath knife such as those sailors still make use of—a weapon more formidable perhaps and at least as deadly as any pistol. For even at close quarters a bullet may still go astray, but a knife-thrust is more easily, more certainly aimed.

The accidents of their conflict had brought them nearer that side of the cave where the two great candelabra, one now upon the ground, had burned on each side of that macabre pattern of human bones. Near by, too, lay Coop, very quiet and still save for long shuddering sighs that at intervals shook his supine body. It was chiefly to gain time that Bobby said:

"Dr Maskell, isn't it?"

But Maskell took no notice, did not pause in his slow, wary, deadly advance, his right hand with the knife held in it drawn back ready for the thrust he meant to be the end. Bobby said:

"Notice that lettering on the wall? If the old man were really on the track of a cure for cancer, how many more do you think you murdered when you murdered him?"

This time the question had some effect, for Maskell at least paused, though he never took his eyes off Bobby, though his hand still hung ready for the thrust. It was the urge to justify himself all feel that made him speak. He said:

"Muck. Filthy brews. Poison. That's all." He said: "It was the old fool's own fault. I told him I meant to stop him. He tried to kill me. I had to defend myself. That's all. Now I've got to kill you, too, and the child as well because she says she saw."

"Won't do you any good," Bobby remarked, still watching and hoping for some sign of inattention that would give him an opportunity to run in and attack. "I've left my notes to show it was you. You told me that yourself, you know, the very first time I saw you."

Dr Maskell came a little nearer, cautious and prepared and confident, for though he had knowledge now that Bobby was a dangerous fighter, yet he knew the advantage his poised knife gave him, and scarcely regretted the loss of the revolver.

"Or how could you have known," Bobby went on, "that it was human blood on the exhibit I took from the floor of the hermit's hut unless you had spilt it yourself? Because when you said that, you hadn't even broken the seal I put on that exhibit."

"I wondered if you noticed," Maskell said then, pausing for a brief moment in his careful approach, "when I saw the way you looked at me. Just as well I have you where you'll never get the chance to tell."

He drew another step nearer, grim and purposeful. His every movement proclaiming his intention to run no risks now, to 'mak siccar' as the Bruce's friend said so long ago. As he advanced, so Bobby drew back step for step, movement for movement, still hoping for his opportunity, ready the moment he saw it, or without it if it did not offer, to make his last spring and final effort. After it was all over he was able to say he had had no sense of fear, even though he knew well that in this struggle his chance of survival was small, with the odds so heavily against him as they must be when the unarmed man faces armed. All he knew was the tense energy of conflict as he waited, for now he had his back to the cave wall and could retreat no farther. Then came that opportunity for which he had so long waited, so desperately hoped. Shattering the silence that had fallen on Maskell's last dark threat there thundered once again the reverberating echoing roar of a pistol shot, so hugely loud in that small closed space.

In that instant Maskell's attention wavered as momentarily he glanced over his shoulder. In that moment Bobby leaped, hurling his fists, right and left with swift following blows, in them all the fury of his heart, all the fierce power of his knowledge that it was for his life he struck. Beneath those tremendous blows, perfectly timed, behind them every atom of Bobby's leaping body and the full tension of his nervous energy, Maskell's face seemed, as it were, to disintegrate, to change from human features to an unrecognizable and bloody mask. Yet another blow came, aimed with the same savage intensity. Maskell fell; and where he fell, he lay motionless, for his senses had left him.

It had happened so quickly at the last, the victory had been so swift and instantaneous, that the echoes of the pistol shot still rumbled in the corners of the cave above. Yet it seemed to Bobby that he was still alone, and who it was had fired he could not at first imagine. He stooped and made sure that Maskell was in no condition to resume. For safety's sake, for he had had enough of over-confidence, he took possession of Maskell's knife and thought that it was an ugly weapon and was glad he had not experienced the thrust of that sharp, gleaming point. He went across to where Coop lay and bent over him. Coop tried to speak. There was a great, an awful terror in his eyes. It was still there as with a long shuddering sigh, with a sudden straightening and stiffening of his limbs, his spirit fled away to render its account.

No help now that Bobby or any other could give. Bobby went back towards the centre of the cave, remembering Crayfoot and wondering if it had been Crayfoot who had fired that opportune shot which had given him his chance. He could see no sign of him. He supposed he must have made his escape some time during the fight with Maskell. But then he saw a foot protruding from beneath the wooden bench so freely strewn with the utensils used by the old hermit in his researches. Bending down Bobby saw the foot belonged to Crayfoot who, not much of a hero and with the excuse that his nerve and stamina had been exhausted by his time of solitary imprisonment, had sought refuge there and there quietly fainted away. Just for a moment Bobby feared that he, too, was dead, but soon assured himself that it was only a case of fainting. Leaving him there Bobby went across to the alcove.

"Hullo, Loo," he called cheerfully. "You still there? All over now, but, I say, wasn't it a noise?"

There was a pause and then Loo's small white face appeared.

"I've been sick," she said.

"Have you though?" said Bobby. "Better now?"

"It was because of my stomach going all small and tight," Loo explained.

"I know," said Bobby. "So did mine. Tummies are like that. I don't know why."

"Were you sick, too?" Loo inquired with sympathy, understanding and interest.

"Felt like it," Bobby told her. "But you see I was jumping and running about all the time and that rather stops it."

"Does it?" said Loo doubtfully.

"All right now?" Bobby asked.

Loo came a little farther from her refuge.

"I saw stepfather tumble down," she said, "when the doctor made that big bang. So I picked it up to make it go bang, too, and it did and I got under the clothes again. Did the doctor tumble down when it went bang?"

"He did," said Bobby grimly, "and now I want you to shut your eyes just as tight as ever you can and then I am going to pick you up to carry you to the cave's mouth where you came in. You know? And then I want you to climb up to the top again and run as fast as you can home and tell mother what's happened and ask her to tell all the neighbours and send them here. Because I must stop to look after stepfather and the others."

But Loo only shook her head and clung tightly to him, her face pressed hard against his shoulder. He guessed the child was still so terrified that now even her familiar forest seemed to her full of dangers and fears that she could not face alone. He was wondering what to do when he became aware of a noise of scrambling, approaching footsteps. Someone evidently had found and climbed down whatever means of descent—rope or ladder—Maskell had made use of, and, presumably, left in position. A moment later he heard a voice he knew for that of Dick Rawdon.

"Hullo, hullo there," Dick was calling, "who's that? What's been going on here?"

"Oh, quite a lot," Bobby answered. "Quite a lot."

CHAPTER XLVI

CONCLUSION

As soon as he felt he could leave the rest of what had to be done for his assistants to attend to, Bobby motored back home so as to prove to Olive by ocular demonstration that he was still alive. He had already informed her of this fact by 'phone, but then, as Olive had remarked, 'phone messages are easily misunderstood and she would like to see for herself.

She had, however, put sufficient faith in the 'phone to have a good dinner waiting; and when he had paid it the full attention it deserved—'full' is here the operative word—Olive induced him by dint of coaxing, cunning and cajolery, mingled with more than a touch of stern wifely authority, to indulge in a few minutes' repose.

So he consented to lie down for five minutes, closed his eyes, and when he re-opened them again was bewildered to find that apparently blackout time had arrived, since the curtains were drawn. Only by the dim illumination provided by a night-light could he distinguish Olive dozing in an arm-chair near.

"I say," he exclaimed, much alarmed, "what's the time? I must get a move on."

"What for?" asked Olive.

"What for?" he repeated, "Why, there's a million things—"

"At this hour of the morning?" Olive asked, and indicated the clock as Bobby switched on the light.

He looked and looked again, stared, gasped, collapsed.

"Twenty to three," he almost wailed. "It isn't, it can't be."

"Time," Olive reminded him primly, "waits for no man."

"Why didn't you wake me?" he demanded heatedly.

"My good man," she assured him, "we did. Several times. Only we could never get both eyes open at once—one open, t'other shut; t'other open, number one shut again. Very trying."

Bobby groaned.

"There's a million things—" he began again, and then he groaned once more for a fresh and different and even more poignant reason. "What's the matter with my back?" he demanded.

"Probably broken," Olive remarked carelessly. "Lie down again and I'll explain."

Bobby was now feeling his head.

"What's this I've got on?" he asked more bewilderedly than ever.

"A bandage," Olive explained. "Now shut your eyes and listen and I'll tell you all about it."

Still too confused to resist, Bobby obeyed, closed his eyes, heard a far-off voice murmuring faintly in a soothing whisper, and when he opened his eyes again it was to find the room flooded with daylight and Olive tickling him softly under the chin, about the only place, she explained, where he wasn't one vast, continuous bruise.

"I thought you would like me to wake you," she said virtuously, "though it does seem a shame. I've put your arnica and a fresh bottle of iodine in the bathroom. The doctor says there are no bones broken except one in the left hand, and he expects that will mend all right, and he's sewn up your ear—he says it'll be practically as good as new—and he's going to write an article for the *Lancet* about your jaw because it ought to be broken and he can't think why it isn't. Oh, and he doesn't think you'll be lame for more than a week."

"Dear me," said Bobby, rather overcome by this long recital which greatly surprised him but at the same time helped to explain much.

"And why," said Olive moodily, "I didn't marry a pair of boxing gloves and be done with it, I don't know."

She went away then to see about breakfast, and in spite of his many bruises and bandages, these last making him feel that he and an Egyptian mummy were brothers over the skin, Bobby managed to devote himself seriously to the meal and to prove that at any rate his jaws were still fully capable of functioning.

Over the 'phone he had already learnt that Maskell was to be brought before the magistrates at noon, and that the inquest on the unfortunate Coop was to take place at three in the afternoon. Crayfoot, he learnt, was in hospital.

"Have you heard how he is?" Bobby asked Olive as he began his breakfast.

"The doctor says he is suffering from shock but will be all right with rest and care," Olive answered. "I rang up Mrs. Crayfoot to ask. She says he'll have to sell the business and retire and they will go to live in the country somewhere."

"I expect it'll take him some time to get over it," Bobby agreed. "He had a pretty tough experience, shut up in that cave. Not that he had any business to go rooting round after those pictures by himself, even though I daresay he had no idea of what had happened. Lucky for him Stone saw him near the quarry and told me. Just the lead I wanted. Mrs Crayfoot told me he had been fond of rock climbing when he was younger. Maskell took the hint, too. I suppose he guessed the old hermit must have somewhere where he kept his El Grecos and did his stuff with his herbs and roots and plants. I wonder how Crayfoot knew where to look?"

"Mrs Crayfoot seems to think her husband had guessed there was some connection between the hermit and his footman grandfather. She thinks it was because of the talk going on about the El Greco pictures. He told her once he had met the hermit in the forest somewhere and had a word or two with him. She never thought of it again, she says, until now."

"That might mean," Bobby said slowly, "if he introduced himself as a grandson of the old man's former footman pal, that he got a more friendly reception than most people. Very likely he even got a hint about the cave in the quarry. Looks as if when he went to the hut that time when Weston followed him into the forest, and Stone followed Weston and he found what we found—signs of a fight having taken place—he went on at once to Boggart's Hole to see if anything had happened to the old man and so got caught in the trap laid for unauthorized visitors."

"And burnt the El Grecos even though he knew how valuable they were?" Olive remarked.

"Their value, either in money or as works of art, wouldn't make much appeal to a man trapped as he was," Bobby answered. "'Skin for skin, aye, all that he hath will a man give for his life', and very certainly he'll give the finest painting artist ever produced. The cancer cure, too. Every bottle smashed and nothing more left, not even a drop, only a faint hint of a smell."

"I wonder if it was really any good," Olive said. "If it was—"

"Yes, if it was . . ." Bobby repeated. "We shall never know. It does make you a bit dizzy though when you think of what may have been lost through Maskell's folly and jealousy—and Crayfoot's panic. Not that you can blame the poor devil I expect anyone would have done anything to get out of the fix he was in."

Thoughtfully Bobby helped himself to the rest of the bacon while Olive looked on, reckoned how long it would be before the next bacon ration was due, and wondered what there would be for breakfast next day. Salt cod very likely, she told herself grimly.

"Do you think Coop really believed Crayfoot was guilty?" she asked.

"I expect so," Bobby answered. "He would think it obvious. I expect he had been watching Loo and that's how he knew about the cave, and Loo was watching him, and that's why she was so quick in taking away the rope he let himself down by. It must have been Coop I saw that morning. At the time I thought it was Maskell walking into the trap—the one I hadn't laid for him but he found for himself."

"I was wondering," Olive remarked, "whether it was he or you walked into that trap—both of you I suppose."

"Well, I don't know about that," Bobby said defensively. "When I told him Crayfoot had last been seen near Boggart's Hole I could see he was interested and when he wanted to know if the place had been properly searched, it was pretty plain he meant to have a look himself. That was when I remembered the marks on the tree at the quarry edge I noticed the first time we were there."

"You always thought it was Maskell, didn't you?" Olive asked.

"Suspected," Bobby corrected her. "The first time I saw him he told me it was human blood on the earth I had taken from the floor of the hut, though my signature on the paper it was packed in hadn't been broken and therefore he couldn't have made his analysis. So he couldn't have known unless—well, unless he did know. Another time I noticed how when he was speaking of the old man he always said 'was'—again as if he knew. The way the body was disposed of suggested someone of exceptional physical strength unless two people were concerned, which didn't seem likely. And Maskell was a strong man all right," and Bobby paused to grin ruefully and feel himself tenderly in various of the more painful places. "I think he knew I suspected something and tried to put me off by making a parade of his dislike of the old man. It was as if he were saying: 'It's a jolly good thing the old scamp's been murdered, but if I had had anything to do with it, is it likely I should say so?' In fact, I've never heard of any other murderer shouting how much he disliked his victim and what a good thing it was he was dead. Then he gave me a most vivid, dramatic story of the hermit's death. I expect it was all quite true, too. He expected me to feel he would never have talked like that if it had been himself he had been talking about. A good bluff and I'm not sure it didn't work to some extent. I've never before heard either of a murderer calmly telling a policeman exactly what had happened and how and why. I think it did put me off a bit, and started me thinking about all the others all over again."

"What will happen to the confession poor Mr Crayfoot had to sign?" Olive asked.

"Filed with the rest of the papers in the case," Bobby answered. "Nobody is going to pay it any attention. You can tell Mrs Crayfoot so if it's worrying her—or him."

"What do you think would have happened," Olive asked, "if you hadn't been in the cave when Dr Maskell got there?"

"I think he meant murder," Bobby answered gravely. "He brought a pistol, remember. I feel sure he expected to find Crayfoot there, and no doubt the El Grecos and the Diabolic Candelabra as well. He was undoubtedly very hard up and he could have got enough money from their sale to get away somewhere where he could have felt safe. If Crayfoot had never been found, then Crayfoot might well have been held guilty of the murder. I expect that's how it seemed to Maskell."

"What will happen to him now?"

"He'll have to stand his trial for the killing of Coop," Bobby answered. "Plain case and certain verdict. If he had had the sense to tell the truth at first, the killing of the hermit might very well have passed as manslaughter and quite possibly he would have got off with a comparatively light sentence. I suppose he couldn't face it. Remembered their feud and the interpretation that might be put on it. Remembered the story of the El Grecos, too, and was tempted by the chance of getting hold of them." Bobby paused and added thoughtfully: "It's possible he was more impressed by the cancer cure claim than he admitted. He may have thought there might be something in it and have wanted to find out. It may be that was what started the quarrel and why Maskell went to the hut. From what you hear of the hermit he would be very likely to lose his temper if Maskell started questioning him. If Maskell made any suggestion about co-operation, he would certainly have refused it—most likely with every insult he could think of. I'm not sure Maskell wouldn't have thought it better that a possible cancer cure should be lost rather than that it should be discovered by an unqualified man. Blow to the profession, he would have thought. But if he could get hold of it and get the credit or most of it for himself, as a medical man, all the better. Personal motive and professional motive as well. Anyhow, I think there was every ground for a fierce quarrel between them and I think, too, that theory explains all Maskell's conduct."

"I suppose it does," agreed Olive. "Do you think it was really Mr Dick Rawdon at the Crayfoots' house the evening Sir Alfred was shot?"

"Oh, yes," Bobby said. "I think we can accept his story. He very badly wanted another look at that portrait and when he couldn't get any answer at the front, he went round to the back, saw the window open Coop had left like that for a quick get-away—if necessary, and nipped in. He had said something to make his uncle guess where he was going. Sir Alfred had a suspicious sort of mind and he thought it was the El Greco paintings Dick meant when he said something about a picture at Crayfoot's house. So he went along, too, and frightened off Dick who cleared out in a hurry when he was scared by a knock at the front door. Coop had been lying low upstairs after he heard Dick arrive. He had a fresh scare, tried to get away, and was caught by Sir Alfred who tried Jo stop him. Coop was a rat all right, but like any rat, he could fight when cornered, and he shot Sir Alfred in order to escape. I thought at first Coop had been hired by someone else to have a look round, but now I know Crayfoot and the old hermit had been seeing each other. I expect Coop knew that—possibly through Loo or from his own observations—and was trying to get hold of the pictures on his own account. It must have been from watching Loo that he guessed about the cave. That's what made it all so difficult. The El Greco paintings meant big money to anyone who got hold of them. A generalized motive, so to say. There they all were, buzzing round the hermit's hut like so many wasps round the honey pot, and which particular wasp had done the stinging was pretty hard to tell. Minor complications, too, like Dick Rawdon falling in love with Mary Floyd and Coop getting money out of him on the strength of it—that is the simple explanation of what seemed Dick's suspicious interviews with Coop. It worried me a bit at first when I heard they had been seen together."

"I wonder what will become of Loo?" Olive remarked. "She is such an odd child."

"I'm certain she'll be much less odd now," Bobby declared. "Had a bad shock and it means she'll be shocked the reverse way from usual—from the abnormal to the normal. She'll not want to go wandering alone in the forest any more."

"I hope they'll leave that cottage of theirs," Olive said. "It will be all different now and perhaps they won't mind so much, though that first day we were there, Mary and her mother seemed to think it would be the end of everything if they had to move. Do you remember how they talked about it in such a desperate sort of way?"

"I remember it sounded jolly suspicious when things began to happen later on," Bobby agreed. He got to his feet, groaning a little as he did so, for movement was still painful. "Do you really think," he asked, "that Dick Rawdon and Mary Floyd are going to fix it up?"

"Why, of course," Olive said, surprised. "It'll make up for those poor dears fifty years ago who weren't allowed, and isn't it a good thing something nice has come out of it all at the end?"

THE END

Printed in Great Britain
by Amazon

45385873R10129